Flare

Paddy Lennon

Legal Notices

This is a work of fiction. All names, characters, places, dialogue and incidents are products of the author's imagination. Any resemblances to persons living or dead are coincidental.

Acknowledgements

Thanks to Miriam Abuin, Jonathon O'Toole, Ronan Lennon and Ben Hennessy. They read earlier drafts of this book s+o you didn't have to.

PART I
Heroes Among Us

Chapter One | Secret Origin

Maria sat on the cheap black leather sofa in her office. She stared at the large brown damp stain that was slowly consuming the substance of her once pristine grey concrete walls. She wished that she had a window and an office that didn't smell of rot. Then she would be able to look out, smell air that hadn't been recycled half a dozen times and gaze at the mountains that she knew were off in the distance. The U.S. Government, even those parts that worked in secret, wasn't supposed to skimp on that kind of thing. But what did you expect from a building hollowed out of a former nuclear shelter? The nicest thing that could be said about her office was that the pile of coffee stained scientific journals on her desk added a much needed flash of colour to a room constructed solely of blocks of grey.

One thing about working underground is that nothing blocks the view, she thought as she poured more of the extremely cheap wine (sold by the gallon, in cardboard cartons) into the glass on the crowded coffee table in front of her. She took a swig of the red wine. The taste was like an explosion of bitterness in her mouth but that was the calibre of wine commonly found in supposedly non-existent Army bases that didn't appear on any maps. The base, her elegantly appointed office aside, was a little light on life's luxuries. Most of her fellow scientists barely noticed their surroundings and were just happy to have three hot meals and a bed to sleep on. Their work sustained them. Undertaking experiments on the cutting edge of knowledge had that effect on high grade nerds like Maria's colleagues. Who needed a nice soft bed or daylight when there was science to be done?

Maria took another generous gulp, barely even bothering to taste it; for fear that savouring the flavour would trigger her gag reflex. The wine wasn't there to be enjoyed. It was there to get her drunk as quickly and as effectively as possible. After all, it wasn't as if she needed a clear head for the morning. The phone call she'd received earlier had put paid to any thoughts of work.

Maria's office was on the middle level of a bunker built in an artificial cave blasted into the Nevada desert during the Cold War. The bunker was positioned in part of three hundred square miles of America that, officially, did not exist. It would disturb most U.S. citizens to know that there was a lot of the country they'd never be able to visit without the necessary security clearance. This base was only one part of a network of similar installations across the USA that only a select handful of scientists and military personnel would ever see. The fence marking the line that separated the real world from the base couldn't be seen from her office, but she knew that it was constantly patrolled by soldiers who had orders to capture or, preferably, shoot anyone who strayed too close. Over the years lost hikers and people looking for flying saucers had all been caught and quietly executed or injected with cocktails of hallucinogens and sent to insane asylums for the crime of being where they shouldn't. Asylums were a natural home for that sort of person. Most of them were going to end up there anyway.

It had worked so far, no one with any sense believed that there were secret bases in the desert, even if it did happen to be completely true. Who'd believe a crazy person about what they supposedly saw somewhere in Nevada? Of course you'd occasionally see articles in a magazine or an item on the news about Area 51. Maria had visited that particular facility on more than one occasion and had met the bunch of oddballs who were stationed there. It was a convenient dumping ground for the eccentrics that the government wanted to keep around just in case they became useful. Maria knew she never wanted to go there on a permanent visit, put out to pasture with that bunch of losers.

There was a knock on her door. She wasn't expecting anyone else to be around. She'd given the rest of the team time off to drown their sorrows. They'd all gone to Las Vegas for the weekend to have one last blow-out before they had to return to the base and pack away their work into steel filing cabinets, never to be seen again. The busload of technicians had left the base an hour before. Agent Benning, the project leader, had informed her earlier that she had better miss this particular excursion. The bus was going to experience a tragic accident somewhere in the desert. Agent Benning didn't like loose ends.

"Come in" she said. Not caring who was at the door, it had to be the only member of her team that was still breathing, and anyway, a foreign spy wouldn't have had the courtesy to knock. Leo Spencer shambled into the room. Leo was a researcher, kept around because he was just useful enough to get the work done but not too useful that his knowledge would be dangerous, the sort of mid-level bureaucrat you find in many organisations. He wasn't good enough at his job to be considered for promotion to management but you couldn't imagine the place functioning properly without him. He was slightly chubby with a bowl-cut hairstyle that was out of date in the nineteen fifties and a pair of eyeglasses that were probably hand–me–downs from his grandmother. He'd missed the bus, possibly because everyone else had forgotten he existed, again.

"Hey Maria." I just wanted to see if you needed anything?" he said quietly, Maria had to strain to hear him. Most of her replies to things Leo had said over the years had begun with: "Pardon me?" or "What?"

"Sit down" she patted the part of the sofa beside her, smiling like the drunken idiot that she was.

Leo sat. "How are you doing?"

"I'm fine… drunk."

"I didn't know you drank."

"I usually don't, I felt like I needed it tonight though."

"It's hard to believe it's all going to be gone soon isn't it? We sacrificed a lot for this project."

"Yes, we did. And they don't care one bit."

Maria remembered the day she'd been recruited for the project. She was sitting on the grass outside the Science faculty in a prestigious university on the West Coast. She had been dressed in an old red sweater, blue jeans and white track shoes. She hadn't gotten used to the whole "colour co-ordination in clothing" thing so her items of clothing invariably clashed with each other. Her long blond hair had been a mess, untouched by a brush for several days. She'd been busy finishing her final project for her Masters in Biotechnology and hadn't been able to find a spare moment for such time wasting activities as basic hygiene, doing her laundry or eating properly. On this particular day her head had been buried in a text book, she hadn't noticed the man in the sharply tailored suit, bright white shirt, polished black shoes and sunglasses approaching until he called her by name.

"Maria Fleming" he had said, it wasn't a question. He was just confirming information he already knew.

"Yes?" Maria noticed the man's outfit and made what seemed to be the most logical conclusion: "You're not recruiting for a cult by any chance, are you?"

"My name's Agent Benning, International Security Agency. I'd like to talk."

Maria carefully placed a bookmark in the pages of her book before closing it and replied:

"Agent Benning... That was actually going to be my second guess. You stand out a mile on a college campus. Not many people wearing dark suits here. You might have noticed? I mean, items of your clothing look like they've actually been ironed recently."

"Sorry. I left my short shorts and t-shirt at home" he said sarcastically. Maria winced at the thought of the middle aged agent in a pair of short pants. She was barely able to hold down her hastily eaten lunch burrito at the thought:

"Short shorts and T-shirt? I suppose that the last time you bought anything other than a suit was sometime in the mid to late nineteen eighties?

"Actually, yes."

"A sense of humour too, the college comedy troupe is always looking for fresh blood you know. Now, I don't want to be rude but shouldn't you be off in Afghanistan or another hole in the ground, trying to find guys in a cave or something?"

"I did that last week, and besides, Afghanistan isn't so bad. Compared to this place, it's fairly civilised."

Benning pointed across the quad to where two members of the college football team were sitting on the grass, knocking back beers and loudly admiring every girl who walked by.

Maria looked at them for a second, made a face and looked back at Benning.

"So, I haven't sold any state secrets or anything, what do you want with me?"

"We read your thesis; you have interesting theories on genetic augmentation."

"You can't have read my thesis, it's barely finished yet and the only other person who's even seen a draft of it is my Faculty Advisor."

"Dr. Cameron. Yes. He passed it on to me."

"Why?"

"Have you looked at the world outside your college recently? The world's changing. Stuff that was science fiction a few years ago is becoming real. We now have people who can fly, outrun a sports car or shoot laser beams from their eyes. Some claim to be good guys, fighting for justice, or their idea of it. Others are criminals. Out to get whatever they can take. The ISA has tried to keep them in check but we don't have the technology to do that for much longer. If their numbers keep increasing; what's to stop them suddenly ganging up on normal people and deciding that they want to run the place? Someday soon there's going to be a situation with them that the government can't manage. We need the best and the brightest to help protect the human race, that's you."

"What's in it for me?"

"Do you really want to spend your career developing drugs that allow people to keep eating cheeseburgers without having a heart attack or do you want to make a real difference? You'll have the best facilities, enough money to set you up for life and the smartest people we can find working for and with you."

Maria had signed up on the spot. Three weeks later, after graduation, the International Security Agency had arranged for Maria to "die" in a car accident. Her car had been driven off a cliff on the Pacific Coast Highway. Her "body" had never been found but she'd been declared legally dead.

That had been eight years ago. This morning she's received a phone call from a person who didn't give their name. The voice on the phone had said that their funding was being pulled immediately. No more money for research was going to be authorised and she had to destroy all that her team had worked on. Her entire working life to date was wasted. The method the government had picked to deliver the project's death blow had really angered her. After all she'd sacrificed her chance at having a family, a life, to the project. She felt she'd deserved more than an anonymous phone call from some faceless bureaucrat piloting a desk in an office outside Washington.

Leo had a similar story to tell. Jack Silverman had been shoving Leo's head into a toilet bowl while two of Jack's cronies, John and Adam looked on, laughing so hard that they were having trouble keeping upright. Benning had burst into the restroom, knocked Silverman out with a punch to the face and shoved Adam's head through a wall, John ran off, hollering like a young girl.

Benning pulled Leo's head out of the toilet, where it had been wedged in pretty tight.

"Why me?" Leo had asked Benning as they walked towards Benning's car after the course of his life had been mapped out for him in an enlightening five minute conversation.

"Because kid, you're a mathematical genius, you love all this crazy science fiction crap and no one will miss you."

Benning was right, of course. Leo had taken to the project like a duck to water. It made it much more difficult for him to just quit. As a member of the project he had purpose, he was important and, he'd met Maria. The woman he secretly loved with all his heart.

Leo said all this to Maria, except the "Love you with all my heart stuff". She nodded.

"And now they're going to take it all away from us." Leo could hear the anger in her voice as she continued: "How dare they?" She refilled their wine glasses, finishing yet another carton. "You know why our research has suddenly become an embarrassment to the government?"

"The stuff on the news" Leo replied. "The world's changed a lot in the last twenty four hours. The Vanguard defeated that squad of terrorists who had planned to assassinate President Morgan."

"Now, the whole country is celebrating these... things. These super-powered show-offs. They do what they like with no regard for who they hurt or what lives they damage in the process. They're all the same Leo. I don't see a distinction between the ones who call themselves heroes and the villains. The heroes are like the ultimate celebrities, people waste their time wishing they were like them, dressing like them, eating like them, reading stupid illiterate magazines about them. The heroes are worshipped like gods among us, people want the heroes to solve all of the world's problems and won't do anything to try make the world a better place themselves. What do we do when The Vanguard have no one else to fight? What happens if they decide they want to run things their way? With the project gone this country will have no defence! We've got access to all kinds of information on the heroes and villains. We know their real identities, their strengths and their weaknesses."

"And we have the Nanotech and weaponry down in the vault."

Maria smiled: "It would be a shame to waste so many taxpayer dollars. Why not take what we've created and use it? If the government isn't going to do what needs to be done then we should."

She stood up, more sure of herself than she had ever been. Her mind suddenly clear of the brain cell killing effects of the wine she had consumed. This was her destiny. She would save the human race from those who had declared themselves to be their superiors.

"Come on, we've got work to do."

She grabbed her key card, left her office and walked towards the elevator. Leo followed behind; the building was deserted except for the two of them. The bases' contingent of soldiers was currently off site patrolling the perimeter or organising a bus crash fifty miles away.

The elevator arrived. Maria hit the button for the 'Vault' level. Buried even deeper underground, it was a space the size of several aircraft hangars, it contained a fully equipped lab, state of the art operating theatre and fully stocked armoury.

They arrived at the vault after less than thirty seconds on the elevator. Maria, as one of the project leaders, had access to every part of the facility. They walked along a metal catwalk and Maria pointed to the operating theatre.

"Set up the Nanotech delivery systems, I'm heading down to the cold storage vault to get the Nanotech and I'll visit the server room to start downloading the files." Leo nodded and ran down a nearby staircase towards the theatre.

Maria jogged over to the cold storage room and put on a pair of thick gloves and a long coat lined with fur that hung on the wall outside the door. She entered, coughing as she breathed the cold air. The main part of the project, the part she'd been most responsible for, was stored in the room at sub-zero temperatures. There was only one sample of the Nanotech solution. It cost too much to synthesise for them to produce more than one batch at a time. She opened the storage locker and took out a large vial of clear liquid. The vial contained millions of nanites, impossibly tiny robots, each no larger than an atom. These tiny machines were to be injected into a person. Once inside they were programmed to make dozens of changes to the test subject's body. They would increase muscle mass, build stronger bones and improve their eyesight. In short, they'd make someone more than just a regular human. The recipients skin would become impenetrable, their muscles stronger and their mind and reflexes faster. That was the theory anyway. They'd never tested the nanites on a living person. The computerised trials and tests on monkeys had all worked well but she didn't know how the Nanotech would work on a person. A series of injections and the lucky subject could be an almost invincible superhuman or very, very dead.

Maria left the cold storage room and took off the coat and gloves. She picked up the vial and walked a hundred metres over to the server room. The room contained scores of refrigerator sized computers, holding all the data accumulated by the team over the past eight years. She began emptying the information files onto a portable infinity drive, capable of storing huge amounts of data. She programmed the computer to delete all other copies of the information on the project servers. That was, after all, what the government wanted. It would take a few hours. More than enough time for them to take the next steps.

Next, she went to the security control room, a small, dark room, lit by the glow of dozens of screens. She logged on to an access terminal and overrode the systems. It was easy; she'd helped design them in the first place. After less than a minute in the systems, she'd programmed the facility to go into lockdown mode. Steel shutters slammed into place all over the building. Not even an army would be able to break into the facility now.

Once she was sure that the data download and destruction was proceeding as expected, she paged Leo:

"How are you set?"

"I'm ready to load the solution once you bring it here, but there's only one dose."

"That's right."

"So who's taking it?"

"I am."

"But..."

"No buts Leo, I'm doing this; I need to visit the armoury first. I'll be there in a few minutes. We'll programme the Nanotech with the information downloaded from the servers as well. They're more than able to store that data and dump it directly into my brain. I'll have access to all of our files on the heroes and villains, as well as the powers I need to destroy them all."

"Yes, Maria."

Maria went back out onto the catwalk and headed to the armoury. She entered her code on the keypad beside the bank vault like door, which opened slowly. The room was large and contained dozens of racks of all kinds of exotic weaponry, most of them invented in the facility. She grabbed a kit bag and packed a small selection of weaponry she figured would come in handy: anti-gravity discs, a seismic mace, an energy shield projector. Once the bag was full, she strained to lift it onto her back. The weaponry inside was just too heavy. After nearly dislocating her shoulder she settled with just dragging it behind her across the floor. Once she'd been dosed with the Nanotech she wouldn't need to worry about how heavy it was.

She left the armoury and went to the main floor. She stood quietly for a minute and took it all in one last time. She had just destroyed everything she had worked for; she had thought that it would be much, much harder. Maybe it came so easy because she was actually going to use the fruits of her labours instead of locking them away forever. Leo called out to her. She turned in his direction and walked to join him.

Leo had programmed the auto-surgeon, the facilities robotic doctor, to inject the mixture into her at several points along her spine, torso, arms and legs. They inserted the vial of Nanotech solution into the auto-surgeon and Leo ran a cable from the infinity drive into a USB port on the side of the machine. The Nanotech began downloading the data from the drive. Maria stripped down to her underwear and lay face down on the operating table. Leo looped the straps of the operating table around her arms, legs and back. Maria closed her eyes.

Leo spoke: "You're sure you want to go through with this?"

"It's a little late for that: half the army must be trying to get into the facility now. The guards would have received an alarm as soon as I accessed the storage room; it was hardwired into the system. I couldn't bypass it."

"Yes. They're on their way now... Maria, this could be dangerous, if we made a mistake when we made the Nanotech, you'll die. Or worse."

"We're the best Leo, we didn't make a mistake."

Leo turned on his heel and left the room, walking quickly to the glass and steel observation room next door. He sat at a large console and hit a sequence of buttons.

A set of needles lowered slowly from the front of the auto-surgeon and clicked into place.

The four inch long titanium needles moved towards Maria's body and penetrated her skin, moving deeper into her muscle tissue and bone marrow. The injections began, the Nanotech solution entered her bloodstream and Maria screamed.

Chapter Two | First Day

Ryan sat on the armchair beside the window in his bedroom. It was seven in the morning and his parents were nowhere to be found. That wasn't surprising. He had heard them leave an hour earlier as they raced out the door of the apartment to go to work. Had they managed to forget about today and how important it was? There was no way they were going to be back on time. Ryan decided to get ready for school by himself.

He was already washed and dressed so all he had to do was drag his protesting body off the chair, pick up his school bag and head out the door. He entered the kitchen, opened a cupboard and the fridge and pulled out the ingredients he needed to make a southwest omelette: eggs, butter, ham, onions, peppers and parsley. A normal fourteen year old boy wouldn't have to be able to exist completely independently of his parents. But Ryan's situation in life was far from normal. He listened to music as he prepared and ate his breakfast. Once he had finished, Ryan placed the dirty dishes and cutlery in the dishwasher and then placed a load of laundry in the rarely used washing machine. Ryan's mother, Lisa, never had the patience to wait the eternity it took the washing machine to clean a load of clothes. She washed everything by hand. It was faster.

Once the chores were done, Ryan took the cookie jar down from the shelf and dipped his hand inside to take money out. Ryan's dad wouldn't allow sweets in the house, instead the cookie jar held a few hundred dollars in cash, just in case it came in handy. Ryan took a roll of fifty dollar bills out and slipped one into his front pocket. He'd have to pay for lunch in school today. He didn't have time to cook a decent meal.

He left the apartment and headed for the elevator in the hall. He needed to be at the bus stop in five minutes. The rest of the building was quiet. The other occupants had left at the same time as his parents had. He exited the building and walked to the bus stop. He didn't have to wait long for a yellow and black school bus to turn the corner and pull up at the kerb. He got on board and nodded in greeting to the driver. The bus was mostly full. Ryan shuffled down the aisle as the bus started moving; several of the other kids were staring at him, wondering who the newcomer was. Ryan continued on down the aisle and spotted an empty seat about half way down the bus. As he approached the boy sitting beside the seat placed his hand to guard the empty space:

"Someone's already sitting there. Find anywhere else." The boy said. Ryan sat down on an empty seat near to the back of the bus, beside a girl who didn't even look at him as he sat down. She was too busy staring out the window, trying not to catch his eye. The bus sauntered through the early morning traffic and reached its destination: Jimmy Carter Middle School. The doors opened and the bus disgorged its passengers. Ryan followed his new schoolmates out the door and into the school. The place was noisy and warm as friends who hadn't seen each other in weeks laughed and talked together. Ryan took it all in as he moved slowly down the packed corridor. The school had the usual cliques, the pretty girls hung out with other pretty girls, the sports stars hung out with other sports stars and the quiet kids hung out in small closely knit groups or alone.

It was exactly like Ryan's last school back in Chicago, except that most people here were much better sun tanned. Ryan followed the signs for the Vice-principal's office and knocked on the open door.

"Come in." said a bespectacled woman seated behind a desk.

"Excuse me." said Ryan. "I'm a new student here."

"Name?" She responded.

"Ryan Curtis."

"Ah, Yes." She said as she ticked a box on a printed list that lay on her desk. She smiled at Ryan: "Are your parents with you?"

"No, they're busy."

"Well that's understandable. I'm Angela Williams. Your home room is number fourteen. Take a right when you leave my office and then take a left. It's the sixth door on your right. It's numbered."

"Thanks." said Ryan.

"The Vice-principal asked to speak with you when you arrived. He's in his office, go straight in. I hope you enjoy your time with us Ryan."

"I hope so too. See you again."

Ryan rapped his knuckles on the open door and entered the Vice-principal's office.

The Vice-principal's nameplate on his desk identified him as Mr. Stack. He attempted to smile as Ryan walked in, at least, the sides of his mouth curled up slightly and he exposed his teeth.

"Ryan Curtis. It's nice to meet you. Are your parents here?"

"No. They were called away on business."

"I'm sorry to hear that, I was really hoping to meet them. Never mind, let's have a quick chat before you start class. I like to get to know all my students. Connecting with people personally was a value espoused by the man who this institution of learning was named after: Our thirty-ninth and best President." Mr. Stack leaned back in his chair and pointed up at the portrait of President Carter which hung over his desk.

"That's great." said Ryan.

"Yes, he was great wasn't he? I know it's fashionable for people to mock the man as ineffective in office but he proved them wrong afterwards. Yes he did!"

"I suppose." said a confused Ryan, this wasn't how educators were supposed to talk.

"His approach to life informs everything this school strives for. Have you seen our motto? "Attempt to succeed." Marvellous sentiments, I'm sure you'll agree."

"Yes, I definitely do." Ryan said in an effort to bring the conversation to a close before it became even weirder. "I'd better go to class."

"Yes." responded Mr. Stack as he stood up to shake Ryan's hand. "Best of luck."

Ryan left the office as quickly as was polite. A bell rang, signalling to everyone that they had better get to class instantly. Ryan picked up the pace and got to his new classroom just as the second bell sounded. A desk at the front was the only one still free. He sat down and tucked his bag underneath his desk. He probably had a locker. He'd ask a classmate later on. An adult waltzed into the room and stood at the top of the class.

"Good morning class." He said with a slight lisp.

"Good morning sir." The class chorused in unison.

"Many of you know who I am, I recognise a lot of you from last year. I'm Mr. Ridge. English teacher and the nearest thing this school has to a poet. But enough about me; we'll allow our new classmates introduce themselves. You there!" he said pointing at Ryan. "I don't know who you are. Tell us about yourself."

"What would you like to know?" Ryan asked.

"Your name for starters."

"I'm Ryan Curtis, I moved here nearly a year ago but this is my first time at the school."

"And what did you do for a year instead of coming to our palace of education?"

"I was… home schooled."

"And why did you stop?"

"My parents thought it might be a good idea to meet people of my own age. We used to travel a lot because of my parents job but we're settling down now."

"Very good. What do your parents do?"

There it was: the question Ryan dreaded. The answer he gave would undoubtedly greatly affect the new few weeks and months of his life.

"They're involved in law enforcement."

"Excellent. Who's next? You there, the blonde girl with the vacant expression!" said Mr. Ridge.

Ryan sat back and relaxed. He'd dodged that bullet. He mentally gave himself a pat on the back, saying that his parents worked in law enforcement had been smart. It was partially true and also managed to skirt the issue of what it was they actually did. School life would be difficult enough without letting everyone know on the first day that his parents were Superheroes.

Chapter Three | Octoman

The Darkwing sped across the Atlantic Ocean. The aircraft was barely skimming the crest of the waves. Warfare sat in the pilot's seat, quietly concentrating on flying the aircraft and ensuring that it didn't hit the water. The Darkwing could take punishment that would leave most other aircraft as lumps of molten metal and a short dip in the sea wouldn't actually damage the craft but would it would be embarrassing for him both personally and as a pilot.

Flying any higher wasn't an option as it would be a lot more dangerous than a short dip in the salty, murky ocean. Travelling at a height over one hundred feet would allow the radar on Octoman's sea fortress to find them and give the villain time to prepare for their arrival. Octoman had parked a fortress the size of Manhattan off the Spanish coast. Warfare didn't want to give Octoman any more advantages than he already clearly had.

The fortress was currently located just off the straits of Gibraltar. Octoman was demanding something or other. Warfare didn't care about the specifics. He was sick of super villains, their stupid plans for world domination, their doomsday devices and their childish demands. They were a distraction from the world's real problems. Octoman was one of the worst. He had once been a Marine Biologist and Geneticist who had mixed his DNA with that of an Octopus to start the next phase of evolution. He'd been an occasional thorn in the side of The Vanguard for a decade. Octoman had spent half a decade robbing the money and technology required to build his fortress. He'd demanded recognition as "King of the Seas" in a video address to the European Parliament a week ago. The European

Union had laughed at him, in several languages, sending him back to the seas with his tentacles between his legs. He'd promised revenge on the people of Europe. He hadn't waited long to get it.

Four days ago, Octoman had sunk a dozen fishing boats off the coast of France, a combined British/French fleet of warships had sailed into the Bay of Biscay, looking for trouble. They'd found it. Octoman's sea fortress had risen from beneath the waves and proceeded to destroy the fleet. Hundreds of lives had been lost with scores more captured as hostages.

Finally, after a typically European delay in responding to a crisis, The Vanguard had been called in to offer their assistance. Now they were speeding in an aircraft two foot above the waves to pull Europe's fat out of the fire. The cockpit door slid open. Solarstorm entered the cockpit and sat in the co-pilot's chair, the faint solar powered glow he emitted added to the illumination that the instrument panel provided to the cockpit.

"How long 'till we get there?" Solarstorm asked, looking at Warfare. Solarstorm always thought it was odd that he'd known Warfare for six years and had never seen his face. Warfare wore his helmet with mirrored visor and blue and gold body armour at all times. Solarstorm strongly suspected that Warfare slept in them.

"Four minutes. We should be seeing it any second."

On cue, they saw the fortress on the horizon. The fortress was a floating town comprised of skyscrapers, docking facilities and watertight hangars linked by causeways and suspension bridges. The fortress had been constructed from whatever raw materials Octoman had been able to find on the seabed such as seaweed encrusted pieces of sunken ocean liners or aircraft that had crashed into the sea. The flotsam and jetsam of half a century had been cobbled together into a massive, frighteningly powerful secret base. Anti-aircraft cannons and missile launchers situated on the barnacle covered buildings were firing into the night sky, their flashes clearly visible from the Darkwing's cockpit.

"I guess the firing is because of the French air raid that's supposed to be our diversion?" asked Solarstorm.

"Bloody idiots are two minutes ahead of schedule, never ask French people to be on time, they're genetically incapable of it" grumbled Warfare. "They're going to be torn to pieces, tell the others to get ready and you'd better prepare for an air drop"

"Right".

Solarstorm rose from the chair and exited the cockpit, entering the cramped passenger compartment where Velocity, Mage and Mountain waited, strapped into their own seats. Velocity fidgeted impatiently, as she always did when travelling in any vehicle that was going slower than her top speed.

"How long?" she asked, agitation clearly evident in her voice.

"I drop in thirty seconds. You all go a minute later. Follow the plan and we'll be OK. You all know what you're doing?"

A chorus of positive replies in turn eager, anxious and committed, echoed through the compartment. Warfare's voice came over the intercom.

"Time to go Solarstorm, I've gained as much height as I dare. Any higher and they'll see us".

Solarstorm ran over to the cargo door in the back of the Darkwing, hunkered down and waited for his cue.

"Ready"

The door hissed open and Solarstorm jumped. Turbulence caused by the Darkwing knocked him around but he fell towards the sea face down, eyes closed, relaxing for a few moments. After a few seconds, his eyes snapped open and Solarstorm stabilised himself and floated just above the waves.

"I'm away, heading to the fortress now."

"Acknowledged."

Solarstorm stretched his arms ahead of himself as he lay horizontally, hovering above the tops of the waves. He didn't need to pull such a stereotypical pose to fly, but he did it anyway, the public expected certain things from superheroes and this was one of them. He headed towards the fortress.

"They've seen us." said Warfare from the cockpit as the constant anti-aircraft fire from the fortress began to move in their direction.

"Going evasive."

The other members of The Vanguard hung onto their seats as Warfare flew the plane like a maniac who'd taken a handful of steroids, dodging and weaving across the sky, trying to avoid being hit, all the while moving towards their target. He grimaced inside his helmet as a missile exploded just outside the cockpit.

"I'm going to make a strafing run over the fortress to clear a landing zone for you three. Get ready to go."

Warfare armed the weapons systems and targeted a cluster of missile launchers and cannon at a point on the nearest part of the fortress. The Darkwing shuddered slightly as the weapons fired. The Darkwing's cannon and missiles raked the fortress. Warfare smiled as a cloud of debris flew into the air from the part of the fortress he had targeted.

He banked the Darkwing and quickly brought it in over the patch of land which had now been scythed clean.

"You all have your objectives; I'll meet you in the main chamber when I disable the weapons on this floating junk heap."

Velocity, Mage and Mountain disembarked quickly. Mage doubled over and proceeded to get nosily sick.

"I hate flying." he whined once his stomach had been emptied of its contents. "It's bad enough on a commercial flight, disgusting food, screaming babies, terrible films. I think Warfare flies the jet like that on purpose, just to mess with me."

"Grow up Mage, we've got work to do." said Velocity.

"Sure, I'll get right on that. Just give me a minute to get my internal organs back into their usual places." He groaned "Ohhhh, I swear, my body is ejecting that burger I had last night."

"Serves you right for eating at a place called "Val-u-Burger." grumbled Mountain.

"I had a coupon that was very nearly out of date. Letting one of those go to waste is like burning money!"

"We don't have the time for this." said Velocity.

"You're always so impatient. Is it a side effect of your super-speed or are you just a disagreeable..."

"I'm only ever impatient with you, Mage." snapped Velocity. She sped off to the north, faster than their eyes could see.

The other Vanguard moved off in different directions. Mage slowly staggered away, using his staff as support, hoping for dear life that he wouldn't get sick again. Mountain lumbered off towards his destination: the electrical generators that powered the fortress. Explosions echoed from the other side of the artificial island.

Solarstorm had already begun.

Solarstorm flew towards the south of the floating fortress. This part of the base contained the hangars for Octoman's fleet of interceptors. As Solarstorm was nearing his target, a dozen robot interceptors launched directly at him. Pilotless drones, the size and shape of a small car with wings, the interceptors were pretty stupid but they had strength in numbers. Solarstorm fired a concentrated burst of energy from his hands. His energy blasts could melt steel. The yellow beam of light sliced through the first interceptor. It exploded in a ball of yellow flame and the debris from the explosion badly damaged the second, sending it spiralling down towards the sea. The other interceptors began firing; red and green energy beams stabbed through the dark to his left and right, some of the shots were a little too close for comfort. Solarstorm evaded their fire. He looped around and ended up behind a wing of three of the interceptors, he fired his blasts, hitting the interceptors' dead on. They detonated immediately. This was going better than he had dared to hope. Warfare had been really harassing the team about training regularly and it had started to pay off. Flying quickly and performing aerobatics that no aeroplane could hope to match, Solarstorm was enjoying himself.

Mountain lumbered towards the centre of the fortress. His job was simple enough and matched his talent for mindless destruction; smash any electrical generators he saw. He'd already trashed two and was heading towards a third when a voice rang out.

"I'm really sick of you heroes sticking your noses in my business." There was no mistaking that voice, it sounded like someone speaking whilst gargling salt water. It was Octoman.

"Maybe if you stopped trying to take over the world we'd leave you alone" said Mountain slowly. Witty repartee and speaking in general did not come easy to him.

"I was expecting you to drop by. So here's a little gift I prepared earlier."

The wall of the tall stone building to Mountain's left crumbled as a fifty foot tall robotic crab punched through.

Octoman's voice crackled through the loudspeaker again: "When it's finished with you, they'll rename you 'Pebble'. Goodbye".

Mountain leaped out of the way as the giant green Robo-crab swung one of its huge pincers, hitting the ground, gouging out large chunks of rock. Mountain picked up a piece of stone the size of a desk and threw it at the crab's head. The crab reacted quickly, swinging its left pincer and knocking the slab out of the air, pulverising it in the process. Machine guns popped out of the crab's mouth and fired. The bullets bounced harmlessly off Mountain's rocky skin. Ricochets pinged all around as Mountain raised his fists and charged towards the crab's right legs, He landed a solid punch on one of its knee joints and shattered it. The robot swung its right pincher quickly and Mountain was slammed back into a building, he ploughed through the wall, collapsing it. The rest of the building started to fall in on itself and the roof caved in, burying Mountain under tons of metal, glass and concrete. The dust settled and the Robo-crab let out a hideous shriek of victory which cut through the night air. The rubble of the building moved as Mountain stood up, pieces of masonry slid off his back and shattered on the ground. "Hur Hur Hur, it's been a while since I was hit like that." mumbled

Mountain as he ran with surprising quickness, punched the robot in the head as hard as he could and ended the brief fight. The robot spasmed once and then lay still. He hit the robot in the temple and its head flew off and rolled away.

Mage was sneaking through what he guessed was a barracks for Octoman's troops. He was supposed to be looking for the communication centre but right now he REALLY needed the bathroom.

"Why is it that all these crazy secret bases or science fictionish spaceships are lacking in basic facilities, like kitchens or showers or toilets?" he muttered to himself softly.

Mage's journey so far had been quiet, if it wasn't a cliché, he'd have said too quiet. So far, he'd only encountered a couple of sleepy guards that he'd subdued by hitting them over the head with his staff. Shooting fireballs and turning people into frogs was awesome, but there was something satisfying about cracking a bad guy over the head with six feet of metal. Besides, anyone who could resist being hit on the head with a heavy stick was probably immune to most of his spells anyway.

He turned left, entering a brightly lit corridor, hoping to find a bathroom or the communication hub. He opened a thick metal door by sliding back two enormous bolts and entered the large room on the other side. With a start, he realised that the room was occupied and stopped in his tracks. This particular room must have contained fifty of Octoman's troops. It was their locker room. A handful were half dressed, but most were fully clothed, preparing for the battle. All of them were armed or had weapons within arms reach.

Mage's throat went dry, he wasn't a coward but the sight of lots of surprised armed men was a bit of a shock. He tried to think of a witty hero remark to break the tension:

"This isn't the gift shop!" he announced as he smiled at the soldiers, waved cheerily and turned and ran.

Mage ducked out the door just as the more efficient of the troops opened fire. Bullets smacked against the concrete walls of the corridor as Mage raced around the corner. He cursed to himself softly; he was wearing his brown hooded cape and robes. His manager had demanded that he look like a wizard for marketing purposes, never once thinking about the practicalities of running in the costume. When Mage had brought this up his manager Michael had replied:

"Don't run. Running isn't liked by the demographic you're going after. Teenagers prefer people who walk like they don't care when they get there. Practice that instead. Oh, and don't talk in full sentences."

Mage was going to have a word with Michael, assuming he survived. He hiked his robes up above his shins and mentally urged his legs to run faster.

Ten of Octoman's troops were following him. Shouting obscenities and firing as they ran.

Mage muttered under his breath: "Come on; come on… think of a spell, anything at all… got it!"

Mage turned towards Octoman's men as lightening crackled along his staff. A bolt of energy lanced towards the concrete ceiling above his pursuers. The ceiling cracked and collapsed on top of the soldiers. Mage stopped and caught his breath waiting as the adrenaline left his system and the blind panic of the last few seconds subsided.

"OK Mage, time to get back to work" he said to himself and he turned and walked towards what he hoped was the communication hub.

Velocity was in trouble. She'd raced down to the lower levels with the aim of rescuing the prisoners that Octoman was holding. They had intelligence that Octoman had rescued the survivors of the fleet that he had destroyed the previous day. So far, all Velocity had seen were dozens of Octoman's troops. Octoman hired mercenaries from all over the world, promising them fortunes in return for their service. Over the years The Vanguard had arrested dozens of them. By this stage, Velocity would have thought that there should have been a labour shortage caused by the constant arrests of henchmen. This clearly wasn't the case. Octoman had a small army available to do his bidding, which worried her; eventually The Vanguard would lose the element of surprise and could be overwhelmed by Octoman's forces. She hoped she could release the sailors quickly and that they'd be in a position to fight. European Union troops were on the way but wouldn't be able to land on the fortress until The Vanguard had performed their tasks.

As she sped towards the cell block she spotted two guards standing outside it. She barrelled into the two men at high speed, which was her preferred method of subduing bad guys. Warfare was teaching The Vanguard martial arts, hoping to break them of their dependence on their superpowers, but Velocity loved using her speed and liked to keep things simple. She hit her commlink to talk to the rest of the team.

"Guys, I'm running into lots of soldiers this time out, a lot more than this loser can usually convince to join him, is he offering a dental plan or weekend spa getaways to these thugs as a signing bonus now?" Her commlink crackled as a voice came through:

"Hey. It's me, Mage. In a startling break from form, she may be right, I'm at the communication hub and there are a lot of soldiers hanging around. Also, I'm surrounded by them and they're not very friendly so any help would be greatly appreciated."

Warfare spoke; his voice was calm and confident, as if attacking a massive fortress was an activity he had undertaken often: "I'm reading a large power drain coming from the circular building towards the north of the fortress. Octoman is probably there. Once you're finished your objectives, head towards that building, I'll pick up Mage along the way."

Mage cowered behind a bank of computers in the communication hub, occasionally peeking out to fire a spell at whichever target of opportunity presented itself. The room was a mess of servers, computer screens (most of them now cracked or shattered) and office furniture. The furniture provided Octoman's troops with plenty of places to hide. Mage wasn't having much success in picking them off. The troops had sealed the room as well. Meaning that Mage's preferred strategy, running away, wouldn't work either. The door on the opposite side of the room began to glow bright red, Mage ducked behind cover just as it exploded and Warfare charged into the room. Octoman's troops turned and began to fire at the new threat. The bullets bounced off Warfare's armour and helmet harmlessly. He drew his electron sword, flicked the power switch to eviscerate and slashed at the luckless first soldier to cross his path.

The soldier's gun was sliced cleanly in two. He didn't even have time to react to this before Warfare's fist smashed into his stomach, knocking him out cold:

"Who's next?" Warfare said, genuine pleasure in his voice.

Octoman had closed the hangar bay doors once the last of his interceptors had launched. Solarstorm flew towards them at the speed of sound, ignoring the constant firing of Octoman's anti-aircraft cannon. There was no way that stuff could touch him, not at this speed. The air scorched in Solarstorm's wake as he prepared to ram the hangar doors and destroy whatever was inside. The doors were ripped asunder and the metal screamed, as Solarstorm impacted and tore through. Alarms were sounding throughout the base but no one rushed to fight him. Solarstorm was disappointed. A few more explosions wouldn't go amiss. He thought as he spotted a cluster of fuel tanks, no doubt full to the brim with aviation fuel. Solarstorm took aim and fired two powerful energy blasts. The tanks ruptured and exploded. Streams of flammable liquid sprayed over the area igniting when they met any open flame and turning the area into a raging inferno.

Nice. He said to himself as he wondered what to do next. The hangar was becoming uncomfortably hot. A whirlwind of flame was moving through the area, destroying everything it touched. Solarstorm launched up into the air and punched through the roof to seek his next target.

Velocity had reached the prison cells. The guards hadn't seen her coming and now rested unconscious outside. Well, "rested" wasn't the correct term since one of them hung from the rafters, crying softly and another had been kicked through a wall at two hundred miles per hour. The third guard had thrown down his weapon and ran… for about three metres before Velocity had slapped him gently on the back of the head and sent him spinning across the room to bounce off the wall like a pinball.

The small, square cells of bare stone were empty, every one of them. Velocity sped over to the third guard, grabbed him by the front of his uniform and shook him awake before screaming in his face:

"Where are they?"

"They're gone."

"I can see that, don't play games or you'll join your friend on the other side of that wall."

"Octoman came and took them yesterday night, last I heard, they were being brought to re-processing."

"Where's that and what to do they do there?"

"It's the big round building. The stuff he's doing in there… it's evil."

"Like what? Be more descriptive!"

"Weird stuff, like cloning and making mutants, the sailors and marines we captured yesterday are probably already dead… or worse." the guard started to cry. "I didn't sign up for any crimes against nature. I just wanted the money and the free spa weekend as a present for my wife."

Velocity left the guard and headed towards the round building. Hopefully they could stop this before it was too late.

Solarstorm was standing on the roof of a tall warehouse not far from the circular building. A bluish cloud caused by Mage's teleportation spell began to form to his left; he turned to look at it.

"So, you made it." said Solarstorm as Warfare and Mage teleported in.

"Yeah, no problem. There weren't that many troops surrounding him."

"What are you talking about? There were at least seventy of them!" Mage complained.

"I counted thirty five, a walk in the park." Warfare brushed his hands together to remove the dust.

Mountain appeared, jumping over a neighbouring building and landing on the ground beside the building where the others stood. "We're going in?" He asked.

"Yes" said Warfare. "We're waiting on Velocity, no sense going in at anything less than full strength, we've no idea what's inside."

"The Darkwing couldn't scan it?" Mage asked.

"No, Octoman's installed high grade shielding on that particular building."

A dust cloud approached from the south.

"Velocity's here. Mountain? The door if you please" said Solarstorm.

Mountain grinned and raised his large, stony fists. He ran towards the door, as unstoppable as a lava flow, he crashed into the huge steel door and it buckled. Three swift punches and it groaned inwards.

"I love doing that!" he said as the door fell to the ground.

The Vanguard charged into the massive open space. Octoman stood in the middle of the room, surrounded by machinery and thick translucent power cables. Dozens of seven foot tall transparent metal and plastic containers stood in rows near the centre of the room. They were all connected to the power cables and bolted to the floor. Inside each tube was a partially formed human body, floating in red fluid.

"Greetings, Vanguard. Sorry the place is a mess."

"What are you up to Octoman?" asked Solarstorm.

Octoman put his tentacles in the air. There was no point in fighting The Vanguard; they'd beaten him too often for him to think he could stand a chance against them all.

"Over the years, I've found that robots can be so... unreliable. I've dedicated the three years since my last defeat by your team to building a mass cloning device. Splicing DNA collected from various sources, I can produce two hundred fully grown troops each week. They're ready to fight mere minutes after they have been de-tanked."

Velocity gasped in horror. "That's... disgusting. We'll make sure you spend the rest of your life in prison for this!"

"I was probably going to spend the rest of my life in prison anyway. Sinking a fleet of warships and bombing Spain will have ensured that I think."

Warfare took an energy net from his backpack and threw it over Octoman, trapping the villain.

"What was the point of all this? You must have known we'd tear this place apart, what exactly do you think you've gained?"

"My career is finished and, to date, I've accomplished nothing. Not really. You've beaten me fifteen times, did you know that? Fifteen! I've spent most of my life in prison. I've stolen enough money to buy the third world country of my choice but I would have been forgotten in fifty years. Maybe I would have merited a footnote in the history books, if even that. But now I'll be remembered.

I've invented the means to clone anybody. I've changed the world forever! Once this technology gets out into the world anyone with a few million dollars will be able to grow their own people. Think of the chaos that this invention will bring! A person could clone an army and conquer the world. But not me. I've not got long left. I'm a monster and I'll soon die a monster, but everyone will know my name."

"You're dying?" asked Solarstorm.

"You think being genetically bonded with an Octopus is a healthy lifestyle choice? Sure, the tentacles come in handy. I can breathe underwater and I have super strength but my DNA looks like scrambled eggs. I've checked."

"You could have cured yourself" said Mage.

"Only by removing my powers, which I wasn't going to do. Would any of you make that sacrifice? Leave the lives you have behind and become normal? It wouldn't have made any difference if I had tried to reverse my abilities anyway. The damage had already been done."

"You think that you're better off this way? Dying as a monster?" said Velocity.

"Of course I am! I've secured a type of immortality. How many people can say that? My contemporaries... the other super villains, The Grey Shadow, Timeshard, The Blizzard. They're all dead or in captivity. They've all been captured by you or they died due to any number or natural and unnatural reasons. You've no villains left to fight. I've won simply by being the last to fall and making your team obsolete. Enjoy the down slope of your respective careers Vanguard. This is just the start of your problems!"

"What do you mean?" asked Solarstorm.

"You're going to become completely irrelevant. Say goodbye to the endorsement deals, the celebrity status, and the money. Without criminals like me to beat up people will stop caring about you. Stop noticing you and forget you. You'll be just like any other celebrities whose time in the spotlight has ended. You'll all die forgotten, irrelevant and alone. I can't imagine a worse fate for you. Wasting away, your powers burning out your nervous system. You will all die crippled by the thing that makes you special."

Velocity punched Octoman in the face.

"You're never going to see it." She said. "I'll make sure they throw you in the deepest, darkest cell for the rest of your life."

"Does my work disgust you dear?"

"It's repugnant."

"What did you expect? I'm a villain."

"You're history." said Velocity.

"Well, so are you."

Octoman began to laugh. The noise echoed around the chamber. Soldiers from the European Union entered the building through the door The Vanguard had opened. They moved forward cautiously, their guns pointing at Octoman.

Octoman sat on the ground, breathing heavily, the net still covering him.

"I'll be seeing you."

The Vanguard handed Octoman over to the waiting European Union soldiers and headed home.

Chapter Four | Viva Las Vegas

Captain Ed O'Grady shifted his weight; his leg had been asleep for the past two minutes. He idly wondered how much time he'd spent lying on rooftops in cities across the world. It probably added up to at least a few weeks of his forty years of life. This particular roof was located on the Las Vegas Strip, directly opposite the main entrance to The Sphinx Casino and Resort. It was one of the newest tourist traps on the Las Vegas Strip, The most famous collection of tourist traps in the world.

The Sphinx, like every casino and hotel in the city was designed to painlessly separate the tourist from his or her money in as little time as possible. It had been built to resemble the Egyptian monument it took its name from and was filled with gambling tables, slot machines, shops, swimming pools and overpriced restaurants.

Today it had one other item guaranteed to keep people entertained. A large group of terrorists had seized control of the entire complex just over forty-five minutes earlier. So far, they had made no demands. Instead they'd just sealed off the exits and begun lining the inside of the complex with explosives. There had been no phone calls to the police threatening to execute hostages. No communication at all. Which meant that this wasn't about ransom money or a robbery, unless Ed could think of a plan, a lot of innocent people were going to die.

The world had become a much more dangerous place since Ed had joined the police. He had thought he had seen it all during his tours of duty in the Middle East. He had been glad to return home and join the force in his home town. He'd taken to the work of being a police officer like a duck to water. He'd become the Commander of the Las Vegas Special Tactics Unit just over a year ago. Originally the first such unit in the country, most big cities now had an STU. His team was picked from the best officers on the force. They were all well trained, strong, tough and heavily armed.

It had all started about fifteen years earlier when the first heroes had made their appearance, Solarstorm and Velocity among them. Initially, crime rates across the United States had actually dropped for a couple of years. Criminals were scared straight by the idea of being picked up by some muscle-bound spandex wearer and thrown through a building. After this short period had passed and the criminals had realised that heroes were here to stay, the criminal element of society had responded by becoming more aggressive and dangerous. They carried bigger guns and weren't shy about using them if it meant getting away from The Vanguard or the Blood Hunters or any one of a hundred active heroes. Ed occasionally felt nostalgic about the old days, when a masked guy robbing a bank with a handgun was the worst the police had to handle.

As one of the major tourist destinations in the USA, Las Vegas seemed to attract more than its fair share or weirdoes and eccentrics. After all, doesn't everyone visit Vegas eventually? Las Vegas had learned that even weirdoes and eccentrics have money to spend and, above all, the city loved people who had cash and were going to spend it. Lately the city fathers had decided to try softening the bad reputation the city had acquired over the years and tried to make it more of a place where you'd want to bring your whole family. It hadn't worked, not exactly. The city was a lot safer than before and it had lots of police but there was an undercurrent of danger that the drive to improve the city had only papered over.

As a last ditch effort the previous administration in city hall had invited The Vanguard to set up their headquarters in the city. To the politicians and business people, it was a great idea. The publicity worked wonders for the tourist numbers as The Vanguard were a tourist attraction in themselves. Ed personally thought that the whole idea was a bit tacky if he was being honest. But tackiness was Las Vegas's stock in trade. This was, after all, a city that had opened its arms to both Elton John and Celine Dion at different times in the past.

Vanguard Tower had only recently been completed; it had been constructed in record time, even by Nevada standards. There was one small problem. At this moment in time, The Vanguard were half a world away fighting Octoman. But wasn't that always the way with Superheroes? They were great when it came to defeating a mad person who wore underpants outside their trousers but they were worse than useless against a terrorist armed with an assault rifle and a brick of plastic explosive.

Ed turned to the small team that shared the roof with him. The STU had set up observation posts covering all the entrances and exits to The Sphinx. Officer Sarah Lieber was looking at the building through the infra-red scope attached to the top of her sniper rifle, gulping down the contents of a juice-box through a straw. Sarah was barely twenty and was by far the best shot on the force. She had been picked for the STU almost as soon as she had graduated from the academy. She turned to the Captain.

"Boss, I count twenty packages scattered around the building, looks like plastic explosives with a remote trigger, they got it all set up pretty quick. These aren't the usual type of idiots we get. They're good."

"The hostages?"

"They moved them into the centre of the gambling floor. I count at least fifty."

"Oh, that's just wonderful! Anything else? DJ?"

The tall, thick necked man to Ed's left was crouched over a laptop which was displaying the video feed from the cameras inside the casino, suddenly the feed cut out.

"Naw. They just cut the feed, must have severed the hard lines inside. They would have to pick a casino wouldn't they? No windows and the place is a maze inside, tables and slot machines. Plenty of cover. We go in without a plan and they'll tear us apart."

Ed sighed out loud. casinos were usually designed to have as few windows as possible. The owners didn't want you to notice if it was night or day outside. That way you wouldn't know what time it was and would keep gambling. Great for business, not so great if the police needed to raid the place.

"So, unless they want to talk there's not much we can do without the hostages being killed."

"Don't look like it" said DJ. "Our best bet is probably using a targeted electro-magnetic pulse to fry their detonators and rush them. It's risky for us and the hostages but, since the terrorists aren't talking or making any demands…"

"The hostages are dead anyway." finished Ed. "It looks like we'll have to go in and hope that we can get at least some of the hostages out."

Ed sat back, leaning against the low wall, His forehead glistening from sweat. The heat on the roof in the middle of the day was making them all sweat like crazy, dressed as they were in bulky, bullet-proof body armour.

Ed's communicator chirped in his ear. He touched the side of his helmet.

"Yes…? Mr. Mayor... No, sir... Yes sir!"

Sarah looked up at the Captain with a questioning look on her face. The Captain sighed. "He's calling in The Vanguard."

Night had fallen by the time The Vanguard had returned from Europe. The Darkwing hovered over the STU command post for a few seconds, trying to find a place to land. The Darkwing was a piece of engineering beyond anything Captain O'Grady had ever seen. It was completely silent and extremely fast. It touched down with barely a whisper from its engines and a door on the underside of the craft hissed open. A ramp extended from the doorway and The Vanguard strode towards the Captain and his team. The team members seemed to defer to Warfare when they were on a mission but Solarstorm usually acted as their spokesperson, Warfare wasn't much of a talker. Ed had worked with Solarstorm and Velocity a handful of times before, but he could tell that his team were a bit unnerved by them. Superheroes had a tendency to distract normal folks by their very presence. People seemed to act a bit odd when superheroes were around.

"Captain O'Grady" Solarstorm said as he walked towards them his arm outstretched to shake hands with Ed.

Solarstorm was tall, dark haired, broad across the shoulders and muscled like a bodybuilder. The dim glow he emitted made him look like a golden god striding across the parking lot of the shopping centre that was serving as a temporary base of operations for the police. Ed couldn't help smiling as he shook Solarstorm's hand. Solarstorm had that effect on people. He was so confident, graceful and, above all, nice, that you couldn't help feeling better around him, once you got over the fact that you were talking to one of the most famous people of all time.

"You've been briefed on the situation?" asked Ed.

"Yes, the Mayor told us on the flight over. Warfare has been working on a plan."

Warfare stepped forward and placed a palm sized metallic cube with a lens on one side on the ground. The cube flickered and began to project a holographic blueprint of The Sphinx.

Warfare's helmet amplified his voice so that he could be heard over the hustle and bustle of the command centre: "I'm going to fire an electro-magnetic pulse at the building from the Darkwing. That will shut down all electrical equipment, including the remote trigger for those explosives and the lights."

"That's what I..." DJ began to say before Sarah's arm shot out and caught him in the chest.

"Leave it, big guy." She hissed. "We don't want to start an argument with a dude who could throw us into California from here."

"Ok, so that's the explosives neutralised, what about the small problem of the armed terrorists and the hostages?" asked Ed, trying to get the conversation back on track.

"They'll be in the dark. The night vision gear those terrorists have will be shorted out by the EMP as well. Our equipment won't be. Mage will teleport in and get the hostages out." Solarstorm nodded to Mage, who stood at the back of the small group, his pale, post sickness, face hidden in the shadows created by the hood on his brown robe, the fingers of his right hand were wrapped tightly around his staff.

"Then Mountain crashes through a wall and starts hitting terrorists, it's not like their guns can damage him".

Mountain nodded and smiled the light glinting from his teeth: "My favourite pastime."

Ed noticed how Mountain's teeth shined like diamonds. Probably because they are diamond, he thought.

"Velocity will run the perimeter and make sure we have no escapee's." said Solarstorm.

"When do we start?" asked Velocity, her right foot tapping against the ground.

"Right now. Everyone to their positions. Captain, keep the STU in their current locations and have them back us up if needed. We'll make our move within the next five minutes."

Warfare returned to the Darkwing and powered its engines. It took off towards the casino. A beam of light shot out from the front of the plane and shrouded the entire complex in a silver-blue glow.

Warfare spoke over the team's commlink: "That's it!" Solarstorm and Mountain, get ready." Solarstorm bounded into the air and quickly flew into the sky; Mountain lurched forward surprisingly quickly for a rock monster the size of a truck.

"Mage, go!" said Warfare.

Mage disappeared from the parking lot in a haze of blue smoke and appeared inside the casino on the main gambling floor amongst the hostages, a number of whom screamed at the sudden appearance of a stranger in their midst.

"We're outta here!" Mage said as he raised his staff and slammed the end on it into the floor.

Mage and the hostages were suddenly enveloped in a soft green light and vanished. The terrorists didn't have time to react before the group disappeared.

Mountain pounded towards the foyer of the casino. The casino wall began to crumble even before he hit it.

"Shoddy construction, I knew they built this place too quickly." he roared as he smashed through the wall.

The first terrorist to see Mountain cried out for his mother in terror, wet himself, dropped to the floor, curled up into the foetal position, began sucking on his thumb and whimpered. The second terrorist managed to raise his gun but didn't get a chance to fire as Mountain picked him up and threw him thirty yards across the floor where he smashed into a slot machine. The sirens on top of the machine began to make a loud clanging noise. The machine dispensed its jackpot onto the concussed terrorists head.

Solarstorm and Warfare charged through the hole in the wall left by Mountain. Warfare drew his electron sword and swung it at the nearest terrorist. Solarstorm flew across the room, firing yellow energy beams from his hands. One of the terrorists slung his rifle over his shoulder without firing a shot and ran towards the back of the casino.

"We have a runner! Velocity, darling, beat him up." Solarstorm said.

"I'm on it" she said over the commlink.

The terrorist ran down a set of stairs towards the underground car park. He rushed over to a sleek and expensive looking motorbike parked nearby, took a screwdriver from the inside pocket of his jacket, shoved it into the ignition and twisted it. The engine coughed into life. He clambered on, throttled up, and drove away. The wheels screeched and sent smoke wafting up to the ceiling. The bike powered along the asphalt, smashed through the barrier that blocked the entrance to the garage, exited the building and took off down the Strip. The driver skilfully manoeuvred the bike between the police barricades. Sarah and DJ, manning one of the barricades, ran to a police cruiser and slid into the front seats. Ed opened the back door and joined them.

"What are you waiting for?" Ed slammed his fist on the seat, "Go, go!"

Sarah started the engine, put the car in gear and hammered down on the accelerator as they sped off in pursuit.

"Aren't you forgetting something?" Ed asked from the back seat.

"Ah, sorry!" Sarah replied as she simultaneously hit the buttons for the lights and sirens and then tuned the radio to the local heavy metal radio station.

"That's more like it. You can't have a car chase without the proper soundtrack!"

This guy on the bike is completely crazy. Velocity thought as she ran alongside the police cruiser, easily keeping pace with it. Velocity accelerated, her long silver hair streamed out behind her as she passed the one hundred mile per hour mark.

The terrorist looked behind to see if he was being chased, saw the silver and blue blur that was Velocity approaching him and pulled a handgun from his jacket pocket. He began firing wildly in Velocity's direction. She dodged between the bullets.

"Ha! Guys, this idiot is trying to shoot me, someone who can run faster than he can think! That's adorable!"

Warfare's voice came over the radio. "End this quickly Velocity. He could hit innocent bystanders."

"Innocent bystanders? In Las Vegas?" she replied.

Velocity caught up with the bike and clothes-lined the rider across the back of his head, sending him flying over the handlebars. He skidded along the ground and came to rest in a nearby gutter. Velocity continued to run.

"I need a few seconds to slow down. Can anybody else make pick up on the former cyclist?"

Ed's voice came through on her radio: "We're on it. Nice work."

The STU were on the scene seconds later. They got out of the car and trained their guns on the rider. Red laser targeting dots appeared on his chest and head. He groaned, tried to stand up and was hit in the face with the butt of Sarah's rifle for his trouble.

"Stay down" she said as DJ and Ed grabbed the rider and handcuffed his hands.

Not long after the teams were back at the police command post.

"Not a bad job at all." said Captain O'Grady as he supervised the loading of the terrorists into the back of a pair of waiting police wagons.

"Anyone hurt?" asked Solarstorm.

"One of the hostages had a mild heart attack when he suddenly appeared in the shopping centre car park; the paramedics say he'll be OK. Otherwise we're all good." said DJ.

Reporters had begun to cluster around the police command post.

"You'd better go to your adoring audience" said O'Grady to Solarstorm.

"Hey, we're just the Superheroes. You do what we do without any powers. Tell your team, we'd be happy to have you all over to the tower for a barbeque next weekend. It makes sense that they all get to know us if we need to work together again. I'm sorry if we put your officers to any inconvenience today. Thanks for the support."

"I'll tell them. Look after yourself."

"Same to you, Ed."

O'Grady watched as Solarstorm went to talk to the press.

Either that guy is completely messing with my head or he really is the nicest guy on Earth, he thought.

Chapter Five | Vanguard Tower

Ryan stared at the clock on his bedside table. He couldn't sleep. He'd spent the last hour trying unsuccessfully to drift into unconsciousness, even resorting to reading a maths book in the hope that it would bore him enough to cause him to pass out. Nothing had worked. It wasn't particularly late but he had a busy day tomorrow. What with it being the first proper day in his new school, with classes and homework. He needed to work hard this year. Ryan had more reason than most to be worried about moving school. He'd already changed schools twice in the last three years. The first reason a school could find to dismiss him and he was moved on. It made it difficult to make friends, He'd start in a new school and within days everyone would know who he was. Being the son of two Superheroes had made him pretty famous, not 'major movie star' famous, more like 'supporting actor in a moderately successful TV show' famous. Even so, people always found out who his parents were sooner or later. The other kids would pester him for a while, trying to get him to show off his powers (he didn't have any) or asking him questions about his parents, the fabulous Solarstorm and Velocity, AKA Jake and Lisa AKA dad and mom.

Ryan would play along for a while, but sooner or later the other children would lose interest and he'd be left alone or else they were too scared to talk to him at all. It all made for a lonely life. But he was at least as happy as any other fourteen year old. His parents, though usually busy out saving the world, weren't bad. They hadn't been needed as often this past year and Velocity was attempting to make up for twelve years of being an absent mother by smothering him with attention. Ryan wasn't sure which was worse.

Ryan heard the Darkwing returning to the tower and landing in the hangar fifteen stories above. The Darkwing flew silently but Ryan could hear the hanger door open and close. He decided to abandon his fruitless attempts at getting rest, got out of bed, put his slippers and nightgown on and went to the living room of the apartment. He sat down on the gigantic couch and waited for his parents to come in. He'd seen what they had done today on the news but he always liked hearing about their adventures. It was a little childish, he knew. But he didn't care. His mom and dad were Superheroes. He had the right to be a little nerdy about it.

Velocity and Solarstorm entered the apartment.

"All I'm saying is that Octoman was right about one thing, there's no one left to fight. We should consider slowing down and focusing on the charity work."

"You're asking the world's fastest person to slow down? After fifteen years together, do you know me at all?"

"We were talking about having another child a year back, why not consider it now. We're still young, relatively speaking."

"We'll talk about it later, I need a shower."

"I was sitting beside you on the flight back, you need two showers."

Velocity punched Solarstorm in the shoulder softly.

"Remind me why I married you again?"

"It was my broad shoulders, wasn't it? Admit it!

Velocity saw Ryan on the couch: "Hey sweetie, did we wake you up?"

"Not really. Are you two thinking of retiring?"

"We'll talk about it tomorrow. We're tired and you need to get to bed too. See you at breakfast."

"She's right" said Solarstorm. "Let's get some sleep and leave the life changing decisions for the morning."

"How was Spain?"

"We didn't get to see a whole lot over there, what with the explosions, the life threatening situations and all that stuff." said Solarstorm.

"So… no presents then? Is that what you're hinting at?"

"No, there weren't a lot of gift shops on that floating fortress; I think Mountain brought you back pieces of a robot he destroyed though."

"Really? The giant crab thing they showed on the news? Cool!"

"You can get it from him tomorrow after school. Now, go to bed."

Next day, Velocity sped into the kitchen in her dressing gown to put the coffee on. Mage was sitting at the table with a full breakfast already prepared.

"Morning!" he said cheerfully.

"Mage?! What in the name of heaven are you doing?" she tied the belt of her dressing gown tighter, making sure she was completely covered up. "Since when do you get up this early? How did you get in here?"

"I can walk through walls when I need to."

Velocity covered her face with her hands, it was too early in the morning to be dealing with this guy: "Why did you 'need' to walk through ours first thing in the morning?"

"I need a small favour. Tiny, you could even say its infinitesimal. My new line of wholesome, healthy foodstuffs is getting its official launch today. Photographers, TV cameras, all that good stuff. I could use backup. It'd be good PR for the team!"

Solarstorm entered the room dressed in a navy suit, a blue shirt and tie.

"This is the same 'wholesome' stuff that you complained gave you diarrhoea last month?" He asked.

"The very same. The doctor actually said it was chronic diarrhoea, by the way. I have a sick note." Mage picked up a box of breakfast cereal from the table. "Check this out. It's called 'Mages Choice' and it's worth a lot of money to selected charities."

Velocity examined the box, which had a picture of Mage smiling and giving a thumbs up as he used a spoon to scoop up cereal from a bowl.

She laughed: "Do these 'charities' include the local bars, restaurants and clothes stores?"

"Oh, what's this? I'm getting harassment from the woman who endorsed those running shoes that are made by five year olds in a sweatshop."

"Those allegations were never proven!" Velocity retorted.

Solarstorm raised his voice to try and stop the developing argument: "We're not interested Mage. Buying a lot of fancy food from your company won't make people healthier or thinner, why not just tell people to eat fruit and vegetables and exercise if they want to be healthy?"

"Because" Mage said slowly, as if speaking to a child; "that's… not… profitable. Mage's Choice is more than just a food brand. The very name conjures up a lifestyle choice that means no stress and no effort, just the need to spend money on these 'dried fruit crunchies' that I'm selling."

Solarstorm sat down and poured himself a large cup of coffee.

"Very nice. Was that a quote from the press release?"

"Yes." said a suddenly assertive Mage

"No deal. People are told to buy useless junk by companies all the time; we're not getting involved in that."

"Fine, ok. But what about that reality show that my agent is trying to set up over at the TV network? Can't you at least sign off on that?"

"Not happening. We're private individuals. We don't like seeing our faces plastered everywhere."

"We're the world's greatest heroes. We're going to have our faces everywhere whether we want to or not. Am I the only one who wants to make a moderate amount money off of that?"

Solarstorm sighed: "We're well looked after by the government. Velocity and I love to do the charity work but we're not in this for the money. In fact we're thinking of stepping back from all this."

"You're breaking up the band?!" asked Mage, surprised.

"We've been talking about it."

A tear appeared in Mage's eye. He fell off his chair and got down on his knees:

"Please, please do this for me! For us! For the good of humanity! Couldn't you at least wait until my brand has established itself in the marketplace?"

"That was much better than usual, have you been practicing your grovelling technique?"

Mage began to cry: "I don't want to die poor! I don't want to!"

Real tears continued to streak down his cheeks as he pounded his fist on the floor and wailed.

"We're not needed Mage." Velocity cut in, "Yesterday was the first action we've seen in six months. Our family deserves a normal life. We've been superheroes but not great parents for a long while now.

It's time for us to fix that."

Mage got to his feet and wiped the tears from his eyes: "Thanks for that rousing speech, Yoko Ono. You two are a disappointment!"

Mage strode to the door, opened it and slammed it loudly, for effect. He turned around to face Velocity and glared angrily at her for a few seconds. He finally left the apartment by passing through the wall as if it wasn't there.

Solarstorm looked puzzled: "How is it that he can enter our apartment and make breakfast without making a sound but he always makes sure to slam the door when he's leaving?"

"Typical Irishman."

Solarstorm tried some of the cereal. It was terrible. He coughed most of the mouthful into a napkin and washed the remainder of the cereal down with orange juice.

"That's awful; I think I'll have toast instead."

Solarstorm picked up a slice of bread in his right hand and pointed his left index finger at it; his finger emitted a soft orange glow, within seconds the bread started to toast.

"Do you want to discuss what we said last night?" asked Velocity "Ryan will be up soon and we should talk to him about it".

"I think we're done. The super criminals are all safely locked away and the police are well able to handle everything else, they could have dealt with that hostage situation in the casino without our help. The Mayor didn't need to call us in for that."

"Yeah, you're right. I've been thinking the same for a while."

Ryan walked into the room, dressed in jeans and a t-shirt, carrying a schoolbag over his right shoulder. Solarstorm smiled at him:

"So kiddo, you ready for your first day of public school?"

Ryan nodded: He had already decided not to tell them that he had actually started yesterday. It would upset them if they realised that they had forgotten the correct date. "Got my switchblade, some notebooks, my laptop and these writing sticks." He said, fishing in his backpack and producing three ballpoint pens.

"Pens? I remember those. Is your switchblade properly sharpened?" Solarstorm deadpanned.

"I think so; Warfare gave it to me last Christmas. He doesn't usually give inferior sharp objects as gifts."

Solarstorm looked across into the living room to see the display of old fashioned weaponry that Warfare had given the family over the years, battle-axes, swords and even a mace were displayed in various locked cabinets. Warfare had odd ideas about what people could receive for birthdays and Christmas, but his heart was in the right place.

"Honey, leave that at home!" said Velocity

"Mum, I don't really have one." said Ryan, a little exasperated, "I asked Warfare but he said I wasn't ever going to need one."

"He's right; this is a public school you're going to, not Iraq."

"Ok, but if I come home covered in bruises…"

"Could you try to avoid that kind of thing? We're running out of schools to send you to."

"Tell the kids to stop picking on me just because my dad can knock buildings over and my mum can run faster than anyone else on the planet. Things are a lot different to when you two were in school."

"Hey" Velocity cut in "We had it hard growing up too!"

"You had powers, I don't."

"You still might. You're only fourteen."

"I'd prefer not to get any, thanks. Am I supposed to grow up to be a super-powered accountant or lawyer?"

Solarstorm grabbed his car keys from the kitchen counter: "Come on, I'll drive you to school. We still have plenty of time to ruin your life for you. You're our responsibility until you turn eighteen."

"Yeah, you two go on ahead" said Velocity. "This apartment is a pigsty; I'm going to clean it."

Ryan looked around the spotless apartment; "Mum, we really need to get you a hobby. I hear that knitting is a lot of fun."

"I already tried it. I can knit a jumper in forty seconds. Your dad has a wardrobe full of them from when we started dating."

"I never wear them because they're so special." said Solarstorm. "It's definitely not because they're in garish colours that make my eyes bleed."

"We're going to be late!" said Ryan, checking his watch.

Solarstorm smiled: "See Lisa? He gets that from you. We'll speak to Warfare when I get back."

"Sure, go. I'll see you in an hour or so."

Ryan sat in the passenger seat of his dad's car as they drove through the traffic on the way to school.

"Listen Ryan. Your mom and I are worried. Are you going to be OK in this new school? You've had a lot of trouble fitting in everywhere."

"Having superhero parents doesn't lead to making friends easily."

"I can understand that. It's difficult to make friends at all. You'd be surprised how few we have. Outside of the hero community, I mean."

"Because you have powers?"

"That's part of it, but it's more like regular folks don't really approach us as people. We're icons, like famous actors or singers. People see the glitzy public façade but not what's inside. The fact that we're famous makes our relationships a bit on the superficial side. People want to be friends with you for what you can do for them. Not necessarily because of the person you are. We don't want that for you. If there's a chance for you to be a normal person, unaffected by all the craziness that this life brings, then we're going to take it."

"Which means what exactly?"

"It means we want you to study and talk to kids your own age, your best friend at the moment is a walking pile of rocks that likes to smash robots."

"I'll try."

"Good, I'm not sure that I'll be able to pick you up, you can get the school bus home if neither your mother nor I can make it. I've a feeling that the meeting with Warfare is going to take time. Enjoy your day. Try to talk to other teenagers, preferably ones who aren't members of a gang."

Mage was in heaven. He had teleported directly from Vanguard Tower onto the lush red carpet leading to the entrance of the nightclub. It wouldn't do for him to roll up to the club in a limo like the normal celebrities. He had to be seen arriving, His PR people had told him so. Exposure was what it was all about. A few pictures in tomorrow's paper and the tabloid celebrity magazines would be great free publicity for his brand. It was the launch party for his range of wholesome foodstuffs: he needed to talk and act like the biggest star in the world. This evening, the inside of the Velvet nightclub in Monte Carlo was heaving with musicians, actors and models. All invited and promised the night of their lives so that they'd turn up for a few minutes and garner him plenty of free advertising. It would be the crowning achievement of their empty little lives.

I could get used to this. He thought as he waved at the crowd of screaming fans, some of whom were being paid by his manager to do exactly that. Mage meandered along the red carpet, pausing to take pictures with the public and sign copies of his best-selling autobiography A Magical Life. Entertainment reporters from across the world queued up to exchange a few words with him. He spoke; answered questions and name dropped Mage's Choice as often as possible. He performed magic for the crowd, casting illusions and conjuring up fireworks from his staff.

He entered the club. A DJ was playing electro music at a volume just this side of ear-splitting, the crowd was dancing and drinking, reporters and paparazzi were everywhere and everyone was having fun!

He liked the other members of The Vanguard, after a fashion. They were boring and dependable. Exactly what you needed when facing super villains but they weren't the type to party. Solarstorm and Velocity kept to themselves when not on a mission, Warfare didn't really speak to anyone and gave the worst presents. Mountain meditated a lot. None of them liked to party and Mage suspected that at least two of his team-mates were unable to.

These were his people, the rich and famous. They all looked up to him, no matter if they had a number one album or earned a million dollars for standing in front of a camera for a few weeks, there were fewer than one hundred active heroes on Earth and he was one of the elite. He was one of The Vanguard. He was important. No matter how successful the other party attendees were, they'd be forgotten in a generation or two. Not him. Mage's name would live on for eternity, of that he was sure.

Mage worked the room, he posed for photographs with other celebrities, drank a glass of champagne with that guy who played the vampire in that movie and danced with a couple of models. His attention was drawn to a woman dancing on her own in the middle of the dance floor. She was gorgeous; her long blonde hair swirled in circles as she moved gracefully around the floor. Mage walked over to join her, a glass of wine in his hand. The dance floor throbbed underneath his feet, it moved in time to the music, pulsing to the bass line coming through the speakers. Mage had to shout to be heard:

"Thirsty?"

The woman didn't stop dancing but smiled at him and delicately took the glass from his hands. She drank the wine in one long gulp.

"It's pretty good isn't it? French I think." said Mage

"Better than I'm used to." she replied, throwing her arms in the air then wrapping them around Mage's shoulders.

"So, you come here often?" Mage asked.

"First time, I never usually get out much."

"That's a shame, why did you come here tonight?"

"To meet you, of course."

Mage smiled:" Why is that?"

She grabbed his arm and pulled him over to the side of the dance floor.

"To get to know you better."

"You know: you're awfully strong." said Mage, wincing at the vice like grip she had on his arm.

"I know."

"So let's get to know you better." Mage said confidently "What's your name?"

She looked into his eyes as she prepared to kiss him. Her lips met his for a long second.

"Do you want to go somewhere more private? My car's parked nearby." She said, once her lips left his.

"Yeah, why not? I've done enough mingling. My picture will definitely be in the paper now."

They left the club by a side door and stepped into an empty alley. Mage looked both ways and then turned towards the girl.

"Where's your car?"

"The other end of the alley."

"So... You never told me your name."

Mage didn't see her dip her hand into her handbag and pull out the syringe but he felt it bite into his neck. He looked at her stupidly, his hand rising to the puncture the needle had left behind, not believing what had just happened. She removed the now empty needle from his neck and threw it onto a pile of rubbish bags. Mage's world began to spin; his brain struggled to think coherently:

She's tranquilised me. Mage thought as he slumped onto the ground. His staff slipped from his fingers and disappeared in a flash of dazzling green light.

The woman blinked her eyes to get rid of the afterimages. She hadn't expected that to happen. She shrugged her shoulders and looked back at Mage, who was moving his lips. He was trying to speak. Mage tried to whisper the words of a spell to teleport away. It wouldn't work. His powers had left when his staff did. He was trapped.

She smiled at him as he lay paralysed on the dirty bricks of the alley: "My name is Maria."

It was the last thing Mage heard as the darkness closed in on him.

"You can't quit!" said Warfare as soon as Solarstorm and Velocity told him of their decision. "Our work is too important, there's too much danger still out there."

"There really isn't. Warfare, we've given fifteen years to this job. The world's a better place. Life's too short for us to wait around for danger while life passes us by." said Solarstorm.

"There are plenty of others to take up the slack now, there are nearly a hundred heroes out there and most of them are on your speed dial if there's an emergency." said Velocity.

Warfare sat back in his chair. They were in The Vanguard operations centre. It took up an entire floor of the tower. The centre of the room contained a large, round, wooden conference table with inbuilt screens and a holo-projector. An LCD screen, currently displaying a map of the world, took up on entire wall.

"Is this to do with your personality clash with Mage?" asked Warfare as he drew a knife from his belt and spun it in his hand. It was an affectation he had when he was deep in thought.

"What personality clash...?" began Solarstorm.

"Yes, that's a big part of it." interrupted Velocity. "I have no idea why you asked him to be on the team. He's immature and an idiot."

"We needed a magician. As far as I can tell he's the only one with that specific type of power."

"Maybe so. But have you read that ghost written autobiography of his? He claims he was trained in the magical arts by 'Secret Masters' in the Himalayas. That's nonsense. He found a magic stick in a field after he spent the night passed out in a ditch. He's a liar and he's only out for himself. I don't feel safe on missions with him on the team."

"Lisa, calm down." said Solarstorm. "Leaving my beloved wife's problems out of this for a second. We're tired of this life Warfare. We've never taken a holiday. We aren't even able to go out to dinner without being recognised."

"Leaving the team won't change that. You'll still be famous."

"For a while, and then people will forget about us, other heroes can take our place. There's plenty of talent out there. Wolfhound and Lightbomb would be more than able to take our places."

"I suppose you're right. And it's not like this is a military unit, more's the pity. If it was I'd be able to do something about Mage going off the grid all the time."

"You've lost contact with Mage?" said Solarstorm.

"No surprises there." said Velocity

"Yes, a few hours ago. He was in Monte Carlo and then nothing."

"Monte Carlo?"

"The launch of Mage's Choice. He practically begged Mountain and I to go for the publicity. We refused. Mountain wanted to go to his yoga class and I'd rather swallow this knife than talk to the press."

"You're not worried?"

"He often turns off his tracer and communicator. It's usually when he's in the cinema, or a concert or where-ever."

A warning light flashed on the console in front of Warfare. He pulled up the display and hit a few keys on the keyboard.

"That's Mage's signal now. According to this he's in Florida and his life signs aren't too good. Slow heart rate. Very little brain activity."

"No change there then." said Velocity.

"This is different, he could be in a coma." said Warfare. "I think he needs our help."

"Let's go!" said Solarstorm. He held his right hand up against his ear, touching his earpiece "Mountain! Mage is in trouble. Meet us at the Darkwing."

Velocity was already at the Darkwing when Mountain, Warfare and Solarstorm joined her.

"Engines are warming up; we'll be airborne in a minute. This better not be his idea of a practical joke. Or a ruse to get us all to show up at a press conference." she said "Where is he exactly?"

Warfare checked the computer built into his helmet: "The tracer is coming from an airport outside of Homestead in Florida."

"What's he doing there? That's a long way from Monte Carlo."

"Who knows?"

They launched from the hangar. Velocity piloted the Darkwing as it sped off in the afternoon light.

They arrived at the Homestead airport within ten minutes.

"Where is he exactly?" asked Velocity from the cockpit.

"Just off the runway, near the swamp and the waterway"

Velocity made the Darkwing hover near to the location Warfare described. Velocity put the Darkwing on autopilot and joined the others.

"Come on!" said Solarstorm as he jumped out of the hatch in the Darkwing's underbelly and landed on the dirt road near the bridge. Mountain and the rest of the team followed.

"I don't like this, it feels wrong. Why would he come here?" said Mountain.

"Expect a trap." said Solarstorm.

They walked over the bridge. Warfare led, drawing his electron sword with one hand and using his computer to follow the tracer. He saw what looked like a small pile of rubbish near the far end.

Velocity ran past Warfare and knelt down by the pile. It was Mage. She touched his neck with her fingers, looking for a pulse. He was dead.

"He's gone". She said. She had tears in her eyes. "I'm going to find whoever did this and hurt them very, very badly!"

A voice echoed across the open space from the other side of the canal: "You won't have far to look."

"Who's there?" said Solarstorm.

A woman stepped forward. Her long blonde hair tied back in a ponytail. She was wearing a black armoured suit. Futuristic devices of all kinds hung off the web gear draped across her shoulders. In her right hand, the woman carried a heavy looking mace which emitted an electrical glow.

"Who the heck are you?" asked Solarstorm.

"I'm your executioner."

Chapter Six | The Battle of Homestead

The Nanotech in Maria's body sang to her like a choir of mechanical angels. She felt a rush of adrenaline as her mind kicked into overdrive; time seemed to slow as the army of microscopic robots in her bloodstream made calculations, trying to predict the reactions of The Vanguard based on their behaviour in past battles.

Velocity moved first, as always. She jumped over Mage's corpse and ran straight towards Maria, ready to wring her neck.

The information that she had downloaded in the facility flashed through Maria's head. She doesn't reach maximum speed and reaction time for four point two seconds.

Maria's hand moved faster than the eye could see as she unclipped an anti-gravity disc from her belt. The disc was smaller than the palm of her hand, a tiny grey circle with a red button, the back of the disc was coated with a super strong adhesive. Maria slipped to the side as Velocity ran towards her; Velocity was a black and silver blur to normal eyes but not to Maria's enhanced senses. Velocity missed her by less than an inch. Maria hit the red button and stuck the disc to the small of Velocity's back. Velocity shot upwards into the sky, faster than a rocket.

"Lisa!" cried Solarstorm as he launched himself into the air to chase after Velocity who was accelerating into the atmosphere.

Maria pulled a black, oval shaped, grenade from her belt and tossed it at Solarstorm before he could fly out of range. It hit him on the chest and exploded. Solarstorm found himself caught in a web of electricity. He roared in pain as the blue waves of current raged through his body. He flew recklessly, struggling to break free as the power surged through him. He convulsed and hit the ground several hundred metres away from the bridge. Dirt and water flew skywards as he gouged a crater out of the earth when he crash-landed.

"Well" Maria said: "That's three of you dead already. You had better call for reinforcements, Warfare."

"Mountain, I'm going to fall back to the Darkwing and call in the cavalry. Do what you have to, just slow her down and keep safe. I'll be back in two minutes."

"Right!" growled Mountain.

Warfare started to walk backwards, keeping his eyes on Maria all the time.

Mountain moved forward slowly. His arms raised in a boxers fighting posture. His eyes darted to the left and right, looking for an opening.

Maria raised her mace as the Nanotech analysed this new threat and fed the data directly to her brain and muscles:

"Mountain. What do I know about you? Let's see. Incredibly strong, tough, able to withstand a lot of punishment and you have no idea who I am."

"I know you're arrogant. Only someone who's overconfident talks when they're supposed to be fighting."

"Very true, shall we do this?"

Mountain closed the distance between them. He threw a swift jab. She ducked under it and rolled to his left. She planted herself on the ground and lashed out with her right leg at the back of his left knee. Mountain heard a sharp crack as a piece of his rocky skin was chipped off and flew away.

He'd never been chipped before. Not by Octoman's robots or any of the villains The Vanguard had fought over the years. He turned towards the woman, who had rolled away and gotten to her feet. She stood a few metres away in a fighting stance. Her legs bent, hands guarding her face, mace at the ready.

"Would you like to try again?" she asked.

He ducked his head as he ran towards her. She stood her ground until the last second and stepped away with a flourish, swinging her mace in an unstoppable backhand stroke as she did so. The mace hit Mountain on his left fist, shattering it.

"Aggghhhhh!" he roared.

"This isn't a regular weapon." Maria taunted: "It's called a seismic mace, It's powerful enough to cause localised earthquakes or pulverise rock, as you've just seen. This fight isn't going to go well for you."

Warfare had made it back to the Darkwing and entered the cockpit. Velocity hadn't been exaggerating when she had made the joke about him having every Superhero in the world on his speed dial. He would hit this woman who'd killed his friends with so many brightly attired heroes that she'd be knocked through time to next Wednesday. He hit the buttons on the Darkwing's communication console that would sent out a broad wave to every hero he knew.

"This is Warfare. The Vanguard have engaged an unknown villain on the outskirts of the Homestead Airport in Florida. She's... she's killed Mage, Velocity and Solarstorm. Every hero who receives this message, please head to our location at top speed. We'll try to hold out as long as possible."

Warfare set the message to repeat. Hopefully help would be here shortly. Warfare drew his sword again and set it to 'Carve'. This woman, whoever she was, was about to enter a world of pain.

Mountain was not doing well. Two minutes into the fight and she'd already managed to inflict serious damage. Parts of him were chipped, cracked and crushed. He hadn't been able to lay a finger on her. The pain from where his destroyed hand had been was dulling his senses. She was too fast and well trained. Mountain was a brawler, used to letting his raw strength do all the work. He was so much stronger than those they usually fought that he often was able to end the fight by landing one solid punch. If only he could land one now.

"So, is this your first fight?" she asked.

She was mocking him, trying to get a reaction. He swung his remaining fist in her direction. He was too slow. She weaved under it, danced away and swung her mace again, Mountain felt a sharp pain as the mace crunched into his side, a piece of rock the size of a dinner plate fell off his body. He fell down, landing on his chest.

"Come on, I've been fighting you at half speed here and you haven't even gotten within two feet of me." She said.

"Aggggh!" screamed Mountain in defiance as he rose.

Maria swung the mace underhand. It crashed into Mountain's sternum. The impact of the mace caused a sandstorm as the wind that the blow displaced whirled around them. Mountain staggered backwards and looked down at his chest as a crack appeared. Yellow light from inside his body poured from the crack. She'd broken him open. Mountain gasped. She swung again. This blow caught

Mountain on his right bicep. He was knocked to the ground by the force of the strike.

Maria pivoted as Warfare ran towards them. He had his sword in hand as he rushed her. The blade of his electron sword glowed a deep crimson.

"So, time for the next round is it? I was worried that I'd get bored pummelling your rocky friend into the ground. I could use a change of pace. This fight just keeps getting more interesting."

"It won't be so interesting when I start carving pieces off you."

"Try it."

Warfare slid forward, testing her reactions. She parried his blade with her mace. He threw his sword from his right to his left hand and slashed at her left side. She didn't try to block it, Warfare's blade should have sliced her arm off but instead it bounced away and cut a rock on the ground cleanly in two.

"Forcefield?" he asked

"Yes."

She was going to give him a lot of trouble. Her mace came down as she swung it diagonally, trying to hit him between the shoulder and the neck. Warfare shuffled backwards. The mace missed him by inches but she used the momentum to raise it above her head and hit the ground. The earth below Warfare's feet buckled from the force of the blow. The nearby bridge broke in two as a ten foot high wall of dirt rippled out from where the woman stood. Warfare was flipped into the air by the giant wave, landing in the canal. He swam under the surface of the water, hoping that the dirty brown liquid would obscure him from her sight for long enough to get his breath back. He needed to get some distance on her to give him time to prepare himself to fight her again. He swam swiftly downstream. An object broke the surface of the water directly in front of him. It was a small silver grenade. Time seemed to slow down as Warfare stared at it, it felt to him like it took an epoch for the explosion to come, he could have sworn that he saw the stress lines appear on the face of the grenade as it exploded in a flash of bright white light that swallowed him whole.

Solarstorm awoke to the sound of Warfare speaking in his ear. He listened groggily, not really hearing it. The message was playing on a loop. It sounded like a distress call. Solarstorm lay at the bottom of the crater that his unplanned descent had caused. Every part of his body ached, half buried as it was under a mixture of mud, water and his own blood.

He lifted a pile of debris off his body with his arms and managed to push himself upright. He jumped and tried to fly and found that he couldn't. Whatever that unknown woman had hit him with had drained his powers. He depended on a healthy charge of sunlight to power his stronger abilities like the energy blasts and flight. He was still able to move though. One way or another, he promised, he'd get revenge on the woman who'd killed his wife. He dragged himself over to the crater wall and began to climb by digging his fingers into the dirt and bracing against the soil to gain traction. It was agonising. He gasped in pain but carried on inching his way up. He eventually reached the top. It was pitch dark, even the light of the moon was obscured by think clouds of acrid, black smoke.

No chance of a recharge I guess. He looked around. The area was sombrely lit by numerous fires. Far away to his left he saw the Darkwing on the ground, slit open, burning brightly. Small explosions peppered the night air as the ammunition on board detonated. He heard the distinctive sound of pulse blasts behind him. He turned; sure enough he could see someone firing in the distance. Another figure was dodging the shots and laughing. The laughing figure threw a long and shiny piece of metal at the shooter, who let out a harsh scream and collapsed.

Solarstorm walked forward slowly and tripped on a rock, his feet slipped on some gravel. He fell heavily; the wind was momentarily knocked out of his lungs. Spots flashed in front of his eyes as his ribs complained from the rough treatment. Solarstorm was pretty certain that at least four of them were broken, one in particular rasped in his chest, cutting deep into his flesh. He stared at the rocks closely as he got back up. They weren't rocks. It was Mountain's body. He had been shattered into pieces.

Crossing the field seemed to take a lifetime. Everywhere he looked, Solarstorm saw victims of the battle. He stepped over the body of a young woman in a white outfit he recognised:

"Lightbomb." He whispered. She was obviously dead; her eyes were wide open, looking at the sky with an expression that conveyed utter terror. Solarstorm noticed that her arms were missing, removed at the shoulders. Solarstorm reached down, closed the young woman's eyes and whispered a prayer for her.

He looked around. Lightbomb was just one of many corpses that littered the area. Solarstorm saw other heroes he recognised, all of them were dead.

The woman, the one who had murdered so many heroes had a man wearing a red and blue uniform in her grasp. Solarstorm didn't recognise the victim. One of the English heroes maybe? He guessed by the Union Jack influenced colours the man was wearing. Whoever it was barely struggled as the woman snapped his neck.

Maria stood and looked at the western horizon. The sun had set; the dull red glow of the waning sun had left the sky minutes before. She had just dispatched the last group of heroes that she was expecting. News helicopters orbited the airport; they'd been there for the previous five hours, the first one had arrived not long after she'd killed the second wave of heroes to show up. The news crews had diligently broadcast the day's events to the entire world. She raised her mace in triumph, it felt good.

Suddenly she felt as if she was being watched: she turned around slowly and saw Solarstorm standing not far away.

"I thought I'd killed you already." she said.

"Who?"

"Who was he? He was Slice, leader of The Bloodhunters, those English soccer hooligans turned "heroes". I always thought they were just a bunch of losers who liked to beat up people. Who am I? I'm the person who just liberated the world from your kind. My name isn't really important."

"Why are you doing this?"

"You've changed the world, Solarstorm. Just by your very existence, you've made normal people feel weak. We don't do anything for ourselves anymore. Instead, we depend on our 'protectors' for everything. People stand on the ground, looking at the sky just to catch a glimpse of you, their heroes. They wish with all their hearts that they were up there with you, never realising that the human race could be so much more if we tried to solve our own problems.

Humanity's progress and evolution has taken a massive step backwards ever since you appeared on the scene. You're venerated as gods come to earth. I'm changing things back to how they once were."

"Do you think killing so many of us will accomplish what you want?"

"Yes, I started with your team. The best and the brightest. Warfare sent out a distress call like I knew he would, calling all of your friends from across the world. I've killed as many as were brave enough to come." She nodded to the sky, towards one of the news helicopters which was circling in the distance: "And I've done it in public. The world has watched as I personally killed eighty-five of your kind. As far as I'm aware, and I'm very well informed, I've slaughtered nearly all of the active heroes on the planet. As far as I know there's only seven left, well, eight including you."

"Eight?" Solarstorm said, dumbfounded. "How did you do all this?"

"I've been studying your kind for years; I helped compile an entire database of knowledge on all of you. How you fight, your powers, your reactions to every given situation. And that database is now in my head."

"And you used it to kill us all."

"Not yet, you're still around. I'm glad you're still alive actually. I was looking forward to killing you up close and personal. Your wife died fifty miles up, gasping for breath. She was no fun at all. I'll take my time with you, if given the opportunity."

"You'll have it. Trust me."

"Of course, I'll also have to find the ones who were too scared or just unable to travel here today as well. I'll have to kill your son too.

Ryan, is it? The only child of the world's greatest heroes. He's too dangerous to let live."

"I won't let you hurt him!" Solarstorm shouted as he jumped at Maria.

She hit him in the face with her seismic mace. Solarstorm felt as if she'd struck him full force with the Titanic. He fell to his hands and knees, too weak to move. She stood over him.

"Goodbye, Solarstorm. You'll be with your wife soon enough. Ryan will join you both shortly." She said as she raised the mace, gripped it with both her hands and smashed it into the back of his head.

Maria stood still, exhausted from the battle. Super powered she may be, but she'd expended enough energy in the last few hours to power a city for a week.

I've done it. I've wiped them all out, The Vanguard, The Bloodhunters. All of them. Maria laughed and raised her mace to the night sky.

"Do you hear me? I've done it. We're responsible for our own futures now! No more heroes or villains interfering in our lives."

A voice rang out from the darkness of the sky: "That not true, baby. I count one more bad guy left!"

"Who?"

"Particle accelerator cannon!!!" the voice screamed.

Maria staggered back as she was hit by an incandescent blue beam of energy. The beam was so intense she was blinded for a few moments. As the spots in front of her eyes began to clear she felt a metallic fist hit her on the right hand side of her face. Her mace slipped from her grasp and flew into the distance. She didn't have time to react before she was kicked in the stomach.

Maria wasn't prepared for the onslaught, besides, the energy blast had actually hurt her and served to taken her shields down. She could feel the skin on her face burning from the heat of the beam. She fell onto her back and saw a suit of black and red armour standing over her. The armour was over twelve feet tall and had rocket pods clamped to its upper arms. The fires all around were reflected in its polished carapace, machine guns and energy blasters of various types bristled on its wrists. Maria noticed rocket boosters on its back and lower legs.

She rolled out of the way as the machine's foot hit the ground where her chest had been. She crouched and ran towards the canal where her mace had landed after it had been blasted from her hand by the newcomer's first attack. She slid along the ground, grabbed the mace in her left hand and got to her feet facing the armoured robot or whatever it was.

"That nice tech you got there, lady" said the voice coming from the armour. "Pity for you mine better."

The armour's right arm reached over its right shoulder and it unclipped a weapon from its back. There was a clanging noise as the figure gripped the shaft of a large double headed battle-axe and hit it against its left palm, as if testing the weight of the weapon.

The Nanotech in her mind sent warning signals through her nervous system:

"I don't know who you are" Maria said slowly, suddenly unsure of herself. She'd won so far because she knew how the heroes would fight down to the last detail and had been able to anticipate their actions.

It doesn't matter. She thought. I've beaten nearly a hundred heroes today, barely breaking a sweat; one more shouldn't be too much trouble.

"I a new hero. I not know who you are either!"

"Don't I at least get a name?"

"My name is Mech, prepare for battle!!!"

Maria head the hydraulics in the suit strain as it sprinted towards her with the axe above its head.

"WAR AXE SLICER ATTACK!!!"

The axe came down so quickly Maria could barely see the blades; she raised the mace to block it. As the weapons clashed there was a clap of thunder, orange sparks and blue bolts of electricity flew in every direction, bouncing harmlessly off or being absorbed by the metal skin of the suit of armour. Maria wasn't so lucky, she received a severe electric shock which nearly knocked her out cold and sent her hurtling backwards towards the canal.

My shields are down; I need to end this quickly. She said to herself when she came to a stop.

Warfare painfully opened his eyes, wondering what had just happened to him.

Oh, right. A grenade. His mind was fuzzy from the after-effects of the explosion.

His armour had taken the brunt of the blast but still seemed to be relatively intact, except for a clutch of nasty deep slashes in his armour. His visor had a handful of small cracks which water was seeping in through. Three of his fingers on his right hand were broken. He swam upwards, towards the surface. As he did so, he could see flashes of light above him on dry land. He smiled inside his helmet:

The battle is still on! Help must have arrived.

He swam upwards towards the surface and the bank of the canal. He stuck his head up to assess the situation. The tactical sensors in his helmet took in information from overhead satellites, news feeds and radar with the result information fed to the display on the inside of his visor. The woman was in a duel with someone wearing a suit of armour. The woman had her back to the canal and was being forced backwards by the thundering blows of her opponent. She wasn't fighting as confidently as she was earlier but she was managing to defend herself. As she leaped backwards to dodge the swinging axe of her opponent, Warfare made his move. He jumped and landed directly behind her, catching her right arm in a lock, leaving her defenceless.

"NOW!" Warfare shouted at the armoured suit "Finish her off."

The armoured suit back flipped, its thrusters pushing it backwards to gain distance on Warfare and the woman struggling to break free in his arms. The armour dropped onto one knee and prepared to fire a rocket.

"Nanotech storm missile!!!" Mech shouted as he fired.

The missile launched and flew directly at Maria. It shattered against her chest. She grabbed Warfare with her left arm and elbowed him sharply in the chest. Warfare released his grip and fell down, gasping for breath. Maria looked down at her chest where the missile had hit.

"Was that supposed to do something?" She asked.

"Wait for it!" Mech replied.

Maria prepared to attack Mech again, raising her mace. Suddenly she felt a horrific pain in her head, she screamed. Her brain felt as if it was on fire. The agony was vicious and unbearable. Her scream changed pitch, growing louder before it abruptly petered out. She collapsed to the ground and stopped moving.

Mech walked over to where Warfare lay.

"You OK, buddy?" Mech asked.

"I've had worse." Warfare attempted to stand up; Mech placed one of his giant hands on Warfare's shoulder and steadied him.

"What did you do to her?" Warfare asked.

"Nanotech storm missile."

"I understood that much, but what did it do?"

"It releases thousands of machines into her bloodstream to activate all her pain receptors at once. It very painful. Most people probably die. Her? I don't know. Shut down her brain and put her into coma maybe. She have serious upgrades."

"Well, I'm glad it's finished. Where are the other heroes? I called everyone I know but I don't recognise you."

"I new at this, it first time I take suit out. I see battle on TV and come as soon as I could. Other heroes all dead or too scared to come fight I think. Look around you."

Warfare looked around; he saw the bodies of his fellow Vanguard and scores of other heroes. For the first time in his life, Warfare didn't know what to do. The world still needed saving but there was no one left to do it.

Chapter Seven | Kidnapped

Aimee was bored. She was sitting outside the women's changing rooms in Carísimo, a world famous clothing store in Rodeo Drive, Los Angeles. It was world famous in the sense that everyone had heard of it but very few had actually bought anything from it. This particular store charged ten thousand dollars for a pair of blue jeans. Which Aimee thought was insane. Aimee's mother, Barbara, shopped here a lot. Well not "shopped" exactly. Shopping was too crassly commercial for what went on behind the doors of Carísimo. This was supposed to be an experience. So far, the only thing Aimee had experienced was acute boredom. The younger shop assistant, a girl who looked like she had walked off the set of a soap opera about the lives of the stupid, had tried to entertain her by talking about shoes. The girl had given up when she realised that Aimee couldn't have cared less about them. Aimee had been sitting here for what felt like seventeen years as her mother had tried on her size of almost every item that they had in stock.

Aimee's family had money, too much of it probably. Her Dad was CEO of DeWitt Industries, a multinational electronics manufacturer and defence contractor. The main difference between the rich and poor, Aimee had decided, was that rich people had more interesting ways of being bored. Take this afternoon, for instance: Aimee was being forced to spend her time staring at the white walls of a shop where they did a credit check on you before you were allowed in. How many shoes did Barbara need anyway? She must have a few thousand pairs. Aimee had four pairs, including sneakers. Barbara DeWitt, Aimee's mother, had been a beauty pageant winner and model back before Aimee was born and still liked to look the part. She spent a fortune every year on new clothes which were worn maybe once or twice and then discarded. Aimee thought that it was all a bit of a waste to be honest. The differences didn't end there either. Barbara DeWitt was a blonde, blue eyed cartoon princess. Aimee took after her father and had permanently ragged brown hair and dressed like a tom-boy, always in a hoodie, Vanguard t-shirt and combat trousers, whatever the weather. Barbara wanted her to be a "normal" girl, with dresses and fancy shoes, which was why she brought Aimee along on these shopping expeditions to places where an average wage could be spent in less than twenty minutes. The expeditions hadn't worked so far. Barbara wanted Aimee to look pretty and grab a well-connected (i.e. rich) husband, just like she had. Aimee wanted more from life than being a bored socialite and had already tried to explain this several times to her unhearing parents.

Finally, it was time to leave, her mother had spent the equivalent of the aid budget to Guatemala on clothing and all was well with the world. Their limo was waiting patiently down the block and Barbara waved to the chauffer to come collect them. Why walk a whole fifteen steps when you had paid someone to wait on you hand and foot? The car pulled up to the kerb in front of them and stopped. Jason, their driver, didn't get out to hold the door open. Barbara sighed in dramatically enhanced exasperation. She waited a few seconds and opened it herself with great theatricality, as it if was the most difficult thing in the world. Barbara placed the bags of new clothes carefully on the seat. Aimee climbed in behind her without saying a word and shut the door. Barbara tapped sharply on the window that separated the front compartment from the passengers.

"Jason! Jason? What are you doing?"

The window rolled down. The occupant of the vehicle wasn't Jason. It was a man Aimee didn't recognise. He was looking over his shoulder at them and holding a snub nosed revolver.

"Shut up and sit down." he said.

Barbara, shocked into silence for the first time in her adult life, sat down. The rear door opened and a man in a smart grey suit, carrying a black briefcase stepped into the Limo. Aimee immediately didn't like him. He had greasy brown hair and a feeble attempt at a moustache. He sat down opposite Aimee and placed the briefcase on his lap. He touched the clasps which opened with a sharp click. He reached inside and pulled out a silver pistol.

"This is a gun." He said in a harsh German accented voice. "A Glock 17 to be precise. The gun means that you are going to do what I say. The first thing I'm going to say is this: shut up. I don't want to hear a peep out of you. If you try to call for help, I will shoot you in the head. If you try to escape, I will shoot you in the head. In fact, if you do anything except sit down and shut up, I will shoot you in the head. Are we clear?"

Aimee nodded. Barbara had either already fainted or was pretending that she had.

"Good." The German continued: "Now, we're going to sit back and enjoy the drive. I've never been in a limo before."

They drove for about two hours. Aimee sat beside the window and tried to remember the route they were taking, the driver was staying off the freeway and was using back roads whenever possible. Aimee was lost.

"What do you want with us?" Aimee asked the grey suited man.

He made no response; he just continued to stare at her blankly.

"Why won't you talk? Where are you taking us?"

"I said for you to shut up." He finally responded, pointing the gun at her to emphasise his point.

It was dark by the time they arrived at their destination. It was a small estate of abandoned warehouses, most only partly finished.

The limo slowed to a stop and the driver got out to open the sliding shutter of one of the warehouses. The shutter creaked loudly. He then got back into the car and drove them inside. The car stopped and the grey suited man spoke:

"Get out"

Aimee did what she was told and she exited the car followed closely by the grey suited man. He walked her over to a store room, took a bunch of keys out of his pocket and unlocked it. All the while keeping his gun on Aimee.

"You'll be spending the next couple of days in here"

"No! You can't..."

He grabbed Aimee by the front of her hoodie, pulling her closer to him as he put the gun to her temple:

"This says I can do anything I want. Now get inside!"

He turned her around roughly and pushed her into the storeroom. At that moment, the driver opened the car door to carry Barbara from the car; she hadn't moved a muscle since she had fainted earlier. She moved now. Barbara shoved past him and made for the door, which was still open. She was attempting to run in high heels

92

and had only made it a few metres before he caught up with her and cracked her over the head with his gun, knocking her to the ground:

"That's enough!" He shouted "Any more of that and we'll kill you!" Barbara began to cry. He grabbed her by the shoulder and forced her to stand up by digging his fingers into the inside of her arm underneath her armpit. He walked her over to where Aimee and the grey suited man stood. The driver pushed Barbara into the store room first. She fell onto the floor in the corner of the room furthest from the door. The man then took a pair of handcuffs from his back trouser pocket and cuffed one of her hands to a pipe.

The grey suited man did the same to Aimee, cuffing her to the outlet pipe for the small, cold radiator that was in the room. The driver closed the door and locked it without a word. The sound of their footsteps disappeared into the distance. A minute passed. Barbara whispered to Aimee.

"Are you OK honey?"

"I'm OK. Are you hurt?"

"Just a split lip and a cut on the head. It looks worse than it is."

Aimee looked at her mother, there was a lot of blood on Barbara's forehead.

"What do you think they want?"

"Money." She said quietly. "It's always about money. You'll see. They'll ask your father for money, he'll pay and we'll be released."

Aimee was having her own thoughts on that. Why would the two men show their faces if they were just going to let her and Barbara go after a ransom had been paid? Aimee decided not to worry her mother and just said:

"Yeah, that makes sense".

They stopped whispering when they heard one of the men walking towards the storeroom. He paused outside the room for a few seconds and continued walking.

"Don't worry about them Aimee. They're just idiots with guns."

Aimee thought about her dad. Paul DeWitt was an extremely shrewd individual. He had built up DeWitt Industries from his parent's suburban garage to a billion dollar company in less than twenty years. He'd married late in life, more to provide an heir to the company than for any other reasons, such as, for example: love. He'd hoped for a son and was mildly disappointed to receive a daughter. Barbara had gained financial security and an invite to all the best parties. Paul DeWitt was a talented businessman but was distant to people on a personal level. He rarely spoke to Aimee. Paul DeWitt wasn't the kind of man to pay a large ransom for a wife he didn't love and a daughter he'd rather not have had.

After an hour of sitting on the cold floor, Aimee heard someone approach their room. The driver entered, carrying a tray with paper plates of sandwiches and two bottles of water. Aimee and Barbara ate and drank with their free hands. Tuna sandwiches. Aimee despised Tuna and everything else that swam in the sea. Why would you want to eat something that ate worms? Still, it was better than nothing. They ate hungrily, finishing the food in a few seconds and gulping down the water with enthusiasm. Barbara was still bleeding from her scalp.

"Mum..." Aimee began.

"I know honey; it's not as bad as it looks, really."

They stopped talking as they heard footsteps approach across the concrete floor of the warehouse. The driver unlocked the door to the storeroom and entered, this time he was carrying blankets and pillows, his gun was tucked into the front of his trousers. He threw the blankets at the woman and girl, turned around without a word and left the room again. Barbara grimaced when she smelled the bed clothes. They were filthy and stank to high heaven. The driver closed the door to the storeroom and locked it.

Aimee lay on the pillow and looked around the room. Barbara had managed to fall asleep, being kidnapped had taken a lot out of her. The walls of the room were bare except for the pipes and radiator that they were handcuffed to. The floor was uncarpeted and had a number of small puddles, caused by a leaking roof. There was a single small window high up near the roof which let in orange light from the streetlight outside and a little sliver of light crept in from underneath the door. Aimee couldn't hear anything outside. There were no cars or other traffic, no voices from the street, not even the sound of airliners flying through the night at thirty five thousand feet.

Aimee concentrated and tried to ignore the sound of her mother snoring. She could just make out the sound of the two men talking; they were keeping their voices low:

"Spoke to our employer... not paying... saying we weren't supposed to take the girl." said the German.

"It's not our fault. She was supposed to be in class instead of out shopping!"

"I'll go talk to the client in person now. I will be able to stop him panicking and going back on the deal. Keep an eye on them."

"What if he says for us to kill them?"

"Then we kill them, that was the plan all along."

"I wasn't told that!"

"You were hired to drive and play babysitter, you didn't need to know."

We have to get out of here. Aimee looked around the bare room, trying to find a way out. There was only one. Through the door they came in. She heard a car start and the shutter of the warehouse open and close. The German must have gone. She waited a few minutes to make sure that he had left.

"Mum?" she whispered.

Barbara didn't respond. Aimee looked closely at her mother. Barbara still had a small trickle of blood coming from the side of her head. She'd been injured worse than she had admitted. Aimee started to panic. She pulled sharply at the handcuff. It was strong, there was no way she'd be able to break it. But the pipe it was attached to didn't seem to be fixed to the wall particularly well. Aimee braced her legs against the wall, one on either side of the pipe and pulled with all her strength. The pipe moved slowly but began to pull away from the wall. She had to move slowly. If the driver heard anything he was sure to come in and catch her. After a few more attempts, the pipe broke away from the radiator and Aimee was able to slip the handcuff off the pipe though it was still clamped firmly to her wrist. She was free.

Aimee crawled slowly, her legs were cramping from sitting on the hard floor all day. She made it over to the wall where her mother was chained. Barbara was breathing, just barely. Her breaths were very shallow and she had lost a lot of blood, judging by the large dark pool on the ground next to her head. Aimee stood up. She would have to fight the driver the next time he came in the door. She looked around, the trays that the driver had used to bring in the food and water lay on the floor and she had the handcuff attached to her wrist. She could use those to hit him. She picked up one of the trays and hid behind the door to the storeroom.

"Help! Help! My mother isn't breathing! Help!" she shouted.

Aimee listened as hurried footsteps approached. She tensed her muscles, raising the tray above her head. She heard the sound of a key in the lock of the door and the door opened. The driver stepped into the room; he was staring at the corner where Barbara lay. Aimee slipped forward silently and hit him across the back with the wooden tray. It broke in half and he cried out in pain. He swung around, trying to draw his gun from his waistband, Aimee hit him again, this time on his right arm as he freed his gun, he dropped it on the floor between himself and Aimee. She kicked it away from them and it slid across the concrete floor.

"You're not that scary, you're just an idiot without a gun." she said as she swung the half of the tray she still held, putting all of her weight into the blow. She caught the surprised man on the side of his skull. His hands rose instinctively to his head to protect it. Aimee dropped the tray, and ran into him shoulder first. She caught him in the centre of the chest and he staggered backwards. He fell over onto his back and struck his head on the ground. He was out cold.

Aimee knelt down and searched through his pockets. She found a mobile phone and dialled nine-one-one. She hoped the police would be able to track the signal like she'd seen on TV.

"Nine-one-one, emergency. Which service do you need?" asked the operator.

"I need the police. My mother and I were kidnapped. Two men took us when we were shopping. My mother is hurt."

"Ok. Do you know where you are?"

"No idea, somewhere in California, to the North East of LA, I think."

"Ok, sweetheart. Don't panic. We'll put a trace on your call and narrow down your location by the cell towers. Where are the men now?"

"One of them left, the other is unconscious on the floor."

"Good girl, what's your name honey?"

"Aimee. Aimee DeWitt."

"Ok, Aimee. We have your location. Police and an ambulance will be there inside ten minutes. Stay on the line. I'll be here if you need anything."

Aimee ran to her mother. Barbara was in bad shape. Her long blonde hair was sticky with blood. Aimee shook her to wake her up.

"Mum? Mum? Can you hear me?"

Barbara opened her eyes a fraction of an inch and coughed.

"Aimee… baby. I'm sorry." Barbara said: "I shouldn't have dragged you out today. You were meant to be safe at home."

"It's OK. The police are coming. We'll be fine."

"Sorry, I'm sorry…"

Barbara's voice faded and she stopped breathing. Aimee held her mother's head in her hands and cried.

She heard a moan from the unconscious victim. He was waking up. Aimee felt the rage build inside her. Dark thoughts flooded into her mind. He killed my mother.

She stood up and walked slowly over to where he lay. She kicked him in the stomach as hard as she could, again and again.

He cried out, groaning louder and clutching feebly at his stomach in an attempt to defend himself from Aimee.

Sirens called out in the distance. The police were coming. Aimee went back to her mother's body and sat down beside her, clutching her mother's quickly cooling hand in her own.

Chapter Eight | Leaving Las Vegas

Ryan had seen most of the battle in Homestead on TV. He'd seen Mountain smashed to pieces by the woman with the mace, seen Mage's body on the ground, seen his dad make one last desperate attempt to stop the woman and watched his dad die in the mud as the woman laughed. The newscasters in the studio had sat there in shock, not knowing what to say after what had just been shown. They'd offered meaningless "analysis" of the situation. No one knew who this woman was. Shortly after she'd been defeated, a fleet of black trucks and SUVs had appeared and whisked the unconscious woman away. He hadn't been able to watch anymore after that. He'd turned off the TV, gone to his room and lay on the bed, looking at the ceiling in a state of numb shock. It couldn't be real. It had to be a crazy ratings stunt. If he just went to sleep, in a few hours he'd be woken up by the Darkwing returning and he would get up and meet his mom and dad in the living room of the apartment. Just like he always did. They'd laugh and talk and they'd send him to bed because he'd have to get up for school in the morning and... and.

Ryan slipped between the sheets, closed his eyes and was asleep within seconds.

He'd slept for less than an hour when he heard a group of people enter the apartment. Whoever they were, they definitely weren't his parents. There were three of them and he didn't recognise their voices. He inched out from under the duvet cover and walked over to the green armchair beside the window, trying to not make any noise. His aluminium baseball bat was leaning against the side of the chair. Ryan grabbed the bat and held it tightly. Someone had come for him: it could be an enemy of his parents, out for a piece of petty revenge. Ryan moved towards the door of his room, it was slightly ajar, with the small crack between the door and frame providing a view of the hallway. Ryan could see torches shining in the apartment. The main lights were off. The voices were coming from the living room now.

"Where is the bloody lights-witch?" an older man's voice, Ryan thought.

"Maybe they have one of those voice activated things?" a young sounding woman replied: "This is a pretty fancy place, after all."

"Nah, it's here." said the second man.

The lights in the living room came on; Ryan tiptoed soundlessly into the hall and crouched behind a decorative table. The hall connected the living room and kitchen to the bedrooms. The hall was still dark. Hopefully, whoever these people were, they wouldn't be able to see him.

"Ryan?" said the first man. "Are you here?"

Ryan didn't answer.

"DJ, Sarah. Check the bedrooms. I'll look in the kitchen and on the balcony."

Two people entered the hallway. Ryan shifted his grip on the baseball bat. They might get him but he'd try his best to hurt one of them. The first figure was a big guy, built like a football player; he loomed over Ryan, casting a long shadow in the hall as he blocked the light filtering into the hall from the living room.

"Yaaaahhh!" said Ryan as he sprang from his hiding place, swinging the baseball bat over his head towards the large figure. The man grabbed the bat with one hand, almost lazily stopping its swing and simultaneously yanking it up into the air, Ryan still had a tight grip on it and followed it upwards, his legs dangled two feet off the ground. He released his grip and landed on the floor, falling onto his backside.

"Ryan! Chill little dude!" said the giant.

"Ryan, we're with the police." said the woman "I'm Officer Sarah Lieber and this is Officer Wyatt."

"Prove it!"

"Fine, you're under arrest for attempting to strike a police officer. Does that prove it? Or we could show you our badges?" she pulled a gold shield from her belt and showed it to Ryan.

"What are you doing here?"

"Our Captain is here with us. We're here to get you into protective custody."

"Why?"

"You know why. The Captain will explain, come on."

Sarah offered Ryan her hand, which he grabbed. She pulled him to his feet and placed her hand on Ryan's back, gently but firmly guiding him into the living area.

The three of them entered the kitchen just as the Captain stepped in from the balcony.

"Ryan. You're safe, good. I don't know if you remember me, my name is Ed O'Grady. I run the Las Vegas Special Tactics Unit. I was friends with your mother and father. I met you a few times when you were much younger."

"I think I remember."

"OK. You've seen the news tonight, I guess?"

"Yeah."

"Then you know what's happened to your parents?"

"I saw most of it."

"I'm really sorry. We came over as soon as we could. Your dad made me promise a few years back that if anything happened to them, we were to protect you."

"What took you so long?"

"Have you seen outside? Come onto the balcony with us."

All four of them walked out onto the balcony of the apartment. The living quarters for The Vanguard were twenty stories above street level.

"What am I supposed to be seeing?"

"Look down." was all Ed said.

Ryan saw it. A crowd had gathered around the tower, there could have been thousands of people out there and more were arriving as he watched. People were lighting candles and leaving bunches of flowers near the entrance. Ryan heard a dull background murmuring made up of the cries, prayers and sobbing of the people on the ground. A line of armed police officers kept the crowd away from the main entrance.

"We practically had to ram our way in past the crowds." said Sarah.

"What are they here for?"

Wyatt spoke: "Most are here to mourn The Vanguard. Some are just ghouls, here to break in and steal whatever they can to sell as souvenirs. Others are here to witness history so they can say they were here tonight in years to come."

"What do we do?"

Ed spoke: "We're getting you out of here as soon as possible. The Mayor and I discussed it. You're going to have to leave the country."

"That's crazy! Why? Everyone I know is here!"

"That's true and everyone down there knows who you are. There are people down there who want to hurt you; your parents still have lots of enemies. Others want to make you kind of a living saint because you're the last connection to the heroes we lost today. Neither of those options would be particularly good for you."

"Where are you sending me?"

"I was thinking of Europe. The Mayor has contacts over there. We'll get you placed into a boarding school out of the way someplace."

"Why Europe?"

"Have you ever been to Europe, Ryan?" asked Sarah, smiling. "No one over there cares about superheroes, at least, not as much as they do here. You'll be able to blend in much easier. A lot of people won't have any idea of who you are."

"That can't be true."

"It is. You're like a baseball player or a NASCAR driver: famous in the USA but practically unheard of everywhere else."

"My thoughts exactly." said Ed. "Start packing. Sarah, help him out. DJ will walk the perimeter and I'll get back to ground level and manage things down there. Don't let him out of your sight."

Ed and DJ left the balcony and walked towards the door out of the apartment.

DJ turned and looked at Ryan and Sarah: "I'll be in the hall, keeping an eye on the stairs and elevators. Give me a call if you need anything."

Ryan and Sarah left the balcony and walked down the hall into

Ryan's room. Sarah carried a bag over her shoulder. She walked ahead of Ryan and checked every corner just in case a motivated mourner had managed to sneak in unnoticed. Sarah opened the door to Ryan's bedroom, looked around the room and motioned to Ryan that it was safe to enter. Once Ryan was safely inside, Sarah dumped her bag on the floor. She reached down, unzipped it and took out a shotgun. She pointed the barrel at the floor and made sure to keep her fingers away from the trigger.

"I don't think you need that in here." Ryan said, "This tower is supposed to be impenetrable. Warfare used to say that."

"You never know. Lots of things are supposed to be what they're not."

Ryan started packing his clothes into a backpack. He was unsure what to take with him. How do you pack your life into a couple of small bags knowing that you may never come back? Sarah sat down on the bed, facing the door, holding the shotgun across her lap.

"One thing." he asked "I don't have a passport."

Sarah reached down into her duffel bag. Ryan couldn't help noticing that it was full of different types of guns and ammunition. She pulled out a padded envelope and threw it to him.

Ryan caught it clumsily and opened it by sliding his finger along the flap at the top and shook the contents onto the bed. A passport and two stacks of money, one of dollars; the other of euros, fell out. Ryan picked up the passport and flipped through to read the identity page:

"Who is Ryan Haines?"

"You are, starting tomorrow morning."

"Where do the police get a fake passport?"

"We know all the best forgers, finding a fake is never a problem. But that's a real passport. You'd be amazed the kind of strings that can be pulled when you mention the names Velocity and Solarstorm to the President. She owed them a favour from way back."

"What am I supposed to do for money? That cash won't last forever."

"The Captain has organised things so that money will be provided to you from a fund we use to protect witnesses and pay informants. It'll be hard for anyone not directly involved with my unit to find out where the money is going to."

"I'll still look like me."

"Hair dye will be your new best friend, at least until you get a bit older and your appearance changes naturally"

"I'm really leaving, aren't I?"

"Yes. I'm sorry but it's for your own good. Everything the Captain said is true. You're really not safe here anymore."

Ryan started to cry. It had been a long day and everything had finally hit home, his life as he knew it was over.

Sarah spoke softly: "I know it's a lot to take in. Losing your parents at your age isn't easy."

"What would you know about it?"

"My dad died when I was a kid."

"Sorry."

"I'll tell you one thing: it hurts like crazy now, but everyday it'll hurt a little less. Until the day comes that it doesn't hurt at all. Your parents are heroes. They died doing the right thing. That won't make you feel better now. But one day it will. I promise."

Ryan lay face down on the bed and continued to cry. Sarah placed her hand on his shoulder. Eventually Ryan, exhausted and red eyed, fell asleep and Sarah moved off the bed to the armchair near the window, to keep an eye on the door to the room.

"I promise" she whispered softly as she watched Ryan sleep.

It was late in the morning when Ryan awoke. There were raised voices coming from the kitchen. Ryan climbed out of bed and ran down the hall. Maybe this was a sign that his parents or one of their team mates had returned. He opened the door to the kitchen and his hopes were dashed. A dozen police officers had occupied the apartment. Ryan recognised Sarah, DJ and Ed. Sarah beckoned him over as Ed spoke to the other officers.

"Good morning." Sarah said.

"Hey. What's going on?" asked Ryan.

"Things are a bit crazy here. We're making plans to get you past the cordon of photographers, protestors and mourners outside. You should have breakfast. But take my advice and don't touch that cereal over there. It tastes like tree bark and burnt plastic."

"Thanks for the advice."

"No problem."

Ryan grabbed bread from the cupboard and put it in the toaster. Ed turned around from his briefing and spoke to Ryan.

"Hey Ryan. Arrangements are made to get you out of the country this afternoon."

"Oh. I was hoping that Warfare would make it back and help me out. He survived the battle, right?"

"Sorry." said Ed. "No-one's seen him since after that robot guy saved him from the super villain. We believe, that is, the Florida police believe, that he has disappeared."

"He wouldn't do that!" exclaimed Ryan. "He was mom and dad's friend. He wouldn't just leave!"

"I don't know what to tell you Ryan. We have to plan as if he isn't coming."

Ryan turned his back on Ed and took butter from the fridge to put on his toast.

"So. What's the plan, Captain?" asked DJ.

"We're doing a high speed run to the international airport. The convoy will be two cars escorted by four motorcycles. We don't stop for anything." said Ed.

"The paparazzi will be all over us as soon as we leave the underground car park." said DJ.

"Exactly, which is why Sarah and I will be in a third car with Ryan. We'll leave five minutes after you do. We'll drive without sirens and keep to the speed limit. Ryan will hide on the backseat underneath a blanket. Hopefully, once you draw off the press we can have a clear run to the Air Force Base. A transport plane is on stand by there to take Ryan to Europe."

DJ smiled: "So I'm the diversion. That's sneaky. I like it. What do you want the convoy to do?"

"Try keep as far ahead of the press as possible and lead them on a wild goose chase to McCarran International Airport. It will make our job much easier."

"No problem. One fake out coming up."

"Excellent. Ok. The Convoy leaves in forty-five minutes. Ryan's car leaves five minutes after that. Get your gear ready."

The officers busied themselves preparing for their tasks. Ed walked over to Ryan and sat down beside him.

"I'm sorry this isn't turning out the way you hoped."

"It's OK. I shouldn't have said anything earlier. Thank you for helping me."

"I made a promise and I mean to keep it. Clean up and get dressed. We need to be ready soon."

"Sure thing." said Ryan as he hopped off the stool and ran for his bedroom.

Ryan stopped and took one last quick look around the apartment before he left to get ready. He wondered if he would ever be coming back.

PART II
Five Years Later

Chapter Nine | Discovered

Ryan sat enjoying the sunshine outside of the bar in a small square just off the main street of the village of Arcos in southern Spain. The bar wasn't much to write home about. It consisted of a few tables set out before a door which led to a tiny, dingy bar area manned around the clock by a slightly bored barman and consistently harried waitress. It also had a small kitchen out back containing a loud, red faced cook. Ryan liked it, the food was cheap and filling and actually pretty good. The bar wasn't in the guidebooks and was therefore visited mainly by locals and the occasional knowledgeable traveller. It was situated directly across from a small but extremely pretty church. Ryan watched as a handful of day trippers moved slowly through the square and filed into the church. It was the only interesting thing to see in this part of town. Arcos, though a fine place to visit, didn't get hordes of tourists. It was far enough away from the beaches that the people that did visit came to relax and walk slowly around and take in the sights. The village was perched precariously on the summit of a sandstone ridge with a dizzying thousand foot drop straight down to the plains below and didn't lack for spectacular scenery.

Ryan had been in Spain for five months now. He'd been moving generally south through the Spanish countryside, taking care to stay off main roads and away from larger towns and cities. Crowds always meant trouble for him. If he stayed too long in one place he'd eventually be recognised by American tourists who were convinced that Ryan was famous.

The phrase: "Hey buddy? Aren't you the guy who auditioned on the singing contest on TV a few years back?" was a phrase Ryan heard often. He was usually able to bluff his way out of these confrontations and convince the person who was sure he was famous that he was just a normal student, after all, wasn't the world just full of nineteen year old backpackers? What were the odds that the quiet, unassuming teenager before them was the guy they'd seen on TV somewhere before? After a few minutes of fast thinking and faster talking, Ryan was normally able to put that type of question behind him. It was worrying that people still recognised him. He had thought that the general public's ever shortening attention span would have worked to his advantage by now. Life for the heir of a now destroyed super heroic family wasn't always easy.

It was annoying that he had to be so careful all the time. For the past five years he had lived with the fear that a journalist or a person bearing a grudge would eventually put the pieces together and track him down. Ryan couldn't complain too much though. His only major problem was that he, like a lot of teenagers, had no idea what to do with his life. This problem was made worse as he had no one to advise him. Regular teenagers had a support network of friends and family to help them make the "big decisions" in life about what they were going to do for the next fifty years. Ryan had no-one. Once his exams were over he'd decided to take a year out to go travelling and hopefully figure out what he was going to do with his life.

Since the night his exams had finished, Ryan had spent his time travelling around Europe. He had hoped that learning new languages and customs would help wipe out any trace of his American accent and body language. After four years of the best education money could buy and twelve months of travel, Ryan spoke German, French and Spanish.

Ryan now had significant good will towards the world after a long sunny year of working and travelling around Europe. He hadn't been able to get "official" work as he didn't want to be included on any government databases if he could avoid it. However, Ryan had quickly discovered that there were always people who were willing to pay cash to a young, strong looking kid for farm work like picking grapes. After many long weeks working on farms and vineyards in the area, Ryan had come to the small town of Arcos with enough cash in his pockets to sleep in a real bed and eat decent food. It was a refreshing change of pace from dozing in the hayloft of a barn and working for twelve hours a day.

Ryan ordered food once the waitress, a woman who somehow managed to appear busy and under tremendous amounts of pressure with only five customers to serve, finally came over to take his order. Tapas and a cold beer would make him feel better, though just being in the sunlight made him feel relaxed. After a few minutes the waitress returned with his glass of local beer, a plate of fried calamari and a small bowl of patatas bravas. Ryan ate hungrily and had finished his potatoes with spicy tomato sauce in record time when he heard a voice behind him:

"Mind if I join you?"

Ryan turned around to see a young woman standing not far away. She had red hair and was wearing green Bermuda shorts and a matching t-shirt. Cheap looking plastic sunglasses covered her eyes and a camera on a strap hung around her neck. Her wrists had dozens of small bracelets tied around them, the kind of cheap souvenirs someone might buy for a couple of euro at one of the thousands of beachside arts and crafts stalls that dotted the coast. She was on her own.

"Of course" he said graciously, waving to the chair opposite.

"Thanks, I really wanted to eat a meal but if I sit on my own, half the 'Romantics' in this village will think it's open season and offer me their company, whether I want it or not."

"Happens a lot, does it?"

She smiled "Not as often as I would hope!"

She sat down and pushed her sunglasses onto the top of her head, leaving her handbag on the ground with the strap looped around the leg of her chair.

She moved her hand towards his to shake it.

"I'm Eva."

"Ryan." He said as he shook her hand.

"Not a very continental European name, I would have thought?"

"It's not."

"You look very European, dark hair, suntanned. I thought you were Spanish or Italian at first."

"Well, I speak quietly and don't live at home with my mother, so I'm definitely not Italian."

"You eat like an Italian." Eva said as she looked down at what remained of Ryan's meal.

"That's true, I guess. So, why are you visiting the village? It doesn't get many young people. The visitors are mostly bus loads full of the recently retired."

"My girlfriends and I are travelling before we go back to our final year of college. I'm majoring in Architecture. I'd heard there was a really nice church in this part of town."

"That's it over there." said Ryan, pointing across the square. "It's named San Juan Luis de las Iglesias Preciosas.

"Really? What does that mean?"

"It's named after Saint Juan Luis, patron saint of pretty churches."

"You're such a kidder!" Eva said as she reached for the camera dangling around her neck and snapped a few pictures, making sure to include a couple of good shots of Ryan.

"Where are your friends now?" asked Ryan.

"Sleeping off last night's party. Did you know the clubs stay open to six in the morning here?"

"Yeah, I'd heard, I'm not much of a dancer though."

"Me neither, I came here to walk the countryside and get back to nature. But you try stopping my three fraternity sisters from going out on the town!"

Eva's phone beeped in her bag and she reached down to grab it:

"Hey Katie! You guys awake down there...? OK. I'll see you in an hour then... No, I'm fine. See you soon!"

She placed the phone on the table: "So what's the food here like? It must be pretty good since you finished yours so eagerly."

"It's good, try the calamari. It's the best."

"I will."

The waitress returned and took Eva's order.

"So where are you from?" Eva asked Ryan, once she'd finished ordering her meal and a glass of pineapple juice.

"Oh, I'm from England. A small town called Taunton in Somerset." lied Ryan.

"I'm an American, from Texas." said Eva.

"Barbeques and beer huh?"

"Ha! It's actually not a lot like that. What about… Somerset, you said?"

"It's much the same as Texas, I'd imagine."

"You don't sound very British."

"Not all of us speak like Colin Firth."

"I guess not. So are you doing the same as us? Having an adventure before going back to college?"

"Kind of. I finished high school and I'm trying to figure out what I want to do."

"And your parents aren't mad that you're just sitting outside bars in Europe instead of getting on with your life?"

"My parents… aren't around."

"I'm sorry to hear that. They died?"

"In a car accident a few years back."

"That's a real shame."

Eva's food arrived and she began to eat. Ryan was starting to feel a little uncomfortable. Speaking with women wasn't a strength of his. It was a side effect of attending a boarding school for boys.

Eva picked up on his nervousness: "You seem a little uncomfortable, not used to women making conversation in Somerset?"

"Not many women down the country to talk to. There's lots of sheep though, so you're never really on your own."

"Ha! I guess not. Well, don't worry; I won't be bothering you for much longer."

"You're not." Ryan fibbed. "I'm just getting a headache. It must be the sun. It's very warm today."

"Yeah, I get those headaches too. If you want to leave, go ahead. I'm nearly finished anyway."

Ryan stood up and took a ten euro note from his wallet to pay for the food. Eva raised her hand and stopped him by touching him on the wrist.

"Don't do that. I'll pay, least I can do for you keeping me company."

"OK, thanks."

"See you around, Ryan."

"You too."

"If you feel like it, we'll be at the club at the far end of the village tonight, letting your hair down might do you good."

"I'll think about it. Thanks again."

"No problem."

Eva watched as Ryan crossed the square, passed the church and walked up a set of grey stone steps. Once she was sure he was gone, she picked up her phone and made a call.

"Control. This is Agent Forty-Three. I've made contact with the target. I'm sending you the pictures now."

Eva reached into her green handbag and took out a long black USB cable. She attached one end of the cable to her camera and the other to her phone.

"How are those pictures looking?" She asked.

Eva heard Agent Benning's voice on the other end of the line:

"It's him. He's changed since he was younger but the facial recognition software is giving us a ninety nine percent match. We'll have a team in position in eleven hours. I'm coming for him personally. Make your way to the safe house and prep for a rendition at first light. Did you plant the tracer?"

"Yes, I slipped it onto his shoe as I was making a show of protecting my handbag when I sat down."

"Good, Benning out."

Eva finished her pineapple juice and reached into her handbag. She grabbed her car keys and placed money on the table for the waitress to collect. Eva stood up and swung her bag onto her shoulder. Benning coming to Spain was a big deal; they had agents all over the world searching for Ryan Curtis. She had no idea why the ISA wanted him so much; he was only a kid after all. What possible threat to national security could the son of a couple of long dead superheroes be?

After a brisk five minute walk, Eva arrived at her car and got in. The safe house was a villa about ten miles from Arcos, and could only be reached by driving on poorly lit, unpaved back roads. She needed to hurry to make sure that the safe house was ready for Benning and the team he was sure to be bringing. She'd lied to Ryan, She had no college friends staying in the town. She was on her own. She was part of a squad of a dozen agents spread out across the continent chasing down rumours and leads as to the location of Ryan Curtis. A tourist from New Jersey had posted about an encounter with who he had thought was Ryan Curtis on his blog a month ago. The off handed remark had been included in the middle of a long and boring article about cycling through Spain. The ISA's researchers had noticed the article and, as a result, Eva had been sent to find Ryan quietly without involving other agencies or the local police. She'd spent weeks visiting small towns and villages across Spain, asking around for a male 'friend' of hers who was travelling alone. Two Irish guys she had met in a bar had mentioned running into a man answering the description working at a vineyard about twenty miles from Arcos.

Eva arrived at the local ISA safe house. It was a small white villa which stood alone surrounded by orange groves for a half mile in every direction. The trees hid the villa from the nearby roads. A person could drive by it every day for years and not realise that it was there. She opened the front door and entered. The villa lacked the comforts of home, there wasn't even a couch. Instead, the living room contained crates of surveillance equipment and a weapons locker. The bedrooms were mostly bare except for filing cabinets. Her bed was a mattress on the floor of the smallest bedroom which also contained a wooden chest for her clothes. The life of a spy, despite what those lying movies she'd loved as a kid had told her, wasn't all casinos and expensive cocktails. It mainly involved sleeping in uncomfortable places on those rare occasions when you could sleep, inedible food, bad working hours and jetlag.

Eva logged on to a computer terminal and brought up a map of the area. The tracer she'd placed on Ryan was working perfectly. A blinking blue dot on the map gave his location as a youth hostel not far from where he had left her. The tracer also gave Eva a read out of Ryan's life signs. His pulse was rapid and his temperature was higher than it ought to have been. He must have eaten bad calamari. Satisfied that they would be able to find him, she went to her floor mattress to catch a couple of hours of sleep. She wanted to get some rest; Benning would expect a full update when he arrived. No doubt he'd want to get straight to work when he arrived in a little over nine hours.

Ryan lay down on the bed but couldn't relax. His head was really pounding. His brain felt like it was going to burst through his skull. He'd never felt anything like it. The pain was so intense it was affecting his stomach. He rolled over onto the floor and scooted along the ground to the communal bathroom down the hall. He vomited as soon as he had reached the toilet. The sickness had gotten much worse since he had returned to the hostel. What had started as a bad headache had slowly spread through his entire body until every muscle he possessed was aching. He spend a not particularly enjoyable few minutes crouched over the communal toilet as everything he'd eaten for the past day had come up. He eventually dragged himself upright and painfully staggered back to his room. Ryan fell onto the bed and, his stomach still protesting, forced down two aspirin with a glass of water. The roaring in his head finally stabilised to a dull thumping and Ryan lay back on the bed. He hoped that he'd feel better in the morning.

Benning and his team of eight agents arrived at the villa in a small convoy of three black SUVs. Eva sighed audibly as she watched them approach from the front porch. Benning had a reputation for getting the job done but he had all of the subtlety of a bowling ball being launched directly at your stomach. He and his men were wearing black suits. Even in the middle of the night, the weather was uncomfortably warm, but here they were: the ISA's finest agents, doing their very best to stick out like a sore thumb.

Someone needed to tell Benning that the Cold War was over. Younger agents, like Eva, made the effort to blend in. They often pretended to be backpackers or exchange students. Once you'd obtained undercover work as a waitress in the right restaurant in Paris, you would overhear enough state secrets to have a long and successful career in the espionage agency of your choice. These guys were relics of an earlier age, when a secret agent could waltz around in a dinner jacket and still manage to get the job done. Small wonder it had taken Benning and those like him fifty years to bring down the Soviet Union.

The SUVs pulled up in front of the villa and the agents stepped out of the vehicles. Benning strode towards Eva. He was tall and well built, as were the other agents on his team. They might have been mass produced from the same mould in a factory. Benning had been in the ISA since it was founded over fifteen years before. The only difference between then and now was that he had a little grey around the temples. A relic he may be; Eva thought, but he's still impressive.

"What's the situation, Forty–Three?" asked Benning as he walked up the gravel path to the front door.

"No change from my report at nineteen hundred hours, local time. The target is at a hostel in a village about ten miles from here. He hasn't moved from the building since then."

"Good. We'll be moving on him at first light. I trust you can provide the equipment we will require?"

"Yes Sir, would you care to come inside?"

Eva turned to lead the way and Benning beckoned to his men to follow, leaving one outside to stand guard. The others entered the living room. Eva pointed to the chests located on the far side of the room.

"You'll find tactical equipment in there. Tranquiliser guns, tasers, bullet-proof vests, the lot."

"Excellent." Benning turned to his men. "Team! Suit up. It is zero five hundred, local time we will have the target in our custody by zero six thirty."

"Sir, yes Sir!" The agents responded in unison. They quickly dispersed around the room to prepare themselves.

"Agent Forty-Three?" asked Benning.

"Yes sir?" replied Eva.

"A word."

"Yes sir."

Benning led the way to the back garden of the villa, sat down on a metal garden chair facing the back door and lit a cigar. He inhaled deeply, held the smoke in his mouth for a few moments and gently exhaled.

"You are aware of the mission parameters?" he said once the smoke had cleared.

"No sir, I haven't been briefed yet."

"We leave here in sixty minutes and head directly for the target's location. Five of our team cut off all of the exits and the other four of us enter the building. We are to silence anyone inside and steal the contents of the safe, to make the operation appear like a robbery. We are to capture the target and return him to this location, whereupon he will be held for eighteen hours prior to transfer to a waiting transport aircraft which will stop over for ten minutes at the nearest airport and then proceed directly to the United States."

"I see."

"What is the target's frame of mind from the conversation you had with him earlier."

"Honestly, Sir? I think he's lonely."

"I don't care which of the seven dwarfs he his! Do you think he's likely to put up much of a fight?"

It's hard to gauge sir, I don't know." replied Eva, quickly changing mental gears and slipping into what she liked to call 'military speak'. "Very well. Get ready. This is the most important operation of your career. Your future in the Agency will be determined on its successful conclusion."

"May I ask a question, Sir?"

"What?"

"Why are we making all this effort for the son of two dead heroes?"

"Ryan Curtis is a dangerous young man. We need to bring him in for the safety of our nation. That's all I'm prepared to say. We move out in fifty five minutes, Agent."

"Yes Sir."

Ryan turned over in the bed and stared at the green numbers on the cheap plastic clock radio on the nightstand beside his bed. It was nearly six in the morning and the sunlight was beginning to creep in through the window. Ryan didn't feel sick to his stomach anymore. His headache no longer made his head feel like he'd been standing beside the amplifiers at a heavy metal concert, it had settled down to just being an uncomfortable stabbing feeling behind his eyes. He could live with that. He sat up and placed his feet on the floor gingerly, hoping that he wouldn't just fall over when he moved to stand up. He pushed himself up and grabbed the nightstand. He could walk again. Miraculously, his muscle pains had disappeared during the night. He grabbed a towel from his backpack and walked to the shower down the hall.

It was time to move on from Arcos. He'd walk south towards the coast of the Mediterranean, before heading east towards the smaller villages beyond Malaga. There were fewer tourists in those areas but enough of them that he wouldn't seem completely out of place. He showered quickly and returned to his room. He didn't have a lot of belongings with him. His worldly possessions barely filled one large backpack. Once he had dressed and packed his clothes he'd go down to the reception desk and pay his tab. He could get breakfast on the road. It was better to start walking early in the morning, stop for a few hours during the blistering heat in the middle of the day and then walk again once the day was cooler. Ryan usually did around twenty to twenty five miles a day. He could go faster; but he was in no rush. He'd take his time, look at the scenery, stop and take pictures and relax. He looked around his room one last time to make sure he hadn't forgotten anything. Satisfied, he lifted the backpack to his shoulder and headed for the exit.

His ears pricked up as a sixth sense he didn't know he had sent warning signals through his body. Something made him feel uncomfortable. There was a noise downstairs, no, not a noise, an absence of noise, an enforced silence. People had come into the reception area. They were moving quickly and attempting to be quiet but their movements were signposted by the air they displaced as they moved. Ryan went to the window and pulled back the curtains. Black SUVs were parked outside and Ryan saw armed men in suits wearing sunglasses standing at either end of the small street. Ryan heard a thumping downstairs and the sound of furniture being knocked over as if someone had been pushed to the linoleum, three floors below, the old man who worked the night shift on the reception desk was shouting in Spanish. Ryan could hear someone speaking;

"The boy in the photo, where is he?"

Someone had found him. Was it a criminal organisation that his parents had fought? It didn't matter; he wasn't going to be captured if he could help it. He opened the window and looked out. The guards that had been left outside weren't looking at the building. They were expecting a threat to come from any other direction except inside. Ryan climbed out onto the tiny ledge of the window sill and levered himself up, grabbing a gutter a few feet above his head with both hands. His heart was thumping in his chest, adrenaline coursed through his veins as he used his legs to kick off the balcony and pulled himself up. It was easier than he thought; all of those hours in vineyards, doing backbreaking work had paid off. He reached the roof and kept his head down, trying to ensure he stayed below the level of the parapet so he wouldn't be spotted from below.

The hostel was located in the old part of the town, no space was wasted and that meant that buildings were, for the most part, built right beside each other with only the occasional small gap of one or two metres wide. These gaps served as the alleyways which linked one part of the old town to another. Ryan started to inch his way across the roof tops when he heard a whistling noise; as a dart flew past his ear, missing him by whisker. A suited man stood on the roof of a house nearby shooting at him with a gun of some kind. Ryan crouched down and tried to use the parapet of the building as cover from the man with the gun, who was quickly moving toward him and speaking into a microphone in the left hand cuff of his shirt. Ryan broke off a piece of slate from the roof he was standing on and threw it at the man, knocking the gun from his hand. The gun skittered across the rooftop and fell down into an alley below. The man ran straight towards Ryan, raised his hands and jabbed at him with his left fist. Ryan avoided the punch and raised his own hands to protect his head. Ryan had never been in a fight before and his opponent seemed to know what he was doing.

The man circled Ryan like a hungry tiger. He had a smile on his face as his eyes flicked this way and that, looking for an opportunity to strike. He stepped forward and threw a left jab and right cross; Ryan tried to deflect them as best he could. The man's right cross hit Ryan in the chest. The man screamed as his knuckles fractured. He moaned in agony as he held his broken right fist in his left hand. Ryan ran as fast as he could to get away.

Eva and Benning were interrogating the hostel owner on the ground floor of the building. Eva winced as Benning held the man on the floor by placing his foot on the man's neck.

"Where is he?"

"Sir, he's saying that doesn't know. The room upstairs is empty."

A voice came through on their headsets: "Agent Vasquez here, He's on the roof. He has injured me but I am pursuing."

"Nothing fancy Vasquez." Benning snarled: "Just tranquilise him and get him down here."

"Roger."

Benning turned to Eva;

"Let's go, we'll follow from the street."

"What about the old man?"

Benning drew his silenced pistol from the holster beside his shoulder and aimed it at the man on the floor. The gun coughed twice. The man stopped struggling as the bullets entered his back.

"There. Problem solved; did you steal the cash-box?"

"Yes."

"Good, the local cops will blame it on our target; after all, he left his room in quite a hurry, didn't he?"

Benning bent over and retrieved the spent casings of his bullets from the floor.

"Let's capture the boy." He said.

Ryan raced across the rooftops of the village, trying to find a quiet spot where he could drop down to ground level; he was too easy to see up here, silhouetted as he was by the rising sun. He came to a gap between buildings and looked down; there was a balcony two floors below him. Ryan knelt down and held onto the gutter on the side the building. He swung his legs over the side and dropped down. He fell onto the balcony and landed on his butt.

"Good going" he whispered sarcastically. "Mum and dad are probably laughing at me right now".

He climbed onto the edge of the balcony and repeated the process, dropping to street level. His best bet was to continue on uphill, the streets were too narrow for cars the nearer one got to the summit of the ridge, the oldest part of the town. He hoped he could outrun his pursuers and disappear into the countryside.

Ryan could hear quick footsteps not far behind him. He jogged away, not daring running for fear that it would make too much noise on the cobbled streets. The village was a confusing warren to anyone who hadn't been there before, which would work to his advantage at least.

He continued on, stopping occasionally to attempt to hear his pursuers. They were still behind him, four men and a woman and, judging by their accents, all of them were American. He jogged more quickly as the voices were getting closer; he took the smaller alleys, keeping to the early morning shadows as much as possible. He was near the highest point of the village when he spotted a third black SUV ahead, four men in immaculate dark suits got out of the vehicle. There was a set of steps to Ryan's right; they led to the main square. Ryan charged up the steps as darts fired by the new arrivals bounced off the walls of the building behind him and the ground beneath. The main square contained the city hall to the right, a hotel directly opposite and a disused church beside the steps where he had entered. There was only one other exit, on the other side of the church between it and the hotel. Two of the men in suits from the black vehicle were blocking that exit and fired at Ryan. There were a handful of cars in the square and Ryan ducked behind one of these, he kept his head down and moved toward the top of the square, which was a dead end. The square contained an observation platform, where people could take in the view of the fields and river far below the ridge.

"Hold your fire!" A man commanded from the alley where Ryan had entered the square.

Ryan turned as a small group of men and one woman entered the square. All of them had guns aimed at him. Ryan recognised the woman.

"Eva? What is this?"

"We're with the US Government. We're here to take you in, Ryan." she said.

"Why? What did I do?"

The man at the front of the group spoke first;

"You're too dangerous to leave just hanging around. We're taking you in for the protection of the world."

"But I'm not dangerous; I'm not like my parents. I don't have powers. I can't do anything that they could!"

Benning laughed; "You think so? My man, Vasquez just broke half the bones in his hand when he punched you. You've ran over half of this town to try and escape. Tell me, are you even a little out of breath?"

"But... no, it's not possible."

"It is."

"Even if I did have powers, that doesn't mean I'm going to do anything!"

The agents walked slowly forward, Ryan kept moving backwards, towards the observation point.

Benning spoke again; "I respect what your parents did for America. They were misguided, but they had their uses. I'll tell you the truth. We're taking you in for study, you're the only pure super human specimen left. Did you know that?"

"What do you mean?"

"Your parents, they were the only two superheroes or villains we know of who had a child together."

"That can't be right."

"Do you know any others?"

"No, but there must be."

"There aren't. Your parents were two of the first superheroes and they were the only ones to get together and remain together long enough to have a kid. The others all married regular people, were sterile as a result of having powers or died five years ago in the Battle of Homestead without having had time to breed."

"So you want to keep me as a lab rat?" Ryan said as he moved a few steps nearer to the summit.

"Only at first. After a while the tests will probably kill you and we'll have our scientists' study what's left."

Ryan saw Eva look at the older agent with a look of shock and disgust on her face.

Ryan spoke; "It's not much of a choice is it?"

"Who in the seven hells told you that you'd have choices in life?"

Benning aimed his gun at Ryan; the other agents except for Eva did likewise. She holstered her weapon and stared at the ground.

Ryan bolted for the edge of the cliff, the agents fired, darts flew through the air. Most missed, two didn't. They hit Ryan, one between his shoulder blades and the other in the left arm. Ryan stumbled and used the waist high wall separating the square from a thousand foot drop to stop from falling. He realised that his headache was gone.

Mum was fast, dad was strong and could fly. He thought as the drugs started to enter his bloodstream. He struggled to keep his head clear. Be a test subject and die or take the biggest gamble of my life and maybe die.

Ryan climbed onto the wall and looked back at the slowly advancing agents. He turned towards the fields and river far below, closed his eyes and jumped. The wind whistled in his ears as he fell. He nearly collided with a flock of herons on his way down; they gave an angry hoot as he passed by.

"Come on, fly, hover, float, whatever. Just stop plummeting to your death."

Ryan suddenly stopped falling and hung in mid-air, nothing was holding him aloft. He laughed joyously and circled the ridge, looking at the agents who stood two hundred feet above.

"Hey idiots! In your face! I can fly!" he shouted as he aimed at the horizon and flew away.

"What the heck?" Benning looked on in shocked disbelief as Ryan, bathed in sunlight, soared through the air. Benning could hear the kid laugh as he looped through the sky, out of range of their guns.

"Are you OK, Sir?" Eva asked.

"I didn't know he could bloody fly!"

"I don't think he knew either."

Chapter Ten | First Night

Aimee sat in the armchair facing her bed, her chin resting on the palm of her hand as she stared at the costume and equipment laid out on top of the king sized duvet. She was beginning to have doubts about what she'd spent the past five years planning to do. It had all seemed so easy back when she'd came up with the idea. Now she thought that actually putting it into practice could involve crossing the line that separates being slightly deranged from being a certifiable raving lunatic.

Five years ago, after her mum died and her dad had decided to become an idiot out of what he claimed was grief, it had seemed almost natural. She had decided she wasn't going to be another victim, hiding from life just in case bad things happened. No, she was going to use what had been done to the DeWitt family as the start of a bigger plan. She would channel her anger at the powerlessness she had felt on the day that she had been kidnapped and make herself stronger, faster, and harder. She would become whatever she needed to be in order to get revenge on the criminals who had made her feel weak and vulnerable.

At least, that had been what she thought. After five years of training and study, the idea of being a masked vigilante scared her. She was fit, intelligent and able kick the snot out of anyone, but it wasn't somehow enough. The fear of being an absolute failure simmered inside her. Who was she to compare herself to true heroes like Solarstorm and Velocity? Then, there were the risks; she could be put in prison for what she was planning to do; that, or a mental hospital. Or she could be unmasked, her secret discovered by a voicemail hacking journalist or the police. And then what? She would be made the punch line of jokes from late night talk show hosts and every college student who fancies him or herself as a stand-up comedian. She could lose everything.

Maybe, she thought I ought to do a trial run? I could put on the costume and go out for a walk across the roof tops, just get used to the idea of wearing it. Take it slowly at first and work my way up to beating muggers and drug pushers. Introduce myself into the world gradually and see how it goes. If things don't work out then I can always quit and find another way to channel my anger and frustration.

Her decision made: she stood up and walked over to the bed. She reached down to pick up the hard black mask and put it on. She slipped the clasps over her ears. The mask covered her face and most of the rest of her head except for her mouth and hair. It would do a good job of concealing her identity.

I wonder what the protocol is when you first put on a costume and makes a decision to prowl the rooftops. She thought. Am I still Aimee DeWitt? Or am I someone else now? Do I change inside until I'm no longer just a regular person?

Aimee stopped hesitating: It's too late for philosophy. It's time for me to stop thinking about this and actually do it.

The green lenses of the eyepieces in the mask allowed Aimee to see clearly in the dark room. She stripped down to her underwear and put on the impact armour. The armour was able to stop a bullet or knife but also flexible enough for her to move quickly and fight. She touched the web gear which lay on the floor and slipped it on over her shoulders. For the hundredth time, she checked the gear stored in the compartments: stun grenades, a hunting knife, throwing stars, plastic explosive. A gas powered grappling gun fit snugly into the holster on her right hip. She opened a plastic box and took out a small, wafer thin, computer that she could clip onto her wrist. Hiroshi had outdone himself with this design, it allowed her to hack into almost any piece of technology that used a computer. Aimee could access any type of network and override nearly every security system in the world with the programs built into it.

Aimee laced up her boots and took the last of her weapons from the drawer beside the bed, a pair of thirty two inch long rattan sticks. She twirled them in the air to exercise her wrists, feeling the weight of them before slipping them into their scabbard on her back. She paused to look at her reflection in the full length mirror on the wardrobe. She was practically invisible, her matte black outline was noticeable only because of the soft green glow of the lenses in the mask. It was the only sign that someone was in the room. She smiled: she looked the part, at least.

She stretched her tendons and warmed up, tonight would be the worst possible time to pull a muscle. Finally, it was time to go out. She crept to the large French windows that opened out onto the balcony and unlocked them. It was late, but this was New York. She was certain that she'd find plenty to occupy her time.

She relaxed for a half a minute on the balcony, taking deep breaths of the cool night air as she stared at the full moon and the stars on this cloudless night and listened to the traffic far below. The honking of horns and the urgent beeps of car alarms down at ground level joined together in a cacophony of noise. It was the heartbeat of the city Aimee currently called home.

This is crazy, what am I doing? She considered as her gaze took in the city lights.

She hushed the doubting inner voice and un-holstered the grappling gun, aimed it at the roof of the building across the street and fired. The gun made a soft, barely audible sneeze as the piton discharged from the muzzle of the gun. The piton, attached to the gun by fifty metres of unbreakable metal cord, embedded itself into the side of the building opposite. A small green light on the handle of the gun blinked twice, meaning that the line was secure. Aimee's natural paranoia made her check it again, just to be sure. She tugged hard on the cord. It held fast. She jumped from the balcony at the same time as she thumbed the lever on the side of the gun that retracted the cord. The motor inside the gun whirred as it rewound the cord, pulling her across the distance between the two buildings in the space of a few seconds. Aimee thrust out her left hand and grabbed the top of the building. She dragged her body up onto the roof. The kernel of panic that had been building inside her chest ebbed away as her brain realised that she'd done it. She had travelled across the gap from one building to another and survived.

She took a deep breath, gathering her wits and courage in an attempt to calm down before she continued. After recovering, She ran south across the rooftops, using the grappling gun when she needed to, otherwise trusting to her parkour training to make it across the skyline. She jumped from roof to roof, rolling on impact to lessen the force of landing. For the first time in years, she felt free. She was high above ground level, where people wouldn't look for her and couldn't see her, even if they wanted to. It was invigorating. But it wasn't enough. Despite all she had done this evening, Aimee wasn't satisfied. She knew that she needed to stop a crime to be a proper hero.

It was a quiet Wednesday night in Midtown Manhattan; there were very few people on the streets. The business people and tourists who swarmed the area during the day had all gone home or back to their hotels, leaving this part of the city to its relatively few permanent residents. No doubt a busy Friday night would present plenty of opportunities for Aimee to dispense vigilante justice but tonight the city was pretty dead. She contemplated just running across the rooftops until she was tired and trying again, another evening.

Suddenly, she heard a piercing scream from a few blocks away. She turned in the direction of the sound and hurried towards it. She landed on a low, flat-roofed, building that had an alley running alongside. Aimee looked down from the roof and saw three men attacking a young woman, they were trying to mug her, or worse.

She dropped from the top of the building, trusting in the shock absorbing technology that Hiroshi had installed in the costume to stop her from breaking her legs when she hit the pavement. It worked; she touched down on the ground soundlessly, like a cat. The three attackers hadn't heard a thing. They were too focused on their task of separating the woman from her belongings. The woman lay on the ground, sobbing, using her arms to try fend off the kicks and punches of her attackers. Her eyes were wide open in shock. The victim saw the green eyes of Aimee's mask. The victim gasped and screamed again, her cry cutting through the frigid air. She must think that another attacker has come to join in. Aimee thought she's right: just incorrect as to whom I'm going to hurt.

One of the attackers turned around and spotted Aimee. She sized him up. He was big, his arms and shoulders were muscular in the way that only someone who's spent a lot of time in a prison gym could be.

"Halloween was a week ago, who the heck are you supposed to be?" He asked.

"I'm the person telling you to step away from the girl" Aimee answered, a touch unsure of what exactly was the etiquette for the situation she was now involved in.

She'd spent hours one afternoon a few weeks back practising her 'vigilante voice' trying different pitches and tones, all in an attempt to try and find the voice that would instil fear in criminals. She'd felt most happy with a raspy, grating "I've got a sore throat" voice before realising that it was stupid and finally settling on using her regular voice. It would save thousands on throat lozenges and no one would ever recognise her solely by the sound of her voice anyway.

The second man laughed. His high pitched, nasal chortle cut through the sounds of the city around them. He was small and thin with greasy brown hair, he reminded Aimee of a giant rat that had now learned to walk upright. She noticed a knife tucked into the waistband of his dirty jeans.

"Get lost, or I'll cut you up." He sneered.

"You won't be able to cut anyone after I smash your fingers." Aimee said as boldly as possible.

"Hahaha." He turned to his muscular friend: "Listen to this mental patient. Let's teach her some manners."

The third mugger was dressed in a ragged green tracksuit and shivered uncontrollably, too much even for the cold autumn evening.

"Yeah" He said as he pulled a syringe from his pocket.

"So it takes three of you idiots to terrify one woman? You must all be very brave." Aimee said, mockingly. "Which one of you wants to be crippled first?"

The muscled one raised his fists and crouched into a fighting stance, he guarded his head and chest with his thick arms.

He isn't just a meat-head. Aimee decided. He's been training.

He moved towards Aimee confidently, and pounced at her once he had gotten close enough to throw his first punch; a wild right hook aimed at Aimee's head with the sole purpose of removing it from the rest of her body. She blocked his punch with her left arm, her impact armour took most of the force of the blow. Before he could react, she swept her right hand up into the side of his throat with a ridge-hand karate chop that would have splintered wood. He coughed deeply, fighting for breath; the blow had taken him by surprise and his hands instinctively moved to his throat in shock. Aimee used the opening created by this to punch him hard in the chest with her left fist and then kicked him in the stomach with a fast right kick. He fell to the ground, desperately trying to get a lungful of air.

Aimee had learned one basic rule of taking on more than one opponent: hurt the biggest one first. It gave a tremendous psychological advantage. Her other opponents were going to be just a little bit more scared of her now and scared people make stupid mistakes.

Aimee stared at the rat, who was in turn, looking at his friend sprawled on the ground. His face was frozen in a delicious mixture of terror and disbelief. Aimee knew he must be close to his breaking point. One more push and he'd run away in panic or come at her in gloriously stupid rage. Aimee decided that she would prefer for him to choose option two. She wanted to mess with his head even further:

"I just mangled your friend in less than three seconds. How long do you think it'll take me to do the same to you?" She said.

The rat grabbed the hilt of his knife, drew it from its sheath and ran straight at Aimee. He had chosen murderous rage as his way of dealing with the situation. Aimee smiled and reached over to her scabbard, she drew one of her fighting sticks with her right hand. He kept coming, screaming loudly in a mixture of panic and anger as he slashed at her with his long knife. Aimee moved to the left as he charged, her stick chopped down diagonally as he came closer. The stick hit him on his right hand with a resounding 'thud'. Aimee felt the impact reverberate through the stick as his knuckles cracked loudly. He cried out in agony as she hit him with a horizontal strike across the hip and stomach and again across the back with the return stroke. The rat tripped over and fell onto his face beside his friend.

The mugger in the green tracksuit took one long look at his friends and said: "Listen, I don't want any trouble!"

"If you didn't want trouble then you should have stayed at home. Drop the syringe and lay on the ground, hands behind your back." Aimee growled.

He did what he was told. Aimee removed a plastic tie from a pocket on her web gear and slid it over his hands, trapping them. She tightened the tie around his wrists. He wouldn't be able to use his hands to do anything now. She pushed him to the ground and into a puddle. She figured that she might as well make him as uncomfortable as possible.

Satisfied that the three were all temporarily disabled, Aimee walked over to the victim and knelt down beside her. Aimee quickly checked her for any injuries. The victim had no broken bones as far as Aimee could see but she was badly bruised and bloody, one eye had closed over from the swelling around it.

"Are you OK?" Aimee asked.

The woman smiled a little, which surprised Aimee: She had expected the victim to be afraid.

"I'm doing much better than they are." The victim croaked.

"Nothing seems to be broken." Aimee re-assured her.

"Thanks to you."

"It was nothing, really. I didn't even break a sweat." Aimee stood up to leave: "The cops will be here in a minute. I'll call them after I leave."

"What's your name?" The victim asked: "Your hero name I mean? You are one of them aren't you? I always knew there was more out there, like The Vanguard."

Aimee mused for a moment: "I don't know, I haven't thought of a good one yet."

Aimee pulled the grappling gun from its holster and fired it at the top of a nearby building. She ascended quickly and saw a pair of police officers enter the alley. They must have heard the screams of either the victim or the attackers and came to investigate. They immediately saw the victim and her attackers. One police officer keyed his radio and called for an ambulance and back-up.

"What happened here?" One of them asked.

The mugging victim replied, slowly: "A superhero. She saved me from these three guys."

"Where'd she go?"

"Across the rooftops."

The attacker in the green tracksuit cried as he lay on the wet ground. "She came, beat us all up and left."

Aimee smiled again as she turned away and started back towards her apartment. She had stopped her first crime. She felt incredible, it was like a darkness that had been inside her had been dispelled. She now knew she had made the correct decision. This was what she was meant to do with her life. The feeling of sheer bliss was indescribable; the adrenaline rush made her feel light-headed. She could get used to this.

Dawn was beginning to arrive as she returned to the balcony of her apartment. She stepped inside her home and began to peel off her outfit. She carefully stored the costume and weapons in a wardrobe and went to the bathroom to take an urgently needed hot bath. The costume, useful as it was, stank to high heaven. She would need to ask Hiroshi to manufacture spares if she didn't want to be constantly washing the thing.

She turned on the faucet and waited for the water to become piping hot. She brushed her teeth in the time it took for the bathtub to fill. The bathroom mirror quickly fogged up as she did so. Aimee used her hand to wipe away the condensation gathered on the mirror and saw her reflection for the first time since she had entered the apartment. Something was different about her. It was just barely noticeable, but it was there: even though she wasn't wearing the outfit anymore. She was no longer just Aimee DeWitt, the girl whose world was changed forever that day five years ago. She was more than that now.

The experience in the warehouse when she had been kidnapped had awoken a desire inside her that tonight's activity had alleviated. She felt like a whole person for the first time in years and she was… happy. The part of her that she had worried was missing had now been temporarily replaced. Aimee DeWitt, carefree teenager, had died when her mother did. The shell of a woman that had walked away from the death of her mother now had a purpose: revenge.

There's a word to describe a creature that returned from the grave to wreak vengeance on those who had wronged it. A Revenant. That's exactly what I have become. She thought as she stared at her reflection in the mirror.

"I'm a Revenant." She said and a smile crept across her face. She had just chosen her superhero name.

Chapter Eleven | Meetings

Aimee awoke at midday to the sound of her alarm clock blaring out someone else's idea of good music. A teenaged pop princess was shrieking about love and how great it was in a particularly tuneless manner. Aimee slowly moved her right hand from underneath the duvet and, without moving her head from its customary position buried deep in the pillows, managed to hit the snooze button on the third attempt. She groaned. Late nights were a killer. She rolled over onto her side and, yawning, threw back the duvet and swung her legs over the edge of the bed. She dragged herself upright, using the bedside table as support and walked like a zombie to the bathroom for her second bath of the day.

Once she had bathed and cleared the cobwebs from her mind she felt a lot better. She wrapped her body in a big white fluffy towel and did the same with her hair. The treacherous snooze button had timed out and the radio played another, remarkably similar song about how great love is from another identikit pop star. She always kept the bedside radio tuned to a pop station, the horrible music would act as a prod to drive her out of bed as quickly as possible.

The Board meeting was today, those were always the least enjoyable days of her year. When she had turned eighteen her dad had stepped down from running the business and gone off to India to find himself. This mainly involved lots of public drunkenness and fist fights with the locals. He had also changed a lot after Aimee's mother had died. The retiring, musty old businessman had morphed into a devil may care idiot. Ballooning around the world, sailing across the Atlantic solo, Paul DeWitt had done it all.

He occasionally sent her an email from a far flung part of the globe with pictures attached of his 'interactions' with the natives. Neither of them had much to say to each other in any event. Aimee wasn't going to go to great lengths to repair their "family bond" which had never been noticeably present in the first place. Aimee had adjusted to not having a father quite easily. It wasn't as if he had been a major presence in her life. As much as Paul DeWitt had changed, she had changed more, from a scared little girl to a confident young woman and, since last night, a part time superhero.

One major part of Paul DeWitt's apparent mental breakdown included him passing his voting rights on the Board of DeWitt Industries to Aimee. The other Board members and senior staff of Dewitt Industries had treated her as a joke at first. After all, she was just the boss's daughter: A young woman who had come in from school to run the company. The staff had changed their mind very quickly once she had proven that she had a flair for business and design. Her colleagues variously described her as 'driven', 'determined' and 'hard working', although those were all basically the same thing. Aimee was as surprised as any of them to find that she was a natural business-woman. That was a scary thought.

Aimee left the bedroom to go to the kitchen. The remainder of the apartment besides the bedroom, gym and kitchen was practically bare. It contained no pictures on the walls, no shelves full of books and very little furniture other than two couches, a large television and a coffee table. The kitchen was well furnished; but that was a remnant of the previous owners' tenure. Most of the cupboards were empty. Aimee couldn't cook and only just managed to keep the fridge stocked with fruit, vegetables, tea, coffee, muesli and yoghurt. She ate out whenever she required more substantial meals. Today, she made a pot of coffee and brought it out to the balcony to sit, watch the city and relax.

Ryan wasn't relaxed. The metal floor of the freight train in which he was currently travelling wasn't exactly helpful when it came to getting a good night's sleep. It had been a month since the ISA had tried to capture him in Spain. It still felt like a dream. He hadn't been able to fly since then so he'd had to return to America the old fashioned way: stowing away on a massive container ship and hiding in a dark, smelly metal haulage container with nothing but crates of Spanish wine for company. It had seemed like the best option at the time. If the ISA were scouring Europe for him then he'd go to the last place they'd look: home.

The ship had reached Baltimore late last night and Ryan had disembarked and slipped away without being noticed in the hustle and bustle as the dock workers began the task of unloading the ship. He'd hung around the freight yard near the docks and had been able to sneak aboard a New Jersey bound train in the early hours of the morning. The train had travelled through the night and was now only a few minutes away from arriving at its destination. Ryan didn't know exactly what to do but he had decided that New York was big enough that he would be able to lose himself for a few days and figure out his next step. The ISA weren't going to stop looking for him, not now that they were sure that he had powers. Ryan had no idea how to go on the run and avoid them. Unless he got help, they would find him eventually. He grabbed his backpack and moved over to the door of the freight car. He watched for a likely spot to jump off the train and head to cover. After a minute he saw a potential jumping off point up ahead, the train began to slow down due to a bend in the tracks up ahead. Not far from the train tracks there was a small cluster of trees, weeds and long grass. He jumped as the train passed the bend and rolled as he landed. He crawled on his hands and knees into the patch of local plant life. After lying in the vegetation for a few seconds, he stuck his head up and looked around slowly, to see if anyone had noticed him. He didn't see anything. The world was empty of curious passers-by and furious railway workers. There weren't even any stray dogs moping around. A rusted chain link fence was the only thing separating the railway tracks from a large, quiet industrial estate. That would be an OK place to hide until nightfall. He crawled over to the fence, pushing his bag ahead of his body as he did so. There was a hole cut into the fence. It was just large enough for him to squeeze through. He stood up, dusted himself off and walked nonchalantly to a nearby warehouse, trying to make it look like he belonged there. The warehouse was old, dilapidated and looked like it hadn't been used in years, weeds grew in the cracks in the driveway and the windows were inexpertly boarded up with plywood. Ryan snuck around back and found a ground level window where the boards had rotted and hadn't been nailed properly to the window frame, he pulled at the lowest board and it broke in his hand. He pulled another and it came away just as easily. Once he'd made a gap big enough to fit through he grabbed a rock the size of his fist and broke the pane of glass. He entered the building and sat down in the corner of the room he'd broken into. It must have been an office at one time as it contained a desk and chair up against the wall. Ryan opened his backpack and pulled out a blanket. Hopefully now he'd be able to sleep for a few hours until it got dark and he could move on.

Aimee arrived at the New York offices of DeWitt Industries just in time for the meeting. The offices were on the fortieth floor of a skyscraper in Midtown. The Board members gathered every three months to complain, argue and eat any free food that was available. Aimee couldn't stand any of them. They were always trying to force her to do things their way. Aimee didn't like to take an active part in the business; they had experienced managers to handle the day to day running of the company. All the Board members seemed to do was interfere in the efficient running of the enterprise. Aimee preferred to let people do their jobs and only occasionally pushed the company in a particular direction, usually to do non-profit, charitable work. The other Board members had always strenuously objected to doing anything so humanitarian and no doubt they'd find a whole new list of objections to throw in her face today as well.

It was hour four of the Board meeting that would never end. Aimee had had to sit through various members of the board complaining about every topic under the sun and then some. They had collectively managed to exhaust the last reserves of her already extremely limited patience over the course of the afternoon.

"And now we come to the next item on the agenda, the Solar Generator project." said Duncan Miles.

Aimee had never heard a sentence pronounced with such vitriol before; Duncan had practically spat the sentence out, as if it was a canapé from the now empty buffet that tasted bad. Duncan Miles was one of the longer serving Board members; he held a lot of resentment towards Aimee as he had thought himself next in line for the top job. He hadn't expected Paul DeWitt to abandon his responsibilities and appoint Aimee, a barely out of high school woman, as the new CEO.

Duncan continued: "To date the company has spent seventy-five million dollars on this fool's errand. They took years to research and develop and when we finally manage to make them work; you give them away for free."

"Not for free; at cost." Aimee replied "There's a slight difference. I thought they would have covered that in Harvard Business School or wherever it was that you're supposed to have been educated."

"Don't get smart with me, young lady. This project represents a significant loss to the company. That technology could have earned us millions in profit."

"We're making plenty of money elsewhere. I made the decision to help people who needed this technology right now. We can make quick bucks with our hundreds of other products."

"That's not the point; we have a responsibility to our stockholders to do what's best for them."

"Last time I checked, I own over fifty percent of the stock. So you can go swivel on it. I have a responsibility to do what's best for the human race. Not just for bunch of people who already have more money than they know what to do with."

"You're treading on very dangerous ground, Ms. Dewitt."

"What else is new? Seriously, what else is new? I'm bored of you already, Mr. Miles. If you don't like the new direction that the company is headed, there's the door."

Duncan sat down with a scowl on his face. Aimee stood up and addressed the other Board members.

"I'm running the company the way I see fit. We need to make the world a better place, not just do what lines out pockets in the easiest way. You all would do well to remember that. Any projects I ask the company to undertake are for the betterment of the human race and that's good for all of us."

Aimee turned on her heel and exited the Board room. Duncan seethed in his chair. The other Board members turned as one to look at him.

"Maybe it's time to consider other options for the future management of this company?" he said.

The others nodded enthusiastically in agreement.

"Any trace of him yet?"

At the sound of Benning's voice over the radio, Eva put the cardboard cup of lukewarm coffee down on the dashboard of her car and picked up the walkie-talkie.

"No sir. The bio-monitor puts him in this general area but I haven't sighted the target."

"Let me now as soon as you see anything suspicious."

"Sir, I'd like to remind you that this is New Jersey. 'Suspicious' is normal for this place."

"Just get it done, Agent Forty-Three."

"Sir, yes Sir."

She'd been sitting in the car for four hours, waiting for the target, Ryan Curtis, to show his face. The equipment back at their Nevada headquarters had picked up Ryan's arrival in the United States a day and a half ago. The readings that the tracer she had placed on Ryan at the restaurant in Spain had given them showed a unique energy signature that they had programmed their computers to search for. The ISA had information provided to them directly from satellites in orbit. They were able to narrow down traces of the signal to the nearest square mile. Which was still a lot of space to cover and they didn't have the luxury of the manpower required to do a full search, not without calling in favours from the other agencies. Benning didn't want the CIA or NSA sharing in his glory and had vetoed the merest suggestion of asking for co-operation from anyone. Eva and three other teams were stationed around the area, hoping to find their quarry. So far, they'd had no success. Eva guessed that Ryan was hiding out in a warehouse. He'd have to come out sooner or later, to get food or just because of sheer boredom and then the ISA would get their man. Benning could stand to wait a few more hours after having spent five years seeking Ryan and the treasure trove of genetic information he contained.

Eva was having trouble coming to terms with what she was being asked to do. Ryan didn't seem like a threat to her, but he had superpowers. There were only a handful of people with powers remaining since The Battle of Homestead, when an apparently unidentified woman had killed nearly all the super humans that they knew about. The senior agents of the ISA knew the truth of course: Maria Fleming had been the head of their secret project to study the heroes. She'd gone mad when the project had been cancelled and decided to take matters into her own hands. Another person with superpowers was a variable that the world could do without. Most of them ended up as villains; at least they had before The Vanguard had captured most of them. Many of the captured villains had died in prison. The real world wasn't like comics books where the villain broke out of the asylum and resumed his rampage without missing a beat. People who got sent to jail for super crimes in the real world generally stayed there. Ryan's parents had been two of the world's greatest heroes, but there was no guarantee that he wasn't going to want to get revenge on the world for what had happened. Even so, Benning's wish to study the kid made her feel uneasy, Eva wasn't entirely sure that capturing him and holding him in a lab for the rest of his considerably shortened life, was the ethical thing to do, even if the defence of the USA was at stake.

Aimee arrived back at her apartment and went on a five mile run on the treadmill as soon as she could change out of her suit and into her gym clothes. She had hoped that the exercise would calm her down but it didn't work. She knew the type of exercise she needed. She had to go out into the city and do vicious things to bad people and all would be right in her head again. She stopped the treadmill and stepped off it, grabbing her towel and bottle of water as she went to her bedroom. She entered the room and walked over to the wardrobe. She slid back the door and stared at the outfit hanging there. Without a second thought she suited up, put on the mask and prepared her weapons and grappling gun. It was dark outside already.

I better not go out in the city tonight, I don't want there to be a pattern of appearances for someone to track me down.

Aimee took the elevator down to the basement. Her car was the only one in the garage. The rest of the building was empty; she'd bought the entire thing via a shell company. The lights in the other apartments were timed to come on at various intervals to make it look like the place was occupied by more than one person. Mail was delivered to a number of the apartments as well, mostly magazine subscriptions to people who didn't exist and so on.

She drove out of the city, through the Holland Tunnel and onto the New Jersey turnpike towards Newark. She had no idea why she'd picked that as her destination, other than a vague feeling that there were plenty of people over there that needed their heads kicked in. After a few minutes of driving around aimlessly, she parked her car in an alley behind an abandoned store and went to the roof tops to see if she could find a task to occupy her time. It didn't take too long for her to find a small time drug dealer who needed frightening.

Jimmy was standing in the shadows beside a long closed convenience store, huddled in a long coat, trying to keep out of the bitterly cold gusts of wind that were chilling him to the core. Business was slow tonight, even discerning marijuana customers knew better than to come out when it was this cold. He decided that it was time to call it a night and go home when he felt another shiver go down his spine, this one had nothing to do with the wind though; he couldn't escape the feeling that he was being watched. He saw a blur of motion to his left just as someone knocked him over onto the ground face first. He felt a weight on his back as his attacker gripped his arm and bent it in a direction it was not supposed to be bent in. A voice spoke:

"I'm debating whether to fracture your spine or not. While I'm ruminating on that ethical conundrum I want you to start telling me why I shouldn't."

"Are you crazy? Who the hell are you?"

"Why does everyone keep asking me that? I'm the person with the means and the motivation to hurt you very badly. Unless, of course, you want me to move up the food chain and leave you alone."

"Stupid... I'm not going to tell you anything."

"Suit yourself." said Revenant.

Jimmy felt the pressure on his back increase as the person shifted their weight, whoever it was had grabbed his hand and was bending his fingers back, the pain was excruciating. He heard a snap and felt his middle finger break at precisely the same moment.

"Gaaah!" he screamed.

"That was one. You have nine more and I have all night."

"Ok! Ok! I'm on my own tonight because the boss needed a few guys to help provide security. He was a big delivery coming."

"What's in the shipment?"

"Grass, blow, guns... Please, I'm only small time. It's him you want."

"Who's your boss?"

"You won't believe me if I tell you"

"Try me."

"It's Cruel-T."

"The not particularly good gangster rapper? They play his songs on the radio all the time. I hate them." responded a surprised Revenant.

"Yeah, that's him. His second album didn't do so well so he's trying to get back in the game. He set up a deal with the Russians."

"Tell me more."

Jimmy talked. Revenant listened.

Cruel-T sat in the back seat of his SUV with his manager, Cecil, and two of his entourage.

"Man. Why have I got to make an appearance at this deal?" he whined.

"You're the one who organised this Cruel-T." replied Cecil.

"Don't mean I actually wanted to go. I got better things to be doing. I'm a star, remember? There's got to be a party on somewhere that needs Cruel-T."

"A star whose last album sold next to nothing. The record label ended up burying one million discs in a landfill in New Mexico. If you want the lifestyle that goes with being rich and famous then you need cash." responded a tired Cecil.

"Wait. Back up. There's a New Mexico? Since when?"

"Nineteen-Twelve."

"How come I never heard anything about it before? Why didn't you all tell me?"

"It's pretty unimportant." said Cecil as he took off his glasses and wiped the condensation from them using the sleeve of his suit. "Cruel. Please pay more attention; this deal with the Russians is important. The leader of their crew is crazy. Try not to upset him."

"I'm a people person. Everyone says so. Watch me charm these guys. There'll be nothing to worry about. "

"Agent Forty-Three. Come in. This is Twenty-Five."

The voice startled Eva; she had started to drift off to sleep. The other units were only to check in if they saw anything going on which may be related to their target. She keyed her walkie-talkie and responded:

"Forty-Three. Go ahead."

"We're seeing activity on the southern end of the operation area."

"The target?"

"Negative, two SUVs. We had a white van pass by about two minutes ago as well."

"That's a lot of activity for an abandoned Industrial estate." Eva said, tiredly.

"Affirmative."

"It's nothing to do with us. Unless the SUVs had our target inside."

"Roger that. I just wanted to keep you informed. Over."

That had been the most exciting thing to happen in hours. Ryan was nowhere to be seen. Eva was getting awfully bored of playing the waiting game.

Ryan heard a number of cars pull up outside the warehouse and the shutter opened. He looked out the window and realised that it was night time. He hadn't intended to sleep for so long. Ryan watched through the narrow crack between the door and its frame as a large white van drove into the building followed by two jeeps. Five men got out of the van and six occupants from the jeeps joined them. The only light in the warehouse was coming from the streetlamps outside. One man hit a switch near the door and the lights in the warehouse came on. They were all armed. This didn't look good.

Two of the men stepped outside the doors of the building to stand guard. Ryan watched as one of the men from the jeeps opened the front passenger door and pulled out a briefcase. He held it up as another of the men snapped it open, showing the guys from the van that it was full of money.

Great, I had to pick the one warehouse in New Jersey to sleep in where a drug deal was going down tonight. Ryan moved away from the door, back into the relative safety of the office. A feeling stirred inside him, his parents wouldn't have liked him ignoring a crime in progress. They'd raised him to be better than that.

Maybe I can do something. Even get the licence numbers and call the cops to bust them. Ryan said to himself.

Revenant drove slowly around the outskirts of the group of warehouses. There were more parked cars around the area than she would have expected but the place was mostly abandoned. She saw activity near a warehouse not far from the railway tracks. The drug dealer she had mistreated hadn't been lying. The loading door had been opened and two men with sub machine guns stood guard outside. They weren't paying much attention. One was smoking and both were talking amiably to one another. Revenant drove on a few hundred yards, parked her car between two garages and got out. She'd scout the warehouse and stop the drug deal. If she managed to hospitalise criminals as well she'd consider it a good night.

Ryan went to the door and opened it enough that he could leave the office without attracting any attention. He used pieces of furniture as cover and moved towards the cars to get a better look.

One of the guys from the SUVs was dressed in designer sportswear and had enough gold draped around his neck and wrists to purchase Idaho. Ryan thought he recognised him from somewhere.

"So, we got a deal?" asked Cruel-T.

"I am thinking we do." replied the leader of the Russian gang. He wore a long black leather coat that looked like it had been dug up from a cemetery over a heavily stained white vest. Twin hatchets hung from his belt. "I am knowing you. Yes?"

"That's right dude. I'm famous. You've heard my number one single Lady Bits. No doubt. I had a number one album too. Cruel Melodies. I got a Grammy award for it."

"Hah! Is true! I am recognising your song! My friends call me Ivan. My enemies call me 'Ivan the Hatchet'. But very few of them are still alive."

"If you want me to sign a CD for you, I'd be cool with that."

"I am saying that I am recognising your song. Not that I am liking it. Let us conclude business and leave. Ivan does not wish to be standing around with guns and drugs in the warehouse. police may catch."

"Oh" said Cruel-T, slightly deflated. "Sure, whatever. You've got the goods and I've got the money."

Revenant watched the two guards from her position hidden in the shadows behind a dumpster about ten metres away from the loading dock door. She pulled two throwing stars from her belt, stood up and threw them at the same time. The guards only had a second to react and had begun the raise their weapons when one star apiece hit them in their necks. The stars were tipped with a powerful tranquiliser. The guards passed out without a word and sank to the ground, unconscious. Revenant walked over to the guards and took their Mac-10 machine guns from them. She released the magazines and ejected the rounds in the chambers. She tossed the guns away to the left of the building and the bullets to the right.

"Try firing those now boys." She muttered as she walked away.

"Agent Forty-Three?"

"Yes, Twenty-Five?"

"I've got more activity here. It looks like a drug deal is going on."

"So?"

"So, maybe the target is waiting in the area for this to happen. He could be here to stop it!"

"Why would you think that?"

"He's the kid of superheroes isn't he? It's the sort of thing he might do."

"I'm either extremely tired or that makes sense I guess." Eva hit another button on her walkie-talkie to talk to all of the units in the area "Converge on Twenty-Five's location. We may have a sighting."

Revenant studied the building for a few seconds, trying to strategize. The best way to win a fight is to use whatever you have that your opponent doesn't have. What advantage do I have that they don't? She pondered: night vision lenses.

Revenant looked around and saw the building's fuse box on a wall on the outside of the building to the left of the loading dock door. She crouched down and ran to the wall and opened the box. She grabbed a multi-tool from her belt and started to cut the wires inside. She spliced in a small explosive charge with a timer. After two minutes the building would go dark. That would leave her just enough time for her to get up into the rafters of the building.

Ryan inched closer to the dealers, hoping to get a better view of the licence plates. They were taking their time, counting the money and checking the boxes of weapons and drugs. They were even laughing and joking as they worked. Movies always showed people double crossing each other at precisely this moment. What is wrong with these guys? Ryan though. It's like a social event. Could someone start a fight and pull a gun so the cops don't have to get involved?

Ryan didn't notice Revenant hiding in the rafters above his head. She watched him for a few moments.

Who's this? He's not involved with the deal or else he wouldn't be trying to hide. A reporter? Or an innocent bystander. He's going to get himself seen and killed, unless I help.

Suddenly, Revenant heard engines outside the building, coming closer. The criminals all looked around nervously or drew their weapons.

Reinforcements? No, from their reactions the dealers weren't expecting anyone either.

Suddenly Cruel-T was shouting hysterically and waving his gun around:

"Hell's this man? You think you can play us like this? No one messes with the Grammy award winning Cruel-T. No one!"

"Is nothing to do with us!" roared Ivan the Hatchet. "Is your "homeboys"! No?"

Three black cars entered the warehouse and screeched to a halt. Four suited men and a woman with red hair emerged from the newly arrived vehicles, pulling handguns from their holsters and aiming at the criminals. The woman pulled a badge from the inside pocket of her jacket and asked:

"We're with the ISA! Where's Ryan Curtis?"

Ivan answered: "I know nothing of this man, ask these men here!"

Cruel-T answered back while gesturing wildly: "Does Ryan Curtis sound like a name I oughta know? I pay Cecil over there to remember names for me!"

Revenant looked down at the teenager hiding behind the packing crates below her as thoughts raced through her mind.

Ryan Curtis! The son of Solarstorm and Velocity? It looks a little like him, I guess. Why would the ISA want him? No-one's heard anything about him in years. I need to get him out of here.

At that precise moment, the lights went out.

Game on. Revenant thought.

Revenant tapped a small button on the right hand side of her mask near her eyes. Her lenses switched to night vision. She could see the inside of the warehouse as clear as day. The dealers and the ISA agents commenced shouting at each other. A couple of the agents pulled out flashlights, for all the good that those would do them in the pitch dark of the warehouse. Revenant took two stun grenades from the pouch near her left shoulder and threw them into the middle of the crowd of agents and dealers. The grenades exploded, throwing off a super-bright flash and creating an extremely loud explosion. Everyone in the crowd was now disorientated, their heads spinning from the effects of the weapons.

One of Cruel-T´s entourage started to fire his sub machine gun wildly, aiming at nothing in particular. Revenant dropped down from the rafters to the ground directly behind him. Even if the people hadn't been blinded by the flash, all they would have seen was a pair of glowing green eyes in the pitch dark warehouse.

Take that shooter first, it's a miracle he hasn't killed anybody yet. Revenant thought as she closed the distance from where she had landed to the man, who was still firing. Revenant grabbed his gun arm at his wrist with her right hand and slammed her left hand, palm open, into his elbow. He shrieked as his arm broke. He dropped the

164

gun. Revenant drove her elbow into his face. He stopped making noise and passed out from the pain. One of the ISA agents, still groggy from the stun grenades, threw a punch at her. She leaned back to avoid it and then darted forward. She threw her right arm around his neck, kicked his legs from underneath him and flipped him over her shoulder.

Another agent, one of the ones with the flashlights, began to point his gun at her:

"Stop… or… I'll… shoot" he said slowly as he tried to shake off the effects of the stun grenades.

Revenant kept moving towards Ryan and, without stopping, slid a throwing star from its sheath on her belt and threw it at the agent. It hit him on the upper right hand side of his chest. He staggered and fell over backwards.

Ivan grabbed the hatchets from his belt and ran at her while screaming a phrase in Russian which she guessed was really offensive, Revenant didn't recognise any of the words but could perfectly understand the emotions behind them. Ivan the Hatchet swung his weapons in circles around his head. Revenant dodged the first and drew one of her sticks to block the other. She grabbed the handle of the hatchet and hit Ivan across the knuckles with her stick. He let go of the handle and she hit him in the face with both her stick and the flat side of the head of his own hatchet. She pivoted and roundhouse kicked him across the back. He toppled over like a falling tree and didn't get up again.

Two of the Cruel-T's crew were all that now stood between Revenant and Ryan. She reached over her shoulder and drew her other fighting stick. Both of the remaining members of Cruel-T's entourage were woozy from the effect of the stun grenades.

Still, can't let them away too easily. Revenant thought.

She struck out at the two men with her sticks whirling in the air, aiming for their arms and legs. Within five seconds she had both of them on the ground nursing various bumps, breaks and bruises. She reached Ryan, who was holding his hands up to his ears. He'd been temporarily deafened by the stun grenades but he had seen the other inhabitants of the warehouse being beaten by a black shape with green eyes. As the apparition came closer to him he raised his hands to try to defend himself. The black shape slid to a halt beside him and hurriedly replaced its sticks in a scabbard on its back. Ryan could just make out what it was saying:

"Ryan Curtis?"

Ryan nodded, realising that the person in the costume was a woman.

"The name's Revenant. I'm going to get you out of here. Come with me now."

Ryan was too stunned to disagree, Revenant gripped his wrist tightly and half pushed, half dragged him out of the building.

Chapter Twelve | The Morning After

Benning isn't happy. Actually that could qualify as the year's biggest understatement. Benning is enraged. You'd swear he had just been told that five of his agents had, for the second time, made contact with a priority one target and let said target slip through their fingers. Either that or The Berlin Wall has been rebuilt while I was unconscious.

Eva sat on a wooden box in the same warehouse where five ISA agents, including her, had failed miserably in their assigned mission. She was nursing a steaming hot cup of black coffee and hoping that the world would stop spinning any minute now. No such luck. Benning was on the other side of the warehouse screaming at Agent Twenty-Five, promising him a place on every terrible assignment between now and retirement. Benning had been told the story of what had happened late last night by the other ISA agents who were present and wasn't happy. Eva wasn't sure what she could add to the report, other than a woman in black body armour with a mask, who carried enough weaponry to severely mess up anyone's day, had left through the loading dock with Ryan Curtis. Eva had been almost unconscious when Ryan and the woman had exited; a stun grenade had exploded directly in front of her and sent her reeling. Benning was coming to the end of his explosive rant at Agent Twenty-Five. The cleaning of toilets was being mentioned, frequently. Finally, Benning stopped and looked around the room, which was filled with police officers and paramedics either handcuffing drug dealers or preparing them for trips to the nearest hospital.

Paparazzi had surrounded the warehouse, hoping to get a shot of

Cruel-T being arrested for the news. Eva could hear the rapper's high pitched voice loudly complaining as he was pushed into the back of a waiting police van:

"You all can't arrest me; I'm the Grammy award winning Cruel-T. I want my lawyer; I want your badge numbers. You can't…"

The van doors slammed, mercifully cutting off his roars.

Benning started walking over towards Eva, mentally preparing the tirade that he was about to unleash.

Eva felt bad enough, even without the forthcoming lecture. Whoever that woman was last night, she wasn't subtle. Most of the criminals involved in the deal and two of the ISA agents needed serious medical help. She'd torn through them in a few seconds and left with the ISA's target. Eva was fully aware of exactly how completely she'd failed. She couldn't have done worse at the mission if she'd really tried to. Benning pointed at her, the subject of his next tirade, commencing in three… two… one:

"Agent Forty-Three! Forty-Three brain cells! Is that why they gave you that code number? Because from where I'm standing that's what it looks like!" harangued Benning.

"Sir, if I may…?" Eva began.

"If you may, what? Apologise?" Benning interrupted, mocking Eva's voice "Oh dear, I seem to have completely failed at the mission I was told to do, I'm soooooo sooorrryyyy." His voice went back to normal: "Well, I've heard two versions of this same story already this morning. Two of my agents are badly injured, trying to capture a child for the second time! All because I'm surrounded by idiots! Idiots!"

"There were other factors involved, sir."

"Oh yes! A new vigilante happened to show up. That's just amazing! What wondrous news will you bring me tomorrow? Every time I send you to capture this kid, a new hero appears. You're like a jinx. You also somehow managed to get the media involved as well. Do you know how much work we're going to have to do to keep this all buried? A Grammy award winner just got arrested at the site of one of our operations!"

"Cruel-T never actually won the Grammy, Sir. He stormed the stage at the ceremony a couple of years back and stole one from that country singer." Eva interjected.

Benning stared at her in silence. Cold rage burning in his eyes.

"We'll be able to track them down." Eva quickly continued. "There can't be that many people with the time, money or inclination to do what that woman did last night."

"For all our sakes, I hope not." Benning replied "You're confined to base for the foreseeable future. We're moving out immediately. We'll have to take time and consider our next move. We're drawing far too much attention."

Benning turned on his heel and strode out the door back to his car. Eva sipped on her coffee and brooded.

Duncan Miles walked into the dining room of his penthouse apartment in New York. The housekeeper had already set the table and was busy in the kitchen preparing breakfast. Duncan looked forward to his usual breakfast of bacon and eggs. The morning paper was neatly folded beside his place setting. He unfolded it and read the headlines. The door to the kitchen swung open. Duncan didn't even raise his head from the paper.

"I'll have brown toast today, I think."

A German accented voice responded: "There won't be any toast today."

Duncan, expecting his housekeeper to be the only person in the apartment, looked up at the speaker; it was a man in a grey suit:

"Karl!" He exclaimed in shock, his voice turned angry. "What are you doing here? Did anyone see you coming in?"

"Just your housekeeper. She won't be telling anyone."

"Do you know how long it took me to find a decent housekeeper in this city?"

"No idea. How long did it take you to find a decent kidnapper?"

"The last job I gave you didn't go so well, remember? You were supposed to kill DeWitt's wife and make it look like a kidnapping gone wrong. Not let a teenaged girl make a complete fool of you."

"It was a rush job. I had to hire out for a driver at the last minute. Idiot let the girl escape and knock him unconscious. Luckily he didn't know any details of who was behind the kidnapping or my identity."

"I still had to pay quite a sum to have him killed in prison."

"I have to admit that was quite smart of you. I don't like loose ends."

"The grand plan didn't work though, did it? A grief stricken Paul DeWitt was supposed to hand over management of the company to me; instead I'm taking orders from a girl barely out of high school. If things had gone our way, I'd be one of the most powerful businessmen in the world."

"And I'd be very, very rich."

"We both would, but that fool Aimee DeWitt is ruining the company."

"I presume that is the little problem you want taken care of?"

"Yes."

"It could be tricky. She won't scare easily. She's already survived one encounter with me. You realise I'll have to kill her? Nothing else would work. It'll take time as well. I'll need to keep a watch on her for a few weeks. I'll have to monitor her schedule so I can pick the opportune moment."

"Fine, do it. Make it look like a mugging gone wrong. Whatever you do, I don't want it to come back on me."

Karl poured a glass of orange juice for himself and drank greedily. Once he had finished the glass, he slammed it on the table:

"Don't worry about that, no one suspected you of anything last time, did they? Pay me enough to make it worth my while and your reputation will remain spotless. I will expect half my usual fee to be transferred to my Swiss bank account by this evening and then I will commence my work. You will pay me the remainder upon successful completion."

Ryan stood on the balcony of the weirdest apartment he'd ever been in. The place, though clearly a nice apartment, with high ceilings and an amazing view over the city, was practically empty. It held only a few pieces of furniture. He'd tried the door out of the apartment earlier. The room was locked tighter than Fort Knox and he didn't think that the door was made of wood. It was too tough: he'd practically dislocated his arm when he'd tried to break the door down with an inexpert shoulder charge. He could feel a bruise forming as he sat down on a beanbag and waited to see what else would happen today.

He heard a key in the lock and the main door opened slowly. A young woman, dressed in black jeans and a grey hoodie entered the apartment carrying two cups of coffee in a cardboard tray and a large paper bag full of food.

"Hope you like bagels!" she said, a lot more cheerfully than you would expect from a woman who had spent the previous evening hitting people in the face.

"I'd like to be able to leave. Who are you?" asked Ryan.

"Is that any way to speak to the woman who saved your life last night? My name's Aimee DeWitt, head of DeWitt Industries by day and a masked vigilante at night. I call myself "Revenant" when I'm out hero-ing."

"Why did you drag me out of that warehouse last night?"

"You were about to do something very stupid, attack an ISA squad, the Russian mafia and a hip-hop crew pretending to be bad-asses so they could sell more records. You'd have made far more enemies than a person could ever deal with."

"I wasn't going to attack anyone, I wanted to get the number plates of the drug dealers and call the cops on them."

"Either way you would be dead or in prison now if I hadn't intervened. You're welcome, by the way."

"Thank you."

"There must be pretty weird things going on if the ISA is chasing you. They're not known for acting as openly as they did last night."

"What do the ISA do?"

"No one really knows. I've heard that they study 'extra normal' activities. Superheroes, strange artefacts, that kind of thing. Rumour was that they were the agency responsible for coming up with ways to stop the heroes in case they went rogue. Of course, then that woman did their job for them at the Battle of Homestead."

"And yet, you attacked them all without a second thought."

"Masked vigilante, remember?" said Aimee, pointing to herself. "It's kind of expected that I violently hurt people."

"But why save me, assuming I needed saving?"

"I was the biggest Vanguard fan when I was younger, I had all the action figures, t-shirts, posters, videogames, everything. I guess you could say I was a Vanguard fan girl. They inspired me to become what I am today. Trying to save the world in whatever way I can."

"Thank you again for saving my life. Now, I don't want to seem ungracious but I really need to go, those ISA agents are going to keep looking for me, I should stay on the move."

"Any idea why they've got a mad on for you?"

"They think I've got superpowers."

"Well, do you?"

"Yes… but not exactly, the powers I have aren't working properly. The ISA chased me and I hurt one of their agents accidentally. He hit me and broke his hand. I eventually got away by flying for a short distance. I crash-landed in a field a few miles away from where I jumped off a cliff."

"Well." replied Aimee. "I'm not an expert but it sure sounds like you have powers."

"What's the use in having powers that only work occasionally?"

"Maybe you have to get training to learn to use them?"

"Who can train me? Nearly all the other heroes are dead. There's only about seven left alive after the Battle of Homestead and most of them are the low powered ones. The only big time heroes left alive are Warfare, Wolfhound and Scorch."

"None of them would be much help to you. Warfare has disappeared, Wolfhound is still active in a small way and Scorch retired quietly. I've no idea where to start looking for him."

"So I'm screwed is what you're telling me?"

"Maybe not." said Aimee. "There is one hero who may be able to help. Eat first and then we'll leave. You look half starved. When was the last time you had a decent meal?"

"Spain, I suppose." Ryan replied "I've been living on cans of cold spaghetti hoops and water. Wait, we're leaving together?"

"Sure, no disrespect, but you're going to need my help. You seem like you need a bodyguard. And we'll need to do some travelling to get to the man I want you to meet."

"Where are we going exactly? And who is this guy?"

"He's in Japan. His name's Hiroshi Saito. He used to be called Mech.

"You're pretty quick to assume that I trust you. For all I know you're an ISA agent."

"I'm not."

"I don't know you. I've already had issues with people not being who they claimed to be."

"Ryan. You can trust me. You're the son of two people who I've idolised since I was five years old. I really want to help you."

Ryan was taken aback. She certainly sounded believable. Besides, he didn't have any other ideas. He decided to take a chance.

"When do we leave?" He said.

"Eat breakfast while I pack and then I'll drive us to the airport, my jet will have us in Japan in five hours."

"That's fast."

"I have a very cool jet."

Aimee opened one of the paper bags and used a plastic fork to dish out a pile of salad onto a paper plate for Ryan.

"Sorry about the plastic cutlery." She said. "I only have one of each of the usual eating utensils, and a couple of spare mugs and glasses that the previous occupant of the apartment left behind."

"Yeah, I noticed the place was furnished a bit sparsely."

"I don't like clutter. Too much furniture makes me feel boxed in. I enjoy having space."

"So what exactly happened to you to make you want to become a vigilante?"

"The details aren't important. I just want to do something worthwhile to improve the world."

"And hitting people improves things?"

"A little, it's not a bad start. Can I ask you a question?"

"Can I stop you?" asked Ryan.

"Not really. What made your parents decide to become superheroes?"

"I'm not sure, It's one of the many things I never had a chance to ask them."

"Sorry."

"No, it's OK. They died doing the right thing I guess. Maybe that's all they ever wanted. To do the right thing."

"Not a bad way of looking at it." Aimee said as she took a swig from her cardboard coffee cup. "You really need try your drink. The Brick café on 33rd does the most amazing chai latte. It's not exactly healthy but it's awesome."

Fifteen minutes later Ryan and Aimee were down in the basement of the building. There was only one car parked in the basement garage, a blue, mid-priced, saloon car.

"Huh" muttered Ryan, under his breath.

"What?" asked Aimee.

"I just figured that if you had a very cool jet that you'd have a very cool car as well. Not a regular family car. Didn't you say you were the CEO of a company?"

"What? You were expecting a Revenant-mobile? Would you respect me more if I had a black sports-car with a massive spoiler on the back and rocket boosters and machine guns?"

"Well, yeah."

"That's stupid, everyone would immediately recognise it as my car and it'd be impossible to get parts for. Trust me, this is the best. It gets really good mileage, it's reliable and it's so average looking that no one even notices it."

"OK, fine, whatever you say. You're awfully defensive."

"I just don't like people making fun of my car."

"That's really sad."

"When you own your first car, you'll understand. Now come on. We have a six hour journey ahead of us. I called Hiroshi and let him know we're coming. You can fill me in on the rest of your back story on the way."

Chapter Thirteen | Super Robot Life-Form

In her defence, Aimee really did have a very cool jet. It was currently heading towards Japan at mach 4, much faster than a regular jet could travel. It looked like a sleek silver arrow-head with tiny angular silver wings jutting out from the top and sides.

"How come this plane is so fast?" asked Ryan.

"It uses hypersonic engines. They're much more efficient than regular jets so we can fly at higher altitudes with greater speed. They're really expensive though. I'm the only person who owns a private plane with them. Our biggest customers are the military which uses them for their 'Aurora' aircraft. Mech invented them and he used the prototypes for his suit. My company bought the patent off him, after he retired."

"Why isn't he a hero anymore? He was active for like, two years and then he stopped."

"I'll let him tell you, if he wants to. We'll be landing in five minutes. Look out the window to the right. That's Tanegashima Space Centre down there. It's our destination."

Ryan looked out the cockpit window. It was raining heavily but through the downpour Ryan could just make out a part of a large island which was covered in runways, tall buildings, aircraft hangars and an artificial mountain with what looked like train tracks pointing straight up spaced around it at regular intervals. Ryan realised that the tracks would need to be massive for him to be able to see them from their plane.

"What the heck is all this stuff?"

"The big metallic mountain to our right is the main launch pad.

Space shuttles are fired by huge electro-magnetic catapults along the tracks and into orbit. Hiroshi works at the Shōji Kawamori engineering design works. It's part of this facility."

Aimee looked at the controls in the cockpit. A text message had flashed up on screen.

"Actually, a shuttle will be launching in a few seconds. Look!"

A bright blue glow appeared at the bottom of one of the tracks and shot up towards the sky, Ryan saw a red space shuttle travel up the track at tremendous speed and gain altitude.

"Wow!"

"It's really something, isn't it? They have around ten launches a day from here."

"And Mech runs this place?"

"Not exactly. Sit down and put your seatbelt on. We're going to land."

Aimee landed the plane expertly and brought it to a stop not far from a long, low prefabricated grey building. Aimee undid her seatbelt, stood up and stretched her arms towards the ceiling.

"Aggh, sitting still for so long always does my back in."

She walked into the cabin and grabbed the large black bag she'd brought with her.

"That's an awful lot of luggage, considering you can be back in your apartment in a few hours." Ryan said.

"It's my vigilante gear, just in case. I also brought food and drink for Hiroshi."

"Because food is difficult to find in Japan?"

"Hiroshi can eat Milk Duds and cookies all day. We have a standing agreement that I bring him a few boxes whenever I visit."

Aimee hit buttons on a keypad on the wall of the plane and the door hissed open.

"Welcome to Japan!" she said, pointing out the door and to the building.

Rain sheeted down onto the tarmac as they ran to the low building. They entered through the glass doors. A bored looking security guard handed them a visitor pass and waved them through without taking his eyes off the TV monitor on his desk. He was engrossed in a quiz show where contestants were being asked trivia questions while running on treadmills and being pelted with eggs by an enthusiastic studio audience.

"Not exactly the world's tightest security is it?" asked Ryan as he slipped the lanyard containing the security pass around his neck.

"It looks that way, but if you started making trouble, you'd be tranquilised and put in a cell in less than fifteen seconds. They don't mess around in here. The only reason I'm allowed in is because Hiroshi got the bosses to give me a permanent guest pass." Aimee took her pass out of her pocket and clipped it onto a belt loop on her pants.

Aimee and Ryan walked down a long white corridor, passing by offices containing neat office workers filing neat piles of paper.

"So far, so normal. It could be any office anywhere." mentioned Ryan.

"Look here" Aimee said, pointing to a long window which looked into a well-equipped gym. Inside, scores of men and women in white tracksuits were being drilled in martial arts by a black haired man in a green uniform.

"OK, that's a bit more military. So where's Mech?"

"A few more minutes' walk this way" Aimee pointed straight ahead.

"And don't call him Mech to his face. It upsets him."

Five minutes of walking had them at a security door with a United Nations logo stencilled on it. Aimee pressed a buzzer and spoke to the person on the other end of the line when the call was answered. The door swung open and they went inside. This corridor had shelves on both sides which were covered in robot toys of all shapes and sizes.

"That's a lot of robots." Ryan said, as he looked at the display while walking towards another security door at the end. This door swung open as they approached and they stepped into Hiroshi's lab.

The place was a mess; pieces of metal of every shape and size were piled up against the walls. Electrical wire and fibre-optic cable were strewn about the tables, work benches and floor. Piles of paper lay on every desk, chair and stool. A man with spiked blue hair, dressed in a lab coat which may once have been white, sat on a high stool with his back to them, writing or drawing feverishly on a notepad. A monitor in the corner was showing an animated series with giant robots noisily fighting each other. The man slowly turned to face the new arrivals, a huge smile on his face:

"Ha ha! Aimee, you are here! I think you forget about me now you big time superhero!"

"Hi Hiroshi, I brought you goodies."

Aimee reached into her sports bag and pulled out a smaller paper bag. She threw it across the room to Hiroshi. He opened it and looked inside.

"Excellent! It been a while since I had these. The chocolate here terrible! Budget cuts, pfft!"

Hiroshi realised that there was a third person in the room, stood up quickly and walked over towards Ryan. Hiroshi took a magnifying glass from the pocket of his lab coat and looked suspiciously at Ryan through it. He walked in a circle around Ryan, peering at him. Ryan noticed that Hiroshi's sleeves were covered in ink of different colours.

"Who this?" Hiroshi queried.

"This is the person I told you about over the phone. Ryan Curtis."

"Aha! Yes, son of Solarstorm and Velocity. So long missing and now found!" Hiroshi grabbed Ryan's hand and shook it enthusiastically: "It a real pleasure to meet you!"

"Thanks." Ryan croaked.

"What wrong, pretty boy? I make you shy?"

"No, I just expected you to look different."

"What? You think that the inventor of the first and only working powered armour be a drunken billionaire. Or maybe the military industrial complex?"

"No, it's just that you're a lot younger than I had imagined."

"I get that a lot, cowboy! I fifteen when I finish Suit One and fight at the Battle of Homestead."

"Fifteen?"

"Yeah, I know! I start building suit for a cosplay competition at anime convention. It supposed to be replica of suit from Super Robot Galaxy Team Number Ten!! I really wanted to win so I just keep adding things to it. Lights, sound effects, glow in the dark paint. After a while I forget about competition and I decide to see if I can make it fully functional battle suit. After six months, presto, it finished!"

"You built your suit at home?"

"No, don't be stupid! You think my parents have proper raw materials or tools? I build it in local High School workshop using parts I salvage from scrap-yards and half of ton of Gundanium Alloy I steal from building site. I actually win cosplay competition too!"

Hiroshi pointed over to a trophy standing in a display case amongst dozens of other awards.

"Cool Statue! Isn't it?" He said excitedly.

"That's crazy. How could a fifteen year old build a robotic suit of armour?"

"Not crazy, I super genius after all. But I get sick of superhero life and I retire a few years back. United Nations recruited me shortly after that."

"What do you do here?"

"United Nations Special Astronomical Fact-finding Expedition! They supposed to be leaving for Mars in a few years. I designing the spacesuits that the astronauts wear!"

Ryan thought for a seconds and then spoke:

"Your team's acronym is "UNSAFE"?"

"So what? I think it funny! Hahahahaha!" Hiroshi suddenly stopped laughing and his expression turned deadly serious: "You worried it become self-fulfilling prophecy?"

"I hope not."

"It really cool work though, even if they not give me funding to build weapons into the suits. They say it not necessary, Mars dead planet. Pfft! That no excuse not to have gravity cannons on the spacesuits!"

Aimee placed her hand on Hiroshi's shoulder.

"Now that we're all acquainted. Ryan could use your help. He seems to be developing powers but they're not working properly. They only work for short periods or not at all."

"Really? That very interesting! What powers you supposed to have?"

"I was really strong and could fly. At least I could for a few minutes until I hit the ground."

"Hmmm! Very similar to the powers your father manifested, no?"

"I guess."

"No energy blasts or running fast?"

"No. Not that I've noticed."

"OK!" Hiroshi walked over to one of the desks and typed in a sequence of buttons on a computer terminal keyboard. A six foot long tiled section of the floor just beside Ryan's feet slid back and an examination table slowly rose from the ground.

"Hop up on table like good patient and I take look at you."

Ryan looked at Aimee and then spoke:

"Emmm, do I need to take my clothes off?" he asked Hiroshi nervously.

"Only if you think it make you more comfortable. The table actually part of a body scanner and it work whether you naked or not."

Ryan, fully clothed, sat up on the table and lay back. Hiroshi tapped in another combination on his keyboard and another section of the floor slid open. A robotic arm extended out over the table and shone a yellow light on Ryan. Hiroshi began to stare at his monitor as Aimee peeked at it from behind him. The monitor began to display a scan of Ryan's body and his DNA helix. Part of the DNA strand began to flash amber.

"Ha! You see that Aimee?" said Hiroshi triumphantly, poking at the screen: "His genome sequence not correct. He have the ability to be super powered but his body not fully able to hold it."

"Can it be fixed?" Aimee asked.

"It a strange problem. Probably due to both his parents being really powerful heroes with different abilities. Powers are clashing with each other. Solarstorm's abilities winning out but they not strong enough to work properly. Ryan meant to be able to store sunlight and use it in different ways like his father, but the power is wasted too quickly for it to be useful for long. He like a car with leaky fuel tank, put petrol in and it go. But it run out much earlier than you expect. Only way for him to have powers all the time would be to stand in direct sunlight so he constantly recharging!"

"Ryan, you were in the south of Spain when your powers worked that time right?" asked Aimee.

"Yes." Ryan replied.

"There's your answer, you had enough of a charge to get away from the ISA but it ran out."

"So, what now? I live only in sunny places and don't go out at night because my powers won't work?"

"You could do that, but I'm sure Hiroshi could think of something."

"Why ISA chasing you? You a terrorist?" questioned Hiroshi.

"I've got powers that they'd like to study; I guess I'm worth a lot to them."

"I don't see why. They not need you. They already have that woman who killed your parents in custody."

Ryan sat up suddenly and looked at Hiroshi:

"What do you mean they have the woman who killed my parents? She's dead, everyone says so. The government, the media, the

184

police."

"Oh! If they all say it, it must be true! She definitely still alive. I know because I not kill her. My Nanotech storm missile just knocked her into a coma. The ISA turn up after the battle and take her away in cryogenic tank. They say to public that she dead and they take her away for burial. It not true. The story that she dead all a lie to stop the public panicking."

Ryan jumped off the table and ran at Hiroshi, arms raised, ready to strangle him.

"You lousy little…"

Aimee stepped in between them and grabbed Ryan's arm, using a martial arts hold so he couldn't move. Ryan continued struggling to escape from her grip. Aimee spoke:

"Ryan, calm down. Hiroshi is a good guy, I'm sure he had a reason to go along with the lie."

"I'd love to hear it! Why didn't you tell anyone before now?"

"Ryan" Hiroshi said. "I just a kid when the Battle of Homestead happen. I only a handsome young boy in a metal suit with no experience, trying to be a superhero. I'm sorry I not speak out, but no-one would have believed me if I said truth back then. You know that. Who listen to a kid? People all in state of terror after heroes killed. Panicking, thinking it the end of the world or that kind of junk. The only way to stop people being scared was to make them believe that everything OK. It better they not know that the killer alive, they go back to thinking they are safe."

Ryan stopped trying to escape from the arm lock Aimee had him in. Aimee released him.

"You're right." Ryan said "I'm sorry." He sat down on the ground and put his head in his hands. "What do I do now?"

Hiroshi spoke: "I have ideas. I can make your powers work temporarily."

"What good would that do?"

"The ISA studying superheroes for years, long before your parents killed. It very likely that they have samples of your parents DNA in their files. If you and Aimee retrieve those for me, maybe I can use them to make a medicine to fix your powers permanently."

"And the temporary solution?" Aimee asked.

"Come with me and I show you".

Aimee and Ryan followed Hiroshi out of the lab and back into the corridor with the shelves of robot toys.

"These pretty cool, huh?" asked Hiroshi. "I have hundreds of them; some are over fifty years old!"

"Yeah, very nice." responded Ryan

"I glad you think so, robots are cool!"

Hiroshi led them down another corridor, further into the complex; the lights flickered, dimmed and then went back on to full power.

"Sorry about that, another shuttle launch. Bring materials up into orbit for the Mars ship. We building it up there. It due to be completed in two years but they way ahead of schedule. I have a year to have suits finished and ready for user testing."

"Will you be going to Mars with the astronauts?" asked Ryan.

"No. Definitely not. I not allowed to fly in shuttle. Psychiatrist says I'm grounded."

"Why is...?" Ryan began, until Aimee elbowed him in the stomach as gently as she could.

"Shut up, shut up, shut up." she whispered quickly.

"Where are we going?" Ryan asked, changing the subject.

Hiroshi stopped at a plain white door.

"Here" he said and swiped his identity card through the card reader. The door opened and he motioned with his hand for Aimee and Ryan to go inside.

Inside the room were a half dozen tanning beds and a changing area.

Ryan was surprised: "Why does a UN facility have sun beds? Do you guys get a swimming pool and sauna as well?"

"Of course, this is UNSAFE. We not underfunded back street operation like NASA. We get all the cool stuff. Sun beds are here for a reason though. People's bodies need sunlight, it help the body provide Vitamin D and have a positive effect on your psychology. Direct sunlight hard to find on a spaceship, It too bright out in space. People would go blind. Also, too much cosmic radiation around the place and opening a window not a thing you want to do in deep space."

"So, you're including tanning beds on the Mars ship?"

Aimee spoke: "They're used on nuclear submarines for similar reasons."

"You want me to spend time on the tanning bed to regain my powers?"

"That it exactly, while you doing that, I work on a new suit for you. If you going to ISA headquarters to get DNA samples, you need to look the part. Now strip down to your underwear and climb onto the bed."

Ryan undressed down to his boxer shorts and climbed up onto the tanning bed: "How long will I need?"

"I say give it a few hours, you won't get burned, your body absorb the ultraviolet radiation like a sponge. One of us will come get you later."

"What will I do for a few hours in a tanning bed?"

Hiroshi took his mp3 player from his pocket: "Here; listen to music. All I got synced on it is Japanese psycho pop, sorry."

"Great, I get to spend the afternoon cooking like a turkey and listening to teenaged girls screaming in a foreign language. That sounds like torture to me."

"We can get the security guards to water board you if you'd prefer" said Aimee sweetly.

Ryan sighed, stuck the ear phones on and lay down on the bed. Hiroshi closed the top and programmed the bed.

"See you in three hours buddy. Enjoy yourself! Remember to turn over half way through so you get cooked properly."

Ryan's muffled voice came from inside the bed "That's not even remotely funny!"

Hiroshi and Aimee returned to the lab. Aimee removed a pile of paper from the couch and sat down. Hiroshi went over to a drawer and took out a soldering gun and a number of circuit boards. He plugged the soldering gun into a wall socket and waited for it to heat up so that he could get to work.

"Do you trust him Aimee? He know who we are now. Only four people in total know I used to be hero."

"I can always deal with him if it comes to that. I'd like to be able to trust him though. He's the son of the greatest heroes who ever lived. He needs our help."

"That true. He a bit clueless all right."

"I think he's trustworthy, I wouldn't have shown him my face otherwise. He tried to do the right thing in that warehouse in New Jersey. He's a decent person, just a little overwhelmed."

"It a difficult life being a hero. Many don't survive the experience. A lot do it for a year or two, then quit. It takes determination. That what I didn't have."

"Your experience was different Hiroshi. No one can deny you did great things. You earned your retirement."

"Didn't do enough great things. Not on my last time in the suit."

"You did your best and saved a lot of lives. That counts for a lot."

"Thank you. You think that kid in there able for this?"

"Ryan is his parent's son; I can see that in him. There are not many people who could escape the ISA."

"I guess not."

The bed switched off automatically after three hours. Ryan had eventually fallen asleep in the bed despite the best efforts of the pop musicians to simultaneously keep him awake and drive him crazy. The top of the bed opened and Aimee smiled in at Ryan:

"So, how was it?"

"Ok I guess. Where's Hiroshi?"

"In his lab, he's completed a costume for you to use, I'll let him show it to you and explain how it works." Aimee handed Ryan a towel. "Clean up. There's a shower over there."

"Thanks."

"No problem, meet us in the lab as soon as you can."

Ten minutes later, Ryan joined Aimee and Hiroshi in the lab.

"Hey! How you doing?" exclaimed Hiroshi. "You look much better."

"I feel good, like I had a really good night's sleep."

"Well, it time to find out if my crazy plan worked."

Hiroshi opened a drawer in his desk and took out a large black pistol. He aimed at Ryan's chest and fired twice. The noise of the shots were deafening. The bullets bounced off Ryan and ricocheted away, lodging into a nearby wall.

"What the hell?" shouted Ryan.

"Ha! It work. That so cool!"

"You crazy idiot! You shot me! You had no idea whether that would work or not!"

"I suspected."

"You suspected?!" Ryan shouted: "You could have killed me!"

"Please!" said Hiroshi dismissively. "I genius! My suspicions are more likely to be correct than your facts! Other good news is I create a costume for you. It should help you to maintain your powers for longer. Your performance issues will be thing of the past!"

Ryan calmed down and caught Aimee's eye. She was desperately trying not to laugh. He saw the yellow and brown bodysuit on the table, Hiroshi wouldn't be winning any awards for 'designing most stylish costume' anytime soon.

Hiroshi saw Ryan's face and was a little upset: "What? You think you do better in three hours?"

"No! It's… it's fine. Seriously!"

"Glad you think so. I've built circuitry into the suit to help store solar energy and allow you to use your powers. The suit also bullet proof. But dry clean only. Don't wash with water. It screw up the wiring. So, what you think?"

"It looks awfully... skin-tight" replied Ryan.

"That for aerodynamic purposes." Hiroshi continued: "You very nervous to show off your body. You not have some kind of body image problem, do you? They very serious." Hiroshi placed a hand on Ryan's shoulder to commiserate with him. "It OK, buddy. You perfect as you are. Aimee say not an hour ago that you have great body!"

"That's not what I said!" spluttered Aimee. "I just said that you seemed to be in pretty good shape for someone who's been on the run and not eating properly for the past few weeks."

"Exactly: he got great body." responded Hiroshi. "That what I inferred from your comment anyway."

Aimee buried her head in her hands to hide the emotional mixture of frustration and embarrassment she was experiencing.

"So." Hiroshi continued. "You not have to put it on here if you still embarrassed about this whole topic. Aimee have bathroom on her jet where you can change when you leave."

"Leave? Where am I going now?"

"We've been talking while you were in the sunbed. Hiroshi thinks he may have an idea of where to start looking for the ISA base." said Aimee

"We're really going to go there?"

"Not me! I look like I going to go on suicide mission? I monitor from back here." responded Hiroshi.

"They won't be expecting us, and your powers will work, as long as you're wearing the suit. We'll get in, find the DNA samples and get the heck out of there. Easy." said Aimee.

"OK, so where is it?"

"I know location of an ISA base in Nevada. I interested in them since the Battle of Homestead, so I do research, tracked them down just in case they ever come after me. Also, the U.S. Government specifically warned us not to send shuttles on particular flight paths over that area." explained Hiroshi "That smell really fishy to me. Especially as those co-ordinates not show up on any maps or satellite photos. Conspiracy theory forums on internet all mention this place. Lots of people disappear in the area."

"We're going to find a secret base by paying attention to what a bunch of tin foil hat wearers on the Internet say?"

"Hey! I post on many of those forums! I not have tinfoil hat! I use carbon fibre, works better. My latest model blocks ninety five percent of all transmissions." said Hiroshi.

"Sad to say, when it comes to things like this, the wackos..." Aimee looked at Hiroshi before continuing: "...are often partly correct. I've heard stories about this place from my dad."

"So it's like Area 51?"

"This place is Area 51 squared. It doesn't have an official name."

"Area two thousand, six hundred and one?" suggested Hiroshi, not particularly helpfully.

"So when do we leave?"

"As soon as possible. We can go right now if you want."

"Sure."

"Two more things." said Hiroshi as he picked up two earpieces from one of the desks and a small black palm computer. "Take these communicators. I be able to contact you and you'll be able to keep in contact with each other if you split up for any reason. This black box is a medical scanner, when you find parents DNA sample, scan it with this. It transmit the information I require to fix your busted DNA."

"Thanks for calling my DNA busted. You have amazing bedside manner." said Ryan

"Why I care about that? I not doctor." Hiroshi paused for a split second: "Well, actually, I am, but not that kind of doctor."

Aimee and Ryan put the earpieces in place. Ryan grabbed his new costume and put in into a backpack.

"Let's go Ryan; we'll change into our work clothes on the flight. It'll be four hours flight time to Nevada."

"OK." Ryan turned to Hiroshi. "Thanks for doing this for me."

"It not a problem. I happy to help out. I not a hero any more but if Aimee trust you then I guess I do too."

Ryan shook Hiroshi's hand and followed Aimee out to her jet.

Chapter Fourteen | Night Flight

Aimee piloted the jet over the Pacific Ocean. It was late. The sky and the sea were the same perfect dark blue colour. Every so often, they would see the lights of a ship on the water in the distance or an airliner passing slowly off to one side of their plane but otherwise it was a quiet night. Ryan felt the need to break the silence:

"Why are you helping me, Aimee? This goes beyond hero worship for my parents. This could be really dangerous for you."

"I'm helping you mainly because I idolised your parents, that much is true. But I have other reasons as well. I just feel that this is what I need to do, to prove myself."

"As a hero?"

"Yes, but not just that. I'm trying to make the world a better place. I'm using my father's company to make everyone's lives more comfortable. It's the things that your parents stood for that made me want to do all this. Truth, justice, honour."

"So that makes you want to put on body armour and hit people with sticks?"

"Only to start." Revenant smiled. "I want to show everyone that they can make a difference. I'll do it by encouraging people to stand up for themselves and also by using my family's money to fund worthwhile projects. Becoming a superhero is a good place to start. The heroes were a symbol to many people that one person in a city could change things for the better. We still need those symbols."

"But for now you're just happy to beat people up?"

"Sure, why not? I'm doing other stuff via the company, not a lot though. It's difficult to do what's best when you have a bunch of ingrates trying to stop you. It takes a long time to gain the experience required to really improve the world, if I have to start out by changing it one crippled mugger at a time, then why not?"

"You're the weirdest girl I ever met, Revenant."

"You're not exactly normal yourself Ryan. By the way, when are you going to come up with a codename?"

They both heard Hiroshi's voice over their earpieces: "That exactly what I thinking! I got lots of options. Solarboy! Solarstorm Junior! Velocitystorm!"

"Holy! Hiroshi! Have you been listening in on us all this time?" asked Revenant.

"Well, for the last few minutes. My anime shows have finished for the evening. Boring news is the only thing on. It time to dig out a box set from the pile I think."

"I haven't thought about a codename." said Ryan. "I'm not sure I have what it takes to be a hero in the first place. My parents were special. They knew what they wanted out of life. All I want to do for the time being is to stop these guys chasing me."

"That's not a bad place to begin." said Revenant. "Hiroshi, we're passing the U.S. coastline now. Did you find anything on your conspiracy theory forums that might help us?"

"Well Aimee, firstly, they not 'my' conspiracy theory forums. Just because I founded one or two and I a regular poster and moderator. Secondly, to answer your question: yes. There going to be serious defences around this place. Surface to air missiles and robot interceptors for instance. But there probably only a few dozen troops guarding the place. I would say less than fifty. ISA is small organisation now that the heroes are mostly gone. They no longer have manpower to use people to guard the place properly. That why they have dumb robotic security. It not a problem for you, I think."

"Surface to air missiles?! How are we supposed to avoid those?" said Revenant.

"It easy for your jet. It faster than most missiles. The interceptors will give you problems though. Is your jet armed?"

"It's a private jet, Hiroshi. It's not an F-22."

"That a problem then. I suggest you have Solarstorm Junior distract them while you try land safely. I install kick ass weaponry next time you visit. How you feel about mass drivers or hyper-kinetic warheads."

"We'll talk about that later."

"OK. Anything else you want to say to me before I stop talking?" said Hiroshi.

"Yeah…Hiroshi, stop calling me Solarstorm Junior!" said Ryan.

"Why not? It cool name!"

Ryan's made a sullen face and clenched his fists.

"Hiroshi, we're going to sign off now, before Ryan flies back to Japan to throttle you in your sleep." said Revenant.

"OK, OK! Have a good evening breaking into secure facility."

"We will. This is Revenant signing off."

"So it looks like we'll be picking a fight soon." said Ryan.

"Yes. I'd get changed if I were you. I'll do the same." said Aimee.

Ryan walked to the back of the plane and picked up the bag that his new outfit was packed in. He opened the door to the aircraft's toilet and used the latch to lock it behind him. The toilet was tiny. It barely had enough legroom to turn around in. He placed the bag on the floor and opened it. He took the suit out and shook it to get rid of any creases. The suit was a one piece outfit. It had a zipper on the front from the waist to the collar and looked exactly like a snowsuit that a kid might wear in winter. It was so tight there was no way he'd be able to wear his street clothes underneath. He took off all his clothes except for his underwear. He had never understood why heroes always fought in tight fitting outfits, were they really all so vain that they wanted to show off their muscles in spandex leotards? He had meant to ask his parents but he'd never found a good opportunity.

Ryan opened the zipper and tried to slip his left leg inside the costume. The suit material, an artificial fibre he didn't recognise, screeched like fingernails on a chalkboard. He got his left leg in and then tried to place his right leg inside. He slipped and quickly steadied himself by slapping his hand against the wall. The noise reverberated around the small cabin. He sat down on the toilet seat and tried to pull the suit up his legs. It wouldn't fit. He tugged harder and the suit slowly moved up, screeching all the time. He balanced on the edge of the seat, lifted his legs up and pulled harder. He lost his grip and balance at precisely the same moment and his legs went flying in opposite directions. His left leg jammed up against the faucet in the tiny sink. Somehow, he had managed to get stuck. He placed his right hand on the floor for balance and tried to free his leg. The tap broke in two and water sprayed across the whole bathroom. Ryan managed to free his leg and eventually untangled his body enough to stand up straight. He started to panic. What would Aimee say if she saw he'd drenched the bathroom of her plane? He thought for a second. If he could fire energy blasts like his dad then maybe he could weld the faucet back together?

He picked up the top half of the broken faucet from the floor and placed it on the recently created fountain. The water continued to shoot upwards and splash everything in sight. He placed the halves together and concentrated. Suddenly, there was a knock at the door.

"Are you OK in there?" asked Aimee.

"I'm fine! I'm perfectly fine!" responded Ryan.

"Are you sure? Are you getting nervous? What we're going to do is a pretty big deal!"

"Really! I'm doing great. I'll be out as soon as possible."

"OK."

Ryan waited until he was sure that Aimee had returned to the cockpit.

He pointed his finger at the tap and focused. A dull yellow beam of light shot out from his finger tip. The water turned to steam from the heat of the beam. Working carefully, Ryan managed to do an acceptable job of fixing the faucet by melting the halves together. The flow of water stopped. He finished dressing and tried to dry the toilet up as best he could with tissue paper. Hopefully Aimee wouldn't notice. He left the toilet and joined Aimee at the front of the jet.

Aimee was already dressed in her outfit. In contrast to Ryan, her hair didn't even seem mussed.

"Why does your outfit seem to be easier to put on than mine?" asked Ryan.

"I designed my suit myself. Hiroshi can't figure out women's clothing."

"He's not great at designing men's either."

"Is it too tight?"

"Next time I want to put this thing on, I'll need to smear butter all over my body first."

"Thank you for burning that image into my brain. I'll be sure to send you the therapy bills."

"Don't mention it."

Twenty minutes later, they approached the western perimeter of the secret base. The night remained quiet, with nothing strange on the radar and no buildings or lights on the ground.

"So far, so nothing." said Ryan as he stared out the cockpit window.

"I wouldn't say that." said Revenant, pointing to their left. "We have objects closing on us, They're too small to show up on radar but it's heading our way, fast."

Ryan saw a small black shape in the night sky, just barely visible because it was darker than the background. As he watched as a handful of similar objects appeared alongside it.

"You must have great eyesight. Are those missiles?"

"They could be. But they're more likely to be interceptors, having a look at us before someone on the ground decides whether to shoot us down or not. I think it's time for you to jump out the door and distract the welcoming committee."

"I think you're right. But what if the suit doesn't work? I'll fall and die."

"Well, if you don't then those interceptors are going to shoot this jet down and we'll fall and die anyway. Besides, Hiroshi makes good stuff. He's away with the fairies a lot of the time but I can't fault his mechanical engineering skills. If he thinks it will work then it will."

"Still… I don't suppose you have a parachute on-board do you?"

"Yes. Take one if it'll make you feel better, they're under the seats. But I'm sure you won't need it."

Ryan looked under the seat nearest him and pulled out a parachute. He began to strap it on as Revenant spoke again:

"Of course, if you do jump out, those interceptors are going to start firing and will rip your chute to shreds, so it won't save you. They'll be within firing range in about ten seconds so you may as well jump without it. I wouldn't worry if I were you. Your parents did stuff like this all the time."

Ryan's face went pale: Revenant knew that she had scared him but she also knew that there was no way Ryan would achieve his potential if he second guessed every decision he made.

Ryan dropped the parachute and went to the door. He pulled down on the yellow and black striped lever and the door opened. He jumped out and fell. Revenant sealed the door using the control on the dashboard of the cockpit and pulled up on the control stick sharply. The interceptors opened fire.

Ryan tumbled from the jet, the winds howled and shrieked all around him. Far, far below, the ground was spinning. He felt like he was going to puke. He spread his arms and legs and managed to stabilise his body and the world stopped spiralling momentarily. Something yellow flashed by his face with a 'zinging' noise.

Bullets! He thought. Looks like they think I'm a threat. I'd hate to disappoint them.

Ryan shifted his body weight and turned towards the first interceptor. It was a black triangular shaped drone with rocket launchers slung underneath its thin wings and twin machine guns jutting out of its nose. He pointed at it and concentrated, hoping that the energy he had been able to fire in the jet's bathroom would work again. A beam of orange light shot from his fingertip and hit the interceptor. It exploded in a shower of yellow orange sparks and pieces of metal. "Hahahaha! It worked. This is brilliant!" Ryan continued to laugh. "Now, let's try to fly."

He closed his eyes and thought about floating. He stopped falling and hung in the air. Two of the remaining interceptors had broken off and were chasing Revenant's jet but the others were heading directly for him. Ryan flew towards them and raised his hands, firing energy blasts as he did so.

Revenant was in trouble. Try as she might, she wasn't able to lose the two interceptors that had locked onto her. The Jet shuddered as it was hit by machine gun fire. Alarms screamed in the cockpit as warning lights flashed. An orange light above her head informed her that the Jet's engines had been destroyed. Revenant pushed the stick forward and the nose of the Jet pointed towards the ground. She wasn't able to fight them and she couldn't escape so her best option was to bail out and crash the jet. Any ISA troops below would have to leave the base to inspect the crash site, allowing her and Ryan a better chance of avoiding trouble when they broke in. Once she had set the plane on the correct course, she unbuckled her seat belt and dragged herself to the passenger compartment. The parachute that Ryan had left on the floor was still there. She grabbed it and slipped it on over her costume and weapons.

Time to go. She thought as she pulled the lever on the door and jumped out.

A blast of wind caught her and swept her away from the flaming remains of the jet. The interceptors that had destroyed her plane swung away in an arc and headed in the direction of explosions happening higher up in the atmosphere.

That must be Ryan. Revenant thought as she saw a yellow beam of light scythe through the night.

"Ryan! Can you hear me?"

"Revenant?"

"Yes. I've had to bail out of the Jet. I'm plummeting to the ground to the southeast of where you jumped out. I'd really appreciate it if you caught me before I die horribly."

"I've destroyed the last of the Interceptors; the two that followed you came after me when your plane was totalled."

"Excellent, that's great news. Now… about the catching before impending death?"

"I'm on it. Do you have the scanner that Hiroshi gave us?"

"Of course. Now, could you please hurry up?"

"Sure."

Ryan flew southeast but couldn't see Revenant.

"Revenant, where are you? It's night and you're wearing black!"

"Give me a second."

Revenant reached into a compartment on her belt and removed her torch. She turned it on and waved it around frantically.

"I see you!" Ryan said. "I'm on my way."

Ryan caught Revenant in his arms. He grunted quietly.

"Ooofff! You're heavier than you look."

"Ryan, the last thing you should say to a woman, especially this one, is that she's heavier than she looks. Do you know anything about women?"

"Not really."

"And, I might point out that I'm wearing body armour and carrying an arsenal around on my back. That's why I weigh more than usual."

"Fine, I believe…" an explosion echoed through the sky, in the distance Ryan could see a bright red glow. "I suppose that's your plane."

Ryan and Revenant quietly gazed as the few patches of scrubland below them caught fire.

"I guess I don't need to worry about breaking the faucet in the washroom now." said Ryan, relieved.

"You did what?" hollered Revenant.

"Yeah, I kinda-sorta broke the fixtures in the bathroom. I did my best to weld them so the water wouldn't get everywhere."

"I can't believe you damaged my plane."

"Sorry, I guess I don't know my own strength. Besides, it's a minor problem now that you've crashed it."

"Shot down."

"Sorry?"

"I was shot down. I did not…" Revenant paused for emphasis:"… crash it."

"Whatever. Same result, right?"

Revenant sulked in silence for a few moments: "The secret base is about fifteen miles to the North. Can you get us there?"

"No problem."

"Then let's go, but get a lot lower or they'll see us coming from miles away."

"Yes boss. Whatever you say!"

"Come on, the night has just begun."

Ryan and Revenant travelled northward and down until they were hovering twenty feet from the ground at the supposed location of the secret base. There were no buildings or roads to be seen.

"Where is it? Did Hiroshi have bad information?" said Ryan.

"Put me down on the ground near those cacti."

They landed and Revenant scanned the area through the lenses of her mask. She saw a small building in the distance, almost buried under, and the same colour as, a sand dune. She pointed it out to Ryan.

"There's a building not far from here. It looks like an old cabin."

"If that's supposed to be a technologically advanced top secret base then the economy must really be in the toilet."

"Well, we can check it out at least, lets' move."

"If that's the only building for miles, where did those interceptors launch from?"

"Most likely from a hidden missile silo. My best guess is that the base in completely underground. They built a lot of underground bunkers back in the Cold War; those places were enormous, they're almost like underground cities."

"I'll fly us over to that shack. It'll be quicker than walking."

"OK."

Ryan lifted Revenant up in his arms and they flew over to the shack. Revenant accessed her wrist computer as they flew.

"I can't find any cameras or other sensors in the area."

"That's good, right?"

"It means they're not here, which could mean that there's no base. Or…"

"Or?"

"They're so sophisticated that my on-board sensors can't find them. That's more worrying. We're near the shack. Land here and we'll walk the rest of the way."

Ryan touched down. Revenant slipped out of his arm onto the ground.

"I'm going in." said Revenant "Watch my back."

"Right."

Revenant walked slowly to the door of the wooden ramshackle cabin, it wasn't locked. She pushed the door open slowly and crept in. The place was empty except for an old fireplace, a couple of old chairs and a rotten wooden table. The floor was covered in dust and dirt. Revenant thought that it didn't look quite right.

"Ryan, come here!" she said.

Ryan entered the shack and looked around.

"Empty" he said.

"Not exactly. Look at the floor."

"Footprints! Not yours I guess?"

"No, they're bigger than mine, they go over to the fireplace and they don't come back out, they seem to have been made recently."

Revenant walked to the fireplace and ran her hands over the mantelpiece and walls beside it. There was a loud click and the fireplace slid back into the wall, exposing a shaft down into the earth with a ladder.

"This is it." Ryan said. "What are we waiting for?"

They climbed into the shaft and began their descent.

Chapter Fifteen | Nevada Base

The ladder ended, eventually. Revenant calculated that they were twenty five stories below ground level when they stepped off the ladder into a dark concrete corridor. The shaft had emergency lighting which gave off a dull red glow. Revenant touched the side of her mask and her night vision came on. She removed her torch from her web gear and handed it to Ryan.

"Well, it's certainly a corridor." said Ryan. "Do you think this place is still being used? Or did the ISA move out of here in the late nineteen sixties?"

"These places are never fully abandoned, and an older, off the books facility would suit the ISA's secret study of the heroes. They may not want to have it in a modern complex where there are civilian employees and lots of closed circuit cameras. That sort of thing leads to information leaks."

The corridor was damp with puddles of water everywhere.

"This is a desert, where did all of this water come from?" Ryan said. "This place probably hasn't seen a plumber since Reagan was President. It could just be leaking pipes. There's only one way to find out. Let's follow this corridor and see where it takes us."

"Yeah, even if it's a dead end, we can always return this way."

They walked for fifteen minutes before coming to a junction; one corridor continued straight ahead, another to their right.

"Let's split up" said Ryan.

"No, let's not. Haven't you ever seen a horror movie? Never split up if you can avoid it." replied Revenant.

"Scared?" teased Ryan.

"No, it's just stupid for us to separate, this place isn't abandoned, the top of the range interceptors you fought earlier prove that. We'll need each other's help sooner or later."

"So which way do we go?"

"Pick either."

"We go right."

They continued walking, after a while the corridor started to become less damp and the air felt warmer.

"Feel that?" said Ryan. "We have heating and air conditioning."

"Yes, I'm seeing light in the distance as well."

"Now we're getting somewhere."

The corridor changed from bare concrete to tiles just as they reached the light.

"Be careful Ryan." said Revenant.

"Don't worry, I feel like I'm able to handle anything after that fight up in the sky."

Ryan continued walking; Revenant noticed that one of the tiles in front of Ryan was raised slightly higher than its neighbours.

"Ryan! Don't….."

He stepped onto the tile and there was a hissing sound.

"Pneumatic trigger…" said Revenant as a bright light blinded both of them.

Revenant looked around the room that they'd just been dragged into. A small group of guards had found both of them sprawled in the corridor, knocked unconscious by the flash bomb that Ryan had accidentally triggered. She and Ryan were chained to a wall. Ryan was shackled with thick metal handcuffs that covered his entire arms. Revenant only had standard police issue manacles on her wrists. She felt slightly insulted that their captors had gone to so little effort to restrain her, relatively speaking. Revenant found that she was incapable of focussing due to the after-effects of the flash bomb. She shook her head to chase the cobwebs away and took in their surroundings. The room was large and furnished with a modern looking desk, office chairs and a solid looking metal door that belonged in a bank vault. Revenant realised that her weapons were gone, though she still had her mask.

Ryan was unconscious and still. Revenant decided that he had rested for enough time.

"Ryan!" she shouted "Ryan! Wake up!"

No response. He was out cold.

The bolts on the metal door groaned and opened slowly. The door swung inwards on its hinges with a slow ponderous grinding noise. Two people entered, first an older man with short, greying hair. He wore a sharply tailored black suit and had the tell-tale bulge of a shoulder holster underneath his suit jacket. He didn't have a wedding ring or a watch as far as Revenant could see. The second person was practically his polar opposite, a young woman with red hair; she was dressed in grey trousers, a green top and wore a thin silver necklace with matching earrings.

"So you're the mysterious vigilante who has been terrorizing the New York underground for the past few nights?" said Benning. "We've heard interesting things about you. You put a bunch of muggers in hospital and you removed Ryan Curtis here from our custody, not to mention annoying the Russian mob and that gangster rapper in the process. What shall we call you?"

"Revenant." said Aimee.

"What is it with superheroes and their names? Very good. Well Revenant, my name is Benning. Agent Benning of the ISA. I'm the person in charge of re-capturing your boyfriend over there. I must say, I never thought that he'd be served up to me on a plate like this. I thought we'd lost him forever when you intervened in New Jersey. But fate has a weird way of placing us exactly where we belong, doesn't it?"

"Are you going to torture me to find out who I really am or are you going to keep boasting about how important you think you are? Because honestly: torture would be a nice change of pace. It wouldn't be as boring."

"Why would I need to torture you to find out who you are, Aimee DeWitt?"

Aimee was shocked: "How did you…?"

"Oh please" Benning jeered "Give the ISA a modicum of credit. We knew you were going to be a costumed vigilante before you did. Rich kid loses a parent as the result of crime and swears vengeance on the criminal elements of society? That was old when I was your age. We use statistical probability software to predict the type of person who will become a hero or villain. We started watching you from the hour you walked out of the warehouse where you were held captive and your mother was killed. We monitored you periodically from then on, we saw the martial arts training, the contact with Hiroshi Saito, everything."

"So what are you going to do with us?"

"You? We'll kill you with a bullet to the back of the head or a lethal injection. Whichever suits us and is the most convenient. No one will miss you Aimee, nobody cares. You've got no friends and the directors of DeWitt Industries will be too busy stuffing their pockets with company money to do much investigating. They'll just figure you jumped off the Brooklyn Bridge or crashed your jet into the Pacific. The media will report whatever sells the most papers."

"And Ryan?"

"He becomes our prize lab rat, until he dies from the numerous procedures we put him through. Our resident scientist, Dr. Spencer, has had years to come up with ideas. He's still mighty annoyed that the heroes turned the love of his life into a crazy murderess. He's got several really twisted things planned for Mr. Curtis over there. As long as I get the information I need, I don't care what happens to him. We'll use Ryan's DNA to build an army of soldiers that no one will mess with."

"That was your plan? Is the woman who killed The Vanguard involved in this?"

"You could say that. Dr. Fleming ran our programme for several years, she almost had a working Nanotech delivery system that would give regular people super powers and she hated the heroes. She thought they had become our masters. She wanted to stop them in any way possible. I have to admit, her way was a little extreme. It worked though."

"She was powerful enough to kill The Vanguard and nearly every other hero!"

"But it damaged her mind beyond repair, made her crazy. Even if Mech and Warfare hadn't defeated her, she would have been a vegetable within a week or two. Mech shutting down her higher cognitive functions saved her life. You'd have to be an idiot to use her version of the Nanotech. We had to take our time and fix the flaws."

"So, you've spent five years doing the same thing over again?"

"Yes, But Dr. Fleming was a genius and they don't grow on trees. Thanks to budget cuts and a few accidents, the only scientist I have left is Leo Spencer. He isn't nearly as good as she was. It took Fleming nine years to develop a working prototype, I'm an impatient man and I'm not going to wait that long again. Ryan's blood holds the secret to creating peace and prosperity for this nation. No one will dare screw with us when we have fifty thousand super powered soldiers."

"You're awfully chatty for a secret agent."

"I guess I'm just happy that my life's work is nearly complete. Six months, Ms. DeWitt. Six months and America will be undefeatable!" Benning turned to the red haired woman: "Agent Forty-Three. Tell the doctor that his specimen is ready." He looked at Aimee again "The other agents, the ones you made look like a bunch of chumps in New Jersey; they're playing a game of poker down the hall. The winner gets to kill you. I felt it was only fair to let one of them do it. I've studied your profile, all those charitable works over the past couple of years. You're ashamed of your wealth and want to make the world more democratic and equal. You'll die for what you believe in: we should all be so lucky."

Benning and Agent Forty-Three left the room and sealed the door. Aimee lowered her head; she was mentally and physically exhausted. She didn't see a way out of this situation. She was a loser; any other hero would have broken the chains holding them to the wall already. She told herself she was in over her head.

"Hey!" Ryan's voice was weak.

"Hey yourself. You're awake?"

"I have been for the last few minutes."

"I suppose you heard our mouthy friend?"

"Yes."

"I'm sorry Ryan." Revenant said miserably. "I thought we were ready for this. I got so swept up in the idea of going on an adventure with the son of the two people I idolised that I wasn't thinking straight. I was wrong to have convinced you to come here. We gave them exactly what they wanted."

"We're new at this. From now on we'll only get better. Don't blame yourself. They would have found me sooner or later. If I hadn't set off that trap then we wouldn't be in this mess. We'll find a way to get free."

"Right. So, what now? Can you move at all?"

"No. Everything feels really heavy."

"I think that those gauntlets they have on you may be sapping your strength. They aren't normal restraints."

"Any way I can break them?"

"I don't know."

The door clanked opened again slowly and Agent Forty-Three entered the room. Aimee struggled against her chains, trying to escape.

"You! Ginger-nut! When I get out of here I'll tear your face off and force you to eat it!"

"Quiet down Revenant or I'll shoot you." said Eva. "I've come here to help." Eva walked over to a computer console and tapped on the keyboard. Ryan's handcuffs clicked open and fell onto the floor.

Ryan attempted to stand up slowly. He felt groggy from the after-effects of the energy draining handcuffs.

"Why are you helping us?" he said.

"What Benning believes is not what I believe. He's gone power mad. This whole project can't be about just protecting America from the superheroes and super villains, they're all dead. It's now about making Benning so powerful that no one will dare question him. Who do you think will be leading that army of super powered soldiers? He's planning to become one of the first specimens once Dr. Spencer has a working process in place."

"Benning might have you arrested as a traitor for doing this." said Ryan.

"Benning and his kind think that politics is a kind of stupid competition, winner takes all. He won't ever stop with just protecting America from its enemies. He'll conquer the world if given the opportunity."

Eva took a set of keys from her pocket and opened the locks of the chains that held Aimee to the wall. Aimee rubbed her wrist where the manacle had been.

"Ok, so you've had your road to Damascus moment. I still don't trust you but we've got work to do. Where do you keep the DNA samples of the heroes, like Solarstorm and Velocity?"

"Dr. Spencer has them in his lab, along with the comatose body of Dr. Fleming and his new research."

Aimee thought for a second:

"Ok, we need to get that DNA and get out of here as soon as possible. Agent Forty-Three?"

"Yes? And call me Eva, I'm taking this opportunity to resign before

Benning fires me."

"Where is my equipment? I have a medical scanner that we need to use to get the information we require."

"What information?"

Ryan spoke:" My powers aren't acting properly, I need samples of my parents DNA to compare mine against and hopefully fix the problem."

"So we spent years looking for you to discover if you had powers and they don't even work? I'd laugh if I hadn't just helped waste millions of dollars of taxpayer's money." said Eva.

"Since when do ISA agents have a sense of humour?" asked Aimee.

"I resigned, remember? Your equipment is down the hall with the poker players, they're probably using your weapons as playing chips."

"OK, that's where I'm going. You two head to the lab and wait for me there."

"Didn't you give me a lecture on not splitting up only a few hours ago?" asked Ryan.

"That lab is our goal and the most important place in this complex. Once they find out we've escaped they'll lock it down. You need to get there before that happens. Eva can show you the way."

"Ok" said Ryan "That makes sense, I suppose. Anything else?"

"Yes, Eva, do you have a mobile phone?"

"No." Eva replied sarcastically. "The last decade's worth of advances in personal electronic devices has passed me by... Of course I have a phone! Why'd you want it? There's no signal in here. We're a hundred metres underground."

"I need a weapon. Never use your bare hands to attack someone, a phone is perfect."

Eva put her hand into the back pocket of her trousers and pulled out a small silver phone: "Here."

"Thanks, I'll return it later."

"Don't bother, it's a company phone."

"Time to go." said Ryan "We can't wait around any longer."

Benning used his key card to enter Dr. Spencer's lab. The room had originally been built as a command and control centre for nuclear missiles. It was massive, able to hold sixty technicians and their commanding officers and keep them alive through a nuclear apocalypse. Ancient computers the size of small cars stood around the walls, surplus to requirements in the digital age and left to gather dust. The room had its own generators, powered by hydroelectricity from an underground river. The walls were steel reinforced concrete. It was the perfect location from which to launch a coup.

Once the process was up and running, His agents, each one handpicked for their loyalty to him, would be the first to under-go the procedure. He had only twenty agents he trusted enough to do this, but it would be enough. Twenty invincible troops would be able to defeat the Army and Air Force in a matter of days. He'd planned the next phase of the operation for years, down to the very last detail. He was certain that it would go off without a hitch.

America's leaders had allowed the security and health of the nation suffer, for now that would work to his advantage. A quick surgical strike and America would have a new leader: one who would do whatever needed to be done to save the country from its enemies, internal and external.

Benning had grown up in an era when American cultural and economic dominance was a fact of life. But now every fool with an AK-47 felt powerful enough to challenge his country. Not anymore. Once he had gained power, the list of countries and organisations willing to mess with America would rapidly drop to zero. There would be internal dissent, he knew. But any protestors would fall into line once he'd killed a few thousand of them and imprisoned the rest. Democracy wouldn't be missed. People would quickly realise that their safety was assured under his leadership and would support him. Then the invasions would begin, he'd lead his troops across the world, crushing any resistance and ensuring the protection of his empire from outsiders..

Benning looked up at the cryogenic tank as he walked over to Spencer. Benning could understand why Spencer had betrayed the ISA five years ago. Maria Fleming was a looker, no doubt. Spencer had held a candle for her for years and did everything she asked without question. Spencer had gone on the run immediately after the Battle of Homestead. But, after having lived underground for all of his adult life and being cut off from the real world for so long, he had been easy to recapture. Benning hadn't needed to threaten or cajole Spencer to have him recommence his work on the project. He'd only had to promise him one thing: Spencer would get to be with Maria for as long as he wished and work on a cure for the brain damage that the first batch of Nanotech had done to her in his spare time. It was an empty promise. The weapon Hiroshi Saito had used on Maria had performed its function admirably. Benning had seen yoghurt with more brain activity than his former head researcher. Despite this, Spencer hadn't hesitated and had worked like a demon in the intervening years to reconstruct the Nanotech project. Work ethic like that was hard to find: he was just too darn slow.

Benning had hoped to be up and running five years ago with his team, building his army slowly before making his move. Now there was no time. His country needed him. A new prototype strain of the Nanotech was currently waiting testing before the next phase could finally begin. All it needed was test data from a living super-powered subject. Ryan Curtis would be the key to unlocking unimaginable power. Benning was giddy at the thought of, one day soon, leading a super powered regiment into battle.

Spencer was sitting in his usual spot: a chair from which he gazed up at the cryogenic tank which held the comatose body of Maria. Benning thought it was a worrying sign of deeper mental problems but never intervened. Most scientists in his experience were touched in the head and besides, Spencer didn't need to be sane to do his work. Spencer spoke to Maria whenever he believed that no one was around. Telling her about the research, arguing to the air about what the latest batch of test data could mean. Often, he just stared at her for hours at a time, deep in thought. It was like Spencer was worshipping her. She hadn't aged a day in five years, the Nanotech which had granted her super powers and destroyed her mind also served to keep her young as her body was constantly being renewed by the millions of tiny machines in her bloodstream. The ISA could have made a fortune licensing the technology to cosmetics companies.

Benning cleared his throat: "Ah hem!"

Spencer spun around in his chair, startled: "I'm sorry, Agent Benning. I didn't hear you come in!"

"I'm not surprised. Aren't you supposed to be working?"

"I am. I've begun synthesising a new batch of the Nanotech to be encoded with the results of our first tests on Curtis. It'll take an hour to complete."

"The boy is ready for your tests as soon as you are. What are you planning to do first?"

"I'll be extracting bone marrow and blood to start. I've ordered special equipment in order to do so. The boy's skin is tough, as Agent Vasquez learned on that roof top in Spain. I'll need specialised equipment to extract what I need."

"When will that be here? I'd like to get started as quickly as possible."

"It'll arrive in our regular supply run tomorrow morning."

"So, tomorrow the boy dies?"

"Yes; and our project will be given a new lease of life."

"Good. I'll leave you to it, Doctor."

"Agent."

Benning turned on his heel and exited the room as suddenly as he had entered it. Spencer watched him leave and, once he was sure he was alone, got up from his chair and paced over to the tank. He placed his hand on the reinforced glass and looked at the face of his beloved Maria, tears in his eyes:

"And, tomorrow, I will finally be able to repair the damage that was done to you five years ago. Did you hear me? Soon, my love, I'll be able to wake you up from your sleep."

Chapter Sixteen | Cell Phone Battery

Revenant left Ryan and Eva and went in the direction that Eva had indicated that her equipment was being kept. The part of the base that they had been held in was much the same as the part she and Ryan had seen before they were knocked unconscious. The ISA clearly had a surplus of grey concrete walls, old fashioned light fixtures, military abbreviations stencilled on every flat surface and pipes of different colours heading in all directions. She heard men laughing in a room not far ahead. She pressed her ear against the wooden door and listened to the men's voices:

"Hey Jones! If you win, and I'm saying "if you win", because you can't play cards, what are you going to do?"

"Dunno. That girl nearly broke my arm in New Jersey; maybe I'll break her arms first."

Revenant heard glass bottles clink as the agents toasted and drank. That was good, drunks were much easier to beat up, they didn't have the co-ordination required to fight properly.

She opened the door silently and stepped inside, holding the phone she'd borrowed from Eva in her right hand. The room was mostly in darkness; the only source of illumination was being provided by a single light bulb over the poker table. It was a big room too, probably a meeting room or lecture hall in a previous lifetime, judging by the blackboard on the wall and small desks scattered around the floor. The poker players didn't hear her enter. She looked around the room and saw her weapons and the medical scanner heaped in a pile on the oak lecturer's desk on the far end of the room, near where the players sat. There were five of them seated in a circle; all of them were drinking bottles of beer. Except for the surroundings it looked like any normal Friday night game with the boys. It was almost a shame to ruin their fun.

"Aren't you the idiots I kicked the stuffing out of in New Jersey?" Revenant said loudly. "Is this a support group for people who've been humiliated by teenage girls?"

As one, the agents looked in her direction. The big bald one pointed at her and spoke first:

"It's her, get her!"

All five of them stood up from their chairs hurriedly. The agent nearest her screamed in anger, trying to get his adrenal glands going, and ran forward. He covered the distance between them rapidly and swung a wild right hook at her head. Revenant blocked his arm with a quick strike of her left hand, clamped her hand around his wrist and pulled him forward sharply to make him lose his balance. She quickly struck the agent twice on the collar bone with the phone. She heard a crack and his scream became louder and changed pitch from fury to agony. She pushed him to the right and he fell back against one of the small desks. It broke underneath his weight and he fell heavily, striking his head on the ground.

"That didn't work as well as you'd hoped, did it? Who's next?"

The small, skinny blonde haired agent plucked an empty beer bottle from the table, smashed it to make an improvised dagger and moved slowly towards her, cutting at the air. Revenant dodged to her left as he slashed and slammed the phone into his fingers, breaking them. He dropped the bottle as Revenant pinned his arm behind his back and put him in a chokehold before spinning him across the room. He slipped and fell onto his back. Revenant ran over to his prone body and stamped on his stomach. He curled up into the foetal position and groaned.

The big, bald man came at her, bellowing like a bull. Revenant raked at his eyes with the phone and then thrust it upwards into his chin. He stepped back. Revenant used the space to spin around and deliver a roundhouse kick to his head; he flew sideways and ploughed into one of the other agents. They both went flying across the room and skidded to a halt ten metres away.

The last agent left standing, Agent Vasquez, was the only one to go for his gun. His left hand was in a cast from his encounter with Ryan in Spain. He'd been the only one with enough sense to go for his weapon. The others had gotten angry and just charged into danger. None of them had believed for a second that an unarmed girl could be a real threat to them. Vasquez had just managed to reach his holster and cock his pistol before Revenant could get near enough to hurt him badly. He placed his gun against Revenant's forehead. She slowly raised her hands in surrender.

"Not so tough now. Are you? You're just a kid. I'm going to decorate the walls with your brains." He sneered.

"Didn't I see you on TV once?" asked Revenant.

"What are you talking ab...?" He began.

Revenant slapped the gun away from her forehead with her left hand and chopped the agents' gun arm with her right. She grabbed the barrel of the gun while hitting him on the collar bone with the phone. He let go of the butt of the pistol. Revenant, still holding it by the barrel and using the gun as a club, hit him as hard as she could in the jaw. Vasquez collapsed at her feet.

The big bald agent was scrambling to get up. Revenant pivoted and launched the gun and the phone across the room at his head as she raced towards him. The flying objects both struck him squarely on the temple. Revenant used the opening caused by his hesitation to kick him in the left shin to knock him back onto his knees. She grabbed him by the collar, pulling him up off the floor and drove her right palm into his face repeatedly until she was sure he was unconscious.

"Bunch of amateurs." She said to herself as she walked over to the big oak desk to collect her gear.

She buckled on her web gear with the stun grenades, her favourite knife, throwing stars and the medical scanner. She placed the sticks into the holster on her back and clipped on her gauntlets. Ready to face whatever or whoever awaited her outside. She collected Eva's phone from the floor as she left. It might turn out to be useful again.

"Where's the lab?" asked Ryan.

"It's not far." replied Eva "We didn't require all the space when we re-opened this facility so we just activated what we needed; the outskirts of the base, like the part you and Revenant entered through, aren't monitored. In total we only have about seventy staff on site. But the base is so big that you'd never even see half of them. Most of the rest of the ISA are spread out around the world, looking for you or chasing down other potential heroes and villains."

"Did you find any?"

"Not yet. Other than the few survivors from your parent's time of course. Most of those are worse than useless now though. There haven't been any new heroes on the scene in five years, until you and Revenant appeared."

"Sounds like boring work."

"It wasn't so bad. I got to travel the world on the government's money. That's what I'll do when this is over. Not that I have much choice. Benning will hunt me down for this. I'd better make myself scarce when you leave here."

"About the woman, Dr. Fleming. Why did she do what she did? My parents were heroes."

"You'd have to ask her. If you could. She's brain-dead now. The other agents told me that she considered them a bad influence on popular culture. Like people didn't look after themselves and solve their own problems because they figured that the heroes would look after the important stuff."

"That's stupid."

"Is it? Lots of people don't save money because they think that they're definitely going to win the lottery in the next few years. Many people always sit back and wait for things to be done for them. I don't blame that on the heroes, it's just human nature. But apparently she thought our reliance on your parents and their friends was stunting our growth."

"That's not how things should be. Heroes aren't supposed to be super powered baby sitters."

"Tell that to the current scientist on the project. Dr. Spencer is his name. He would agree with you. He's looking after Dr. Fleming in his own creepy way. He hates the heroes with a passion for the same reasons that she did. And also because he loves her and he thinks that your parents are responsible for driving her crazy and nearly killing her."

"She started it."

"Everyone has their own view of history. Just be careful what you say around him when we get to the lab, there's no telling what he'll do."

Eva was cut off by the high pitched sound of an ancient speaker in the ceiling screeching and whining as Benning made an announcement:

"All agents, the captives are loose. I repeat: the captives are loose. Terminate with extreme prejudice on sight."

"Bum fluff." said Eva "They know you're out. We need to get to the lab yesterday!"

She put her hand on Ryan's wrist and started to run, Ryan followed along behind her.

Agent Flood stood up slowly. His jaw and nose hurt. The vigilante had broken them. His pretty face had been ruined forever. Benning entered the room.

"Couldn't five of you stop one teenaged girl?" he asked.

"Torry thir." Flood managed to say. "Thee wahz toog ud for uz."

"Take you by surprise did she?"

"Thomethig like dag thir."

"Wake Vasquez and the rest of those idiots up. Those kids are going to tear this place down. I'd rather we weren't here when that happened. Start evacuating all of our men from the facility. Not the normal ISA staff. Just our people. Understand?"

"Yeth thir."

Benning ran from the room. He needed to get to Spencer before Ryan found him.

Benning stormed into Spencer's lab, furiously angry. Spencer was running around the lab in a panic but stopped when he saw Benning:

"You fool, Benning. How could you let them escape?"

"I didn't 'let them' escape. Agent Forty-Three is missing. I think she's gone rogue." Benning wrapped his fingers around Spencer's throat. "Oh, and don't you dare speak to me like that again or I'll kill you. You'd be nobody without me."

Benning let go of Spencer's throat.

Spencer coughed and wheezed: "Curtis must be recaptured if we are to have any hope of succeeding!"

"A blinding glimpse of the obvious, Doctor. But how do you expect me to do that? Half my agents are scattered around the world, I now have less than fifteen men I trust on site."

"If only we knew what they are after. Why didn't you interrogate them properly?"

"Why bother? They were supposed to be dead within the day. And we know why they're here" Benning put his hands on Spencer and spun him around to look at Maria in her tank. "Obviously they came here to kill her! Think about it. Ryan Curtis found out that she was still alive, Hiroshi Saito probably told him. Then he came here to take his revenge on the woman you love. He's on his way here right now to murder her with his super powered bare hands."

"No! I won't allow it!"

"What can you do Spencer? The kid is able to fly, you're just a scientist. Prepare to evacuate the facility, start backing up your files to the secondary site before he gets here. I'll round up my agents and try to delay them."

Benning took out his pistol and checked the clip to ensure it was fully loaded: "Hurry up Spencer!"

Spencer went to his computer and began transferring files to the servers at the backup location.

Once he was satisfied that the work was proceeding as planned, Benning left the lab and locked the door after him.

Spencer sat down in his chair and looked at Maria.

"What do I do, I can't lose you again!" His gaze fell onto a vial of the new Nanotech solution on the desk. He reached out and held it in his hand. It wasn't completely finished, and it could damage him just like it did to Maria all those years ago but... he could use it to give him a chance to stop Ryan Curtis and make Maria proud of him. The vial felt heavy in his hands as he loaded it into a syringe.

Benning ran along the corridor, trying to find members of his team, he turned a corner and spotted two of his agents:

"Cunningham! Robinson! There you are! Where are the others?"

Robinson replied: "Most of them are in the room where you had the DeWitt girl's weapons. Flood is the only one conscious enough to do anything. He's organising the evacuation of our team as you ordered."

"And the rest?" inquired Benning.

"The rest are out of it, Sir. They all need to see a Doctor. She really did a number on them. Her weapons and equipment are gone. She must have taken them." said Cunningham.

"She's just a girl..." Benning began and stopped as Aimee DeWitt appeared in the corridor behind his two agents. "There she is!"

Robinson and Cunningham spun around, pulled their guns and began firing, as did Benning. Their shots ricocheted off Revenant's body armour or missed her entirely. Revenant ran towards them whilst drawing one of her sticks from its scabbard. Cunningham's pistol was empty by the time she reached him and he tried to pistol whip her, she ducked and jammed the tip of her stick into his chest, causing him to double over in pain as she twirled her stick to gain momentum and struck him on the head. Robinson fired at her point blank; the bullet bounced off her armour and hit the wall. Revenant punched him on the deltoid and wrapped her arm around the back of his head, pulling him over and driving her right knee into his face, once, twice. She pushed him away and he dropped to the ground, his nose gushing blood.

"Agent Benning" she said, her voice was different from earlier. She was more confident, like something inside her had changed. "I was hoping I'd run into you again."

"You don't scare me DeWitt. You're just a kid who learned martial arts and likes to play dress up. I fought in Iraq and Afghanistan. I've scraped what was left of scarier people than you off my boots and laughed about it!"

"But that was then and so far away. This is here and now. And I'm not DeWitt. The name is Revenant."

Benning lunged at her; Revenant glided away and kicked him in the hip. Benning staggered back, regained his footing and threw left and right hooks at her head. She blocked him using her elbows, moving in closer with each block until she caught him on the chin with an elbow strike. Benning felt it slam home, stunning him. He snarled and threw another jab. Revenant blocked it with her right hand and drove the base of her stick into his nose. She wrenched his arm out if its socket and pushed back. Revenant hit him on the chest twice rapidly with her stick and then shoved it end first into his teeth. He swung again; Revenant ducked and punched him on the sides of his knees. Benning cried out as he felt his kneecaps dislocate. Benning stumbled and lay on the floor, blood streaming out of his nose. He spat out a bunch of his teeth. Revenant holstered her stick and spoke to Benning:

"And you think you're able to rule the world? I'd reconsider my career choice if I were you. You're just an idiot with a gun." She sneered. "Remember that the next time you try and mess with my friends and me."

Revenant turned away quickly. That had been fun. But there was no more time to enjoy it. Ryan needed the medical scanner. She'd find the lab on her own.

Eva and Ryan arrived at one of the doors of the lab. It was ten feet high, two feet thick and made of steel.

"How do we get in?" asked Ryan.

"We need a key card, Benning or Spencer would have one."

"And without a key card?"

"Can you break the door down?"

"I'll try, stand back."

Eva moved a few steps down the corridor as Ryan planted his legs and hammered on the door. It buckled. He hit it again and again. The thumping noise echoed through the dim corridor. The door finally broke inwards in a shower of dust and rubble. He entered the lab. Eva drew her gun and followed. Ryan stood just inside the ruined doorway and took in the scene. The centre of the room held a large clear vat of liquid, inside, attached to a breathing apparatus was the woman who had killed his parents. A man in a white lab coat lay on a chair. He had passed out with a syringe sticking out of his arm.

"That's Doctor Spencer!" said Eva when she saw him. She ran across the floor to him. "Doctor! Are you OK?"

Leo awoke, raised his head slowly and glared at Ryan.

"That's him? Ryan Curtis?" he said.

"Yes, we're here to…"

Spencer stood up and pushed Eva away forcefully.

Spencer shouted: "I know exactly why he's here. You want to take Maria away from me again. I won't allow it."

"Doctor…" said Ryan "…I just want to get samples of my parents DNA. I'm not interested in revenge on a woman in a coma."

"You're lying! You're just like your parents. Maria hated them and that's why she took a stand. Regular people are in awe of you heroes, afraid of you. But she wasn't. She did what no one else would. She fought back against the oppression of the super powered. She did what I was too scared to do. But not anymore! Everything I am….I owe it all to her."

Spencer extracted the syringe from his arm and held it up above his head.

"Do you see this?" He said, grinning insanely: "This is the weapon I will use to defend her from you."

"Doctor, what have you done?" asked Eva.

"I've injected myself with a new batch of the Nanotech solution that we created to give super powers." Spencer started to shout louder:

"It's beginning! I can feel the changes happening already!"

Ryan and Eva watched as Spencer convulsed, his body shook violently as if he was being thrown around. He fell against his desk and held on tightly. His arms, chest and legs began to swell and grow. His clothes ripped as his muscles expanded. The air filled with the sounds of his bones cracking and breaking as they grew longer and thicker and knitted themselves together again. Bones punched out through his skin on his forearms, shins and back until he bristled with razor sharp spikes. His tormented screams grew louder as his internal organs changed and new ones grew inside his chest cavity. His left eye grew three times the size of his right eye. His skull changed shape and thickened. His face protruded, becoming a massive snout filled with long teeth which glistened like knives. Suddenly: the screams stopped. Spencer began to laugh and the deep bass roar of his voice filled the room:

"I guess my formula wasn't as elegant as Maria's, but it gets the job done."

He stood up and roared, his bellow echoed throughout the base.

"Now, Ryan Curtis. If you want Maria, you'll have to go through me."

"Eva, get out of here! I'll try and stop him! Find Revenant and get the information we need."

Eva ran for the door. Spencer let her go.

"It doesn't matter what information you get, Curtis. You'll be too dead to use it."

Ryan raised his fists: "Bring it on, ugly."

Eva, panicked and out of breath, met Revenant just a short run from the main labs.

"What's going on?" Revenant asked,

"Doctor.Spencer… took Nanotech solution… changed… He's become a monster. Ryan's fighting him."

"OK. I have the scanner, I need to get those DNA samples or that's going to be a really short fight."

Eva took a few long gulps of air and managed to get her breath back; "That stuff is all in the lab, which those two are probably thrashing like it was a speed metal band's hotel room."

"Ryan has to get the Doctor out of there. Ryan will probably need a recharge soon as well. What's the quickest way to the surface?"

"Through one of the decommissioned launch silos. They're empty except for pieces of old equipment but they're built to last. Ryan should be able to punch into one and fly out."

"Ok, so that's what we do." Revenant ran towards the lab.

Eva jogged alongside her: "Wait, you're running towards the smack down in the main lab? Are you completely out of your freaking mind?"

"I've devoted the last five years of my life to becoming a vigilante: what do you think? Besides, Ryan is one of the only two friends I have. I'm going to help him."

The sounds of violence grew louder as they approached the lab. Revenant peered around the door to see the monster that was once Leo Spencer crushing Ryan's throat. Ryan was pounding on Spencer's chest as hard as he could but it was clear that he was weakening from the lack of sunlight, even wearing the suit. The Doctor's breath, which was as hot as a blast furnace, was causing Ryan to sweat profusely. Revenant touched her ear to contact Ryan via the radio link that Hiroshi had provided to them.

"Ryan, I have the scanner but I have to get in there. You need to get him to the surface so you can reach the sunlight and I can scan the DNA. Can you do that?"

"Kind… of… difficult" Ryan responded. "He's… choking… me."

"OK, Ryan, I want you to hit him on both ears as hard as you can as the same time."

"O…K."

Ryan slapped Spencer as he was told. Spencer's eardrums burst and he released his grip on Ryan's throat, screamed and covered his head with his hands.

"Now you have the opening." said Revenant. "Punch him in the face and through that wall behind him. There's a missile silo about four hundred metres away. Use that to get to the surface."

"You got it!"

Ryan hit Spencer in the face and knocked him back through the wall; dust erupted into the room from the pulverised wall and covered the ancient furniture. Ryan flew through the hole and chased after Spencer.

"Where are the samples kept?" Revenant asked Eva.

"There's a cold storage room over there!" Eva pointed.

"Ok, I'll get those. Can we do anything else to help Ryan?"

"Yes, if he can get that monster to the surface, I can launch the base's remaining interceptors with Doctor Spencer as their target. That will buy Ryan time. The controls are on the main console over there."

"Do it."

Revenant picked up the Spencer's discarded key card and ran to the cold room. The door opened smoothly as soon as she ran the card through the reader. Inside the cold room were dozens of stainless steel filing cabinets with hundreds of tiny drawers. Revenant found the drawer labelled 'Solarstorm' and opened it, inside was a vial of blood. She took the scanner from her belt and switched it on, a green laser beam was emitted from the scanner and she passed that over the blood. She touched her earpiece:

"Hiroshi? Can you hear me? Hiroshi?"

"Revenant! How are you? I worried when I not hear from you and Solarstorm Junior." replied Hiroshi.

"I'm sending you a scan of the real Solarstorm's blood. Start doing sciencey stuff to it. Ryan's fighting for his life."

"Sure thing! Get me sample of Velocity blood too. For comparison!"

Revenant finished scanning the Solarstorm DNA and closed the drawer. She found the drawer marked 'Velocity' a few rows down, she opened it and scanned that vial as well.

"Sending the other sample now."

"OK, I got it. I think I can programme a dose of my Nanotech to fix Ryan's problem. I need to deliver it to you though."

"Ryan will be dead by then! You should see the size of the guy he's fighting."

"Tell him to stay alive. I be there in, like, an hour or two!"

"Hiroshi, that's crazy! How can you get from Japan to Nevada that quickly?"

"I worry about that. You help him. Bye bye!"

Hiroshi broke the connection.

Revenant screamed in frustration: "Aggghhh, that… agggghhh!"

She ran from the store room back to the main lab where Eva was busy hacking into the control systems for the base interceptors. She used a picture of Spencer taken post transformation from the security cameras and programmed the interceptors to treat him as their only target. Now she just needed Ryan to get to the surface.

Ryan was not having a good time. His suit was no longer functioning, judging by the red LED's flashing on his right sleeve, bullet-proof it may have been but Hiroshi clearly hadn't designed it to be 'mad super powered monster' proof. Finally, Ryan had forced the Doctor into the silo that Revenant had mentioned. Ryan launched into the air and flew as quickly as he could, which wasn't all that fast, given his weakened state:

"Hey Doctor! Follow me, so I can kick your ass in nicer scenery!"

"Kick my ass? You little punk, I'll beat you down wherever you go, come here!"

Spencer crouched and used his tree trunk sized legs to jump after Ryan. Spencer caught Ryan just short of the roof of the silo but their combined momentum was enough that they punched through to the surface. It was a sweltering Nevada morning. Ryan felt the sunlight on his skin. They landed two hundred metres away from the silo with Ryan bearing the brunt of the impact.

Spencer stood up first and spoke slowly in his deepened voice:

"Just a boy trying to emulate mommy and daddy, aren't you? I didn't like them. Never did. So high and mighty, laughing at normal people from their ivory tower in Las Vegas. I'm glad Maria killed them. I wish I had seen it in person and not just on television! And look at you, their seed. You had so much potential but it's been completely wasted! You're not a fighter or much of a hero at all. You're just the leftovers from a generation of heroes I helped destroy!

"Maybe, but you're still a giant loser, no matter what you did to your body." Ryan said.

"I don't think so. I've finally made something of myself. Doctor Leo Spencer has died and is reborn, as a Behemoth!"

Ryan filled his hand with sand from the desert floor and quickly threw it at Behemoth's face.

Behemoth roared as he tried to remove the grains of sand from his eyes: "Raaaahhh! You little… I'll grind you into paste for that."

Ryan got to his feet, the brief time in the sun had recharged him. He hit Behemoth in the chest: "Try it, nerd!"

Behemoth stepped backwards, wiping the last of the sand from his eyes.

"So" he said. "There's some fight left in you. Good."

Ryan leaped into the air and hit Behemoth, catching him on his misshapen jaw with a right hook. Before Ryan could follow up with his left, Behemoth grabbed his left fist and twisted it. The pain in his wrist caused Ryan to shout in agony. Behemoth kicked Ryan's shins and he slumped onto his knees. Behemoth raised his other arm and smashed Ryan in the face.

"Time to die, Ryan."

Ryan could hear a buzzing noise and the sound of gunfire. Ryan felt Behemoth release his grip as wrist as a stream of tracer bullets connected painfully with Behemoth's back.

"What the heck?"

A missile slammed home directly onto Behemoth's spine and knocked him onto the ground.

"Interceptors!" he said as he rose, turned towards the formation of triangular robot fighters and jumped into the sky to swat them out of the air.

"Curtis!" Behemoth shouted, smashing the robot interceptors like toys in his giant fists: "I'm having so much fun; I've decided not to kill you yet! Once I destroy these irritants from the base, I'm going to bring Vanguard Tower crashing down. I'll let you watch your old home, and any other remaining pieces of your parent's legacy, burn before I finish you off. I can't imagine a worse fate for you. First, I'm going to destroy the site of their last victory. I'll kill my way through Las Vegas. Your hometown will be nothing more than a memory when I'm finished with it. You'll get to see everything you cared about destroyed. You will be begging me to kill you when I'm done." Behemoth leaped off into the morning light towards Las Vegas. He destroyed the remaining interceptors that continued to harass him as he jumped away.

Chapter Seventeen | City of Smoke and Flame

Revenant and Eva reached Ryan less than five minutes after Behemoth had left. They arrived just in time to see his vast bulk disappear over the horizon. Ryan had a cut above his eye that was bleeding heavily. Eva knelt down beside Ryan and produced a first aid kit from her bag. She pulled a roll of plasters from the kit and began applying them to the wound on Ryan's forehead.

"Where's he gone in such a hurry?" asked Eva.

"Vegas. He wants to destroy Vanguard Tower." answered Ryan.

"He'll probably destroy most of the city as well, he doesn't seem to be the type of person who does things by halves." said Revenant.

"I think you're right." said Ryan. "He's an overachiever if ever I saw one."

"What do we do? There's a helicopter in the base but we'll never get there in time, Las Vegas is at least an hour away." said Eva.

"We warn them, I still have your phone." said Revenant.

"How is that not destroyed?"

"Durable things aren't they? We can call the Las Vegas Special Tactics Unit."

"And tell them what? That a rampaging Doctor is going to make a house call? The cops won't believe us."

"Yes" Ryan said "They will, give me the phone."

Captain Ed O'Grady sat at his desk with his feet up. It had been a quiet day so far, Las Vegas hadn't seen a bank robbery or high speed pursuit in weeks. It was the usual winter lull in criminal activity. It was just too late in the year for anyone to try any crimes, except for your garden variety pick pocketing and that sort of thing. Even criminals took a break as things began to wind down in the run up to Christmas. The pattern had become so established in recent years that a lot of the Special Tactics Unit asked for, and received, holiday time. This week, the unit comprised him, Sarah Lieber, (who never took time off unless ordered), Officer Wyatt (who took all of his holidays in summer to spend time with his family) and twenty others. In the normal course of events they would be more than enough to handle most situations. O'Grady was busy reading a movie magazine with his feet up on his desk when one of the duty officers, Olson, stuck his head around the door and spoke in a thick Louisiana accent:

"Captain, we got a caller on line two. Says that there's a super villain on his way to wreck the place."

Ed groaned inside, it wasn't the first occasion that they'd received a message of this type. Kids were usually bored out of their minds in school at this time of the year. A group of high school students calling in a bomb threat in order to get a day off wasn't unheard of.

"I don't suppose this caller gave his name?"

"Yessir, says he's Ryan Curtis and that he knows you personally."

Ed nearly fell out of his chair: "Put him on, immediately."

Ed picked up the phone and pressed the blinking button for the correct line.

"Ryan? Is that really you?"

"Yes. Captain O'Grady?"

"It's me. Now what's all this about a super villain?"

"It's true. He'll be in the city in a few minutes. He's going to destroy The Sphinx and Vanguard Tower."

"An actual super-villain?" asked Ed.

"Big, strong and disgusting looking."

"All the tower is used for is a museum? Why destroy that?"

"He hates my parents and superheroes in general. He needs to be stopped. We're on our way but we won't get there in time!"

"Who's we?"

"It's a long story. I'll fill you in later."

"I'm on it. It's good to know you're around, Ryan."

"Thanks. I'll see you shortly."

Ed got up from his desk and pulled on his Kevlar vest.

"Sarah! DJ! Suit up and bring the biggest things we have in the armoury."

Sarah ran into the office, a big pixie like grin on her face, followed by DJ and a handful of other officers:

"What have we got?" she asked, beaming: "And do you really mean the biggest?"

"Yes I do, I'll explain on the way to the Strip. We need to be rolling in five minutes people!"

The officers dispersed to get their combat gear and move out.

Revenant piloted the helicopter as Eva continued to bandage Ryan's wounds.

Revenant shouted to be heard over the roar of the engines: "I hope they can hold him off for long enough."

"They're good cops" Ryan responded: "They're all the city has for the moment."

Eva looked at Revenant: "What are we supposed to do when we get there, Ryan is hurt and we're not going to be able to do much that the Special Tactics Unit can't."

"I'm hoping Mech can come up with an idea" Revenant touched her earpiece "Mech? Can you hear me?"

"Yes. And why you calling me that?" asked Hiroshi, clearly annoyed.

"I have a civilian on board; I can't use your real name. Do you have anything for us?"

"Yes. I have a Nanotech mixture that solve Ryan's problems and even increase his power levels. I leaving the office now. See you at Vanguard Tower in forty five minutes?"

"Whatever you say. See you then."

Hiroshi had a small problem: how do you get halfway around the world in forty five minutes? Luckily he also had a solution: the shuttles launching from the spaceport could do that trip, albeit it would be a one way journey. A quick trip into orbit and a full burn on the engines would get him to Las Vegas in no time. The shuttle would be irreparably damaged by the journey but would make it there in one piece; or at worst two pieces. The only other issue was that he was banned from ever being allowed near a shuttle thanks to the nervous breakdown he had suffered three years ago after he'd had to quit being a hero.

Getting to the launch site would be easy; he was often called over to consult with the rocket engineers when they had problems that required his special talents. But, if he tried to board a shuttle without permission and reset its pre-planned flight parameters, he would be tranquilised by a security guard and hauled into a jail cell for a few days to sleep it off. Boarding a shuttle would require all of his scientific ingenuity.

He left his lab building and took one of the bases' electric cars over to launch rail four. Shuttle Nine was due to take off in fifteen minutes, leaving just enough time for Hiroshi to drive over, slip past the guards and programme the autopilot to get him to Las Vegas. Assuming nothing went wrong and his calculations were correct.

Hiroshi arrived at the launch rail right on schedule. There were two guards on the elevator gantry that led to the blue and white shuttle. Shuttle nine was unmanned. It was programmed to bring today's 'Groceries' to the engineers in orbit, working on the Mars ship, the Kasei tansa-ki. They wouldn't starve if he commandeered the shuttle, another grocery shuttle was due to launch tomorrow with another supply of fresh food and water and they had plenty of rations in reserve. Their work would be delayed by a few hours as they waited for whatever building materials they had ordered, but so what? Those rocket scientists always got more than they needed, Hiroshi believed. He had to make do with whatever spare parts he could scrounge from them in order to build his prototype space suits.

Hiroshi stopped the car near the elevator to shuttle nine and got out. One of the two guards challenged him in Japanese:

"Saito-san" said one "most apologies but you are not authorised to be in this area. I must, most respectfully, ask you to leave."

"I am aware of my bending of the rules. I wish to see the launch!"

The guards looked at each other. They had no idea what to do. Hiroshi was a project leader. Forcibly removing him could cause them all sorts of problems. The guard spoke again:

"Sorry, Saito-san. But you must leave the area."

"I understand." said Hiroshi, in Japanese, as he pulled the gun he had earlier used to shoot Ryan from its hiding place behind his back and shot both guards. "But science is important. Those were tranquiliser darts by the way. You'll wake up in an hour with a slight blinding headache."

He entered the elevator and hit the button to bring him to the shuttle. Eight minutes to the automated launch. He still had plenty of time to do what he needed.

The Sphinx was burning. Coils of black smoke swept along The Strip, created by the orange and yellow flames that leapt out of nearly every window of the five separate buildings that comprised the world's most exclusive casino. Ed and his squad stood ready behind a line of police cars not far from the main entrance. Behemoth had landed, literally landed, in the main courtyard of the casino less than ten minutes previously. The owners of The Sphinx had built a memorial garden that included a life sized statue of The Vanguard in that courtyard not long after the heroes had been killed. It was as much a part of the city as the Bellagio's fountains or the rancid prawn cocktail in Lucky's on Tropicana Avenue. Its gift shop had been the third busiest in the city. Now, it was all dust, destroyed in the first few seconds of Behemoth's arrival.

Hundreds of people had been in the area when Behemoth attacked. Ed figured that many of them had to be dead, just like the first two squads of police officers to reach the building in response to a handful of panicked 911 calls. Ed had heard the final moments of the second squad over the police radio as he travelled at top speed up Las Vegas Boulevard to the casino. The sounds he'd listened to over the radio were a discordant mess of people screaming, a monster laughing, gunfire, bones snapping and then, finally, mercifully, silence. Ed didn't want to hear anything like that again for as long as he lived. He looked at the entrance to the largest of the casino's buildings, the shopping mall, through his binoculars. No movement. No one living had left the building in a few minutes. There was no other option: they had to go in and try to save who they could.

"DJ! Sarah! Over here now." He shouted.

The two members of his team he had called came running up to him. DJ was carrying a bulky looking, six foot long metal case across his right shoulder. Sarah had a similar, but smaller, case in her left hand.

"I need you to take the rooftop directly opposite. It gives the best line of sight on the area. I'm going to bring Olsen and the rest of squad three into the building to look for survivors."

Explosions rocked the area, coming from the direction of the shopping mall. The police ducked, sheltering behind their cars until the explosions subsided.

Ed continued to talk: "I want you to cover us. If we have to retreat for any reason, you are to try slow that thing down."

"Got it." DJ and Sarah replied in unison.

They took off at a run for the building opposite. It was the same one, Ed suddenly realised, that they had set up a snipers perch on during the hostage situation five years ago. The building was now abandoned and boarded up.

DJ charged through the wooden boards barricading the door, turning them to splinters. Sarah followed hot on his heels. DJ hit the call button for the elevator, saw that it wasn't working and headed for the stairwell instead. It was chained shut, which slowed him down for all of a second as he shoulder-charged the door, knocking it off its hinges. They took the stairs three at a time and raced for the roof. Their boots hammered on the steps as they pounded their way up.

Ed gathered squad three and made for the entrance to the shopping mall. He and the five others in the team moved quickly for the remains of the glass doors which had been shattered. Olsen took point and inched his way across the threshold, broken glass crackled and crunched under his feet. The body of a woman lay not far inside the hallway; she'd been hit by falling masonry less than five yards from safety. Ed knelt beside her and checked her pulse. She was dead.

Someone was laughing further down the corridor. A deep, rumbling laugh; it sent a shiver down Ed's spine. Ed gave a hand signal and the squad continued moving forward, taking care not to make any noise. Ed was under no illusions that they didn't stand a chance against that thing in here. The structure was unstable and using heavy weapons, like grenades, was out of the question in case the entire place came down on their heads.

Their only option was to quietly look for survivors and get them out without making contact with the monster. Once they were sure they'd pulled as many people out as possible, the squad was to withdraw and Ed was to call in an air strike to bury Behemoth alive. The Mayor was on the phone to the Secretary of Defence at that very moment, requesting that the Air Force send in a plane from the nearby Nellis Air Force Base to help complete the buildings transition to a pile of smouldering wreckage.

There were more screams up ahead, coming from the same place that the laughing had come from earlier. They heard a man begging for mercy at the top of his voice and then a hideous scream and a wet thumping sound.

Ed looked at his team; Olsen was crying soundlessly, his mouth opened and closed as he gulped in air. Tears were streaming down his cheeks. None of the others looked particularly happy either.

Ed heard a noise to his left; there was a scrabbling noise coming from the debris up ahead. He moved forward slowly and slung his rifle across his back. He beckoned Officer Washington forward. Washington hunkered down next to Ed and listened. He nodded and they both grabbed a piece of reinforced concrete and moved it. Miraculously, a young girl was alive and unharmed underneath. The rubble had fallen in a way that had protected her from the worst of the collapse. The girl smiled when she saw Ed. He put his finger to his lips to tell her to be quiet. He whispered to Washington: "Get her out of here. Right away. We'll wait for you."

"Yes sir." Washington responded as he picked the little girl up and jogged back the way they had entered.

The screams in the centre of the complex started again. It sounded like a group of people this time. Ed motioned for his people to hold position until Washington had returned.

Suddenly, Olsen got to his feet and sprinted towards the sounds of slaughter up ahead. He disappeared around the nearest corner before Ed had a chance to react. They all heard the sound of Olsen's assault rifle firing for a few seconds until its magazine was empty.

Ed heard Olsen slap another magazine in. Olsen was shouting an incoherent challenge as he fired. Olsen's roars changed from anger to terror as he flew backwards down the hall to land, lifelessly, not far from the squad. His right leg was missing. Ed and the rest of the squad moved backwards slowly, towards the door they had entered. Giant footsteps could be heard approaching from around the corner. Behemoth turned the corner and saw them. He was carrying Olsen's leg.

"I thought I smelled bacon." He said. "If you're looking for survivors, you're too late. I already killed everyone."

The monster started to chuckle. Ed knew at once that the monster was telling the truth. Behemoth's chest was dripping with blood.

"But I've always got the energy for more." Behemoth smiled and started to run towards the squad.

Ed raised his weapon and squeezed the trigger.

"Fire! Try to slow him down! Squad, fall back to the entrance. Move!"

They retreated as quickly as possible while hosing Behemoth with bullets, not caring about whether they made any noise or not. The fusillade of shots from four assault rifles was slowing Behemoth down. The monster continued his charge. Ed and his men fired short bursts to discourage the monster from following them as they retreated. One of the policemen was too slow; Behemoth grabbed him and broke his neck with a sickening snap. It was too much for the other members of the squad, who stopped firing and ran full speed for the door. Ed emptied his clip at the monster and followed. As he ran he took a grenade from his belt.

"Since the place is going to need serious remodelling and I'm probably going to die anyway." he said to himself as he ran.

Ed pulled the pin of the grenade and released the lever. He threw the grenade over his shoulder at the ceiling just in front of Behemoth. The grenade exploded in the monster's face. The ceiling above him sagged and fell, burying Behemoth under a ton of rubble. Ed kept running as the walls and ceiling groaned and continued to collapse. He exited the building just as the hall crumbled completely and the facade of the building fell inwards.

Hiroshi sat back into the acceleration couch on the shuttle. Alarms were going off all over the base; After all, someone was stealing a spaceship. The control tower operators were attempting to override the shuttle launch but Hiroshi had locked them out of the systems as soon as he'd entered the cockpit. The launch track, actually a massive magnetic rail gun, began drawing electricity from the base's power plant and was quickly approaching launch strength. A ten second countdown started. Hiroshi shouldn't have been nervous. He'd helped design the systems, he was sure they would work within their normal parameters, wasn't he? Doubt gripped his mind and a shiver ran down his back, what if it all went wrong? Just like it had in Tokyo that day three years ago? He'd barely survived one catastrophic malfunction. What were the chances that he'd survive another?

Suddenly, Hiroshi didn't have any more time to mull things over. The countdown timer reached zero. Hiroshi was pushed back into the cushioned acceleration couch by the force of the launch. The shuttle accelerated along the track, hurtling towards the concrete and metal mountain four miles away at five times the speed of sound. Hiroshi closed his eyes as the shuttle pointed up towards the sky and continued to accelerate, he wouldn't be going into outer space on this trip. The shuttle was programmed to go just high enough to allow him to travel to the United States in twenty minutes. The shuttle left the launch track and flew straight up into the atmosphere.

Ed escaped the building with no injuries other than a coating of dust from the explosion. He picked himself up from his place on the ground behind a destroyed limousine that he had used as cover as the building came down and sprinted back to the line of police cars on The Strip. He was sure that Behemoth couldn't have survived the building's collapse. He keyed his radio to let the paramedics and fire service know that it was safe to commence search and rescue operations of the area, assuming that there was anyone left alive. Ed hoped that Behemoth had been mistaken when he had claimed to have killed all the inhabitants, the girl Ed's squad had found earlier proved that the monster couldn't have harmed everyone in the building.

There was a sound behind him, coming from what remained of The Sphinx. A repetitive pounding caused the earth to vibrate and shake. Ed took his finger off the radio and turned slowly. A slab of concrete, larger than a delivery truck, flew up into the air and crashed back to earth fifty metres from where he stood.

Behemoth rose up brushing pieces of debris from his arms. He slowly climbed over the mountain of broken masonry and walked towards the exit of the compound. Ed ran, calling Sarah and DJ as he did so.

"I'd really appreciate it if you use whatever you two have planned in the realm of big explosions on that guy. Anytime now would be good, over."

Sarah answered. "DJ isn't ready yet. When I say duck you had better hit the dirt hard, over."

"Roger."

"Duck!"

Ed ducked and kissed the dirt.

On the rooftop, Sarah stared through the telescopic sight on top of her sniper rifle. The rifle was her favourite gun; bought for her by her father not long before he died. Sarah called it 'Daisy', for no particular reason. She aimed at Behemoth's overly large right eye and fired. The booming crack echoed across the city. Sarah used to joke that she could kill a dinosaur with Daisy. Her shot hit Behemoth, who cried loud enough to shatter the glass in the windshields of the police cruisers parked on the street. Sarah fired again, this time at Behemoth's left eye. Behemoth cried even louder. He was in utter agony. Sarah hummed to herself, truly happy, and fired twice more, aiming one bullet at each of Behemoth's knees. He staggered like a drunk and slipped.

"Captain; get up and run! I'll hit him again if he tries to rise."

DJ snapped the last component of his rocket launcher into place and mounted it on the rooftop.

"What did you just shoot him with?" asked DJ. "Those weren't regular bullets. I know that."

"Tungsten rounds. You can punch a hole in the side of a tank with these babies. Even thinking about using them on a person constitutes a war crime under the Geneva Convention. I thought I'd never get a chance to use them." responded a delighted Sarah.

"Better hope the Police Commissioner doesn't find out."

"Does this guy even count as 'a person' anymore? He definitely doesn't look like one. Besides, I'm not sure that they did permanent damage. He seems to be a lot tougher than a tank."

"I'm sure the Police Union Lawyer will be happy to argue the case." Behemoth used his hands to try push himself upright. DJ aimed his rocket launcher and fired.

"Fire in the hole!" he said.

The rocket streaked across the road to Behemoth and exploded on contact. Incredibly, Behemoth was just knocked over by the blast but otherwise uninjured. He glowered at the officers on the roof top, picked up a car by its front bumper and threw it at them.

"Move!" shouted Sarah as she and DJ got up and ran, they jumped to a neighbouring building as the car sailed through the air to crash onto where they had been sitting.

"I think all we did was annoy him." said DJ.

"I think so too. Do you hear something?" asked Sarah.

They both looked up at the sound of engines to see a helicopter approach from the desert.

DJ spoke: "Looks like reinforcements!"

"For him or for us? That helicopter isn't one of ours. It's painted black and there's no registration numbers."

DJ continued to look as a person in a torn yellow and brown costume jumped from the helicopter and landed near Behemoth.

"I think it's reinforcements for us." He said.

"It looks that way." Sarah looked closely at the newcomer through the telescopic scope on Daisy.

She thought that she recognised the young man who was walking towards Behemoth: "Is that Ryan Curtis?"

Chapter Eighteen | Melee

Ryan landed on the pavement not far from Behemoth and strode towards the super villain. He paused not far away from the genetically modified Doctor and circled the monster warily.

"Curtis." Behemoth spat: "I thought that the beating I gave you an hour ago had convinced you to stay away. I was looking forward to hunting you down and snuffing you out once I'd finished teaching Las Vegas a lesson. This suicidal need you heroes have to throw yourself into danger gets old really fast."

"I wasn't about to let you destroy the city just because of your stalled love affair with a murderer."

"Maria wasn't a murderer. She was a soldier fighting a war against your kind. What gave your parents and their cronies the right to impose their moral codes on normal people? Regular folks couldn't hope to stand against The Vanguard. It was up to Maria to put the power back in the hands of the people. She destroyed a group of future tyrants and is feared and hated for doing it."

"My parents weren't tyrants!"

"Not when they died, but how long would it have been before they got bored with the way the world was run and decided to overthrow a government or two? And you know what? Lots of people, fools, would have cheered. The heroes were treated like gods amongst us! So strong, so handsome, so righteous!" He mocked. "It made me sick. I hated the strong using force to impose their will on the weak. That's why I helped Maria five years ago. It's why I'll fight for her now!"

Behemoth swung his right fist at Ryan's head. Ryan evaded the blow and jabbed Behemoth in the ribs twice in quick succession. Behemoth stepped back, winded by Ryan's attack then bared his teeth and forced his hands around Ryan's throat.

Ryan gasped as Behemoth moved forward slowly, pushing him down. Ryan's hands scrabbled in the rubble, looking for an object to use as a weapon. His hands closed around a steel rod used for reinforcing concrete. Ryan swung it as hard as he could and hit Behemoth in the side of the stomach causing him to weaken his grip. Ryan swung again, at Behemoth's legs this time, catching him on the knee.

Behemoth let go. Ryan used an overhand strike, hitting Behemoth's right side and bending the metal bar against the super strong bone jutting out of Behemoth's shoulder blade. Ryan threw the bar at Behemoth's head; he deflected it with a swipe of his arm. Ryan jumped at Behemoth, who backhanded him and sent him flying through the air to land on the wreck of a destroyed car.

Revenant and Eva watched from the hovering ISA helicopter.

"Ryan needs help. Behemoth will wear him down eventually." Revenant said.

"Did you happen to bring a nuclear weapon? We don't have anything big enough to stop him. You have stun grenades and sticks. All I have is a pistol!"

"Take the controls and I'll see what I can get. This is Vegas, there's bound to be things I can use!"

Eva grabbed the control stick as Revenant climbed into the back of the helicopter and opened the door.

"I can't set us down," Eva shouted over the roar of the rotor blades.

"There's nowhere to land."

"Leave that to me." Revenant drew her grappling gun, pointed it at a nearby building and pulled the trigger, the hook fired and dug into the nearest wall. Revenant prepared to jump.

Eva shouted again: "What do I do?"

"Try help with the evacuation. If he kills Ryan and me, well, you know where he's going next."

"Good luck."

Revenant jumped and swung down to ground level using the grappling line.

She surveyed the area as she dropped. She noticed a dead STU policeman to her left and ran over to the body as soon as she had landed safely. The policeman wore a grenade belt. Revenant unbuckled it, taking the grenades with her. She looked around and noticed a car showroom not far away, if she wanted to help Ryan, she'd need transport. She sprinted down the block to the showroom. Scores of people were milling around despite the fact that a mutated creature had spent the last hour destroying everything within arm's reach. It was as if they didn't believe what was happening. Revenant pushed her way through the crowds and ran towards her destination.

The car showroom was a temple to excess. It was the sort of place that not very subtly tries to imply that if you can't afford to own one of their top of the range roadsters then you've failed in life. There were marble floors and columns. Designer Italian tiles adorned the walls. There wasn't a single oily rag or spare car part in sight. The place had recently been abandoned, the owners must have realised that their lives were slightly more important than overpriced aluminium designer rubbish. Revenant picked up a brick from a nearby building that had fallen into the parking lot of the car dealership and used it to smash the biggest window of the showroom. She felt a small spark of rebellion in her chest as she did so. She entered the building and immediately saw the car she wanted; a bright red two seater convertible. She threw the brick she'd used to smash the window onto the passenger seat. She jumped onto the Driver's seat and pulled out a USB lead from her wrist computer. She plugged it into a port on the dashboard. Hiroshi's hacker programme overrode the car's computer and started the engine. Revenant put it into gear and left the building. She steered the car towards the battleground outside the Sphinx.

Hiroshi was thirty thousand feet above Las Vegas. He'd separated the cockpit section from the main body of the shuttle less than two minutes before and was in free fall. He typed a code into the computer and two large parachutes made of golden foil, to the front and rear of the cockpit, deployed. He fell to Earth slowly, the Nanotech solution safe in his hands, he just had to get it to Ryan and everything would be alright.

Ryan was not doing well; he had exhausted his store of solar energy with a blast at Behemoth's head. It had only served to further anger an already irritated villain. Ryan had fought for as long as he was able but now his reserves of strength were tapped out. Behemoth struck Ryan on the side with the jagged bone spikes on his wrist. Blood from a foot long gash on Ryan's side misted into the air and Ryan screamed in pain. Behemoth battered Ryan on the head and knocked Ryan onto his knees.

"It's over, Curtis. Your story ends here. Maybe, if they ever rebuild this place, they'll put a statue of you up beside the one of your parents and their friends. But they usually don't put up statues to failures. How does it feel to know that once I'm done here, I'm going to do the same to Vanguard Tower? Then I'll visit City Hall and do some more remodelling. That blasted Mayor invited your parents to live here after all."

"Someone will stop you."

"You really think so? Look around Curtis. There's no one left. I crushed the police Special Tactics Unit. Your friend, DeWitt, is nowhere. This is where it all ends. Soon you'll be nothing but a trivia question: What was Solarstorm and Velocity's son called?"

Behemoth bent over and picked up a giant metal lion which had previously adorned the lintel over The Golden Hill Chinese restaurant. He raised the statue over his head, ready to deliver the final blow. A car horn beeped, Behemoth looked in the direction of the sound, a red sports car was travelling toward him at high speed.

Revenant wedged the brick onto the accelerator and stood up on the seat, the car gained speed as she aimed it directly at Behemoth. She jumped, back flipped out of the car and landed awkwardly on her feet. Her right hand held the two remaining grenades from the belt she'd taken from the police officer's corpse. The car hit Behemoth and knocked him backwards into a drugstore. The three grenades she'd left armed on the passenger seat of the car detonated, igniting its fuel tank. Blue flames licked the sky. Revenant threw her two remaining grenades into the inferno that the drugstore had become, she ducked as they exploded. Shards of metal and glass erupted outwards and fell into the street. Once the blasts had died down and the fragments stopped falling, Revenant ran to Ryan. He was still alive.

She hoisted him up, leaning him against her shoulder. She needed to get him out into the open, away from the smoke of the burning buildings so that he could recharge.

"Revenant… what happened?" Ryan asked.

"I drove a horrifically expensive car for about thirty seconds and then crashed it."

"Cool." He said weakly.

"Come on, we need to get you to someplace where the sky is clear, sunlight will do you the world of good."

"Revenant… I can't beat him, he's stronger than me."

"It's not always about who's the strongest Ryan. You need to outfight him too."

"Outfight? How?"

"I usually just try to improvise: hit them with whatever comes to hand. That's worked wonders for me so far."

Hiroshi ejected from the shuttle pod and pulled the rip cord of his parachute. He fell slowly but not gracefully. He landed on a rooftop, just behind a couple of police officers.

"Who are you?" demanded the large well-built one, who was suddenly pointing a pistol at Hiroshi's head.

"My name is Hiroshi Saito. I'm friend and advisor to the two superheroes down there."

Hiroshi pulled a business card from one of the pockets of his lab coat. It had embossed lettering that read "H. Saito. Genius Engineer and Hero Consultant".

"Pretty cool huh? The embossing cost me extra but it totally worth it. That a card that says the bearer is a professional." said Hiroshi

"Anyone can make a business card." said Sarah.

"That true. However not everyone can make this!"

Hiroshi opened his hand and showed the police officers the syringe with the Nanotech solution.

"I need get this to Ryan Curtis immediately."

"What's that?" asked DJ.

"It medicine for him, he need it to make stronger!"

"You can't go down there." said Sarah. "Not unless you have a burning desire to be killed or maimed."

"Sarah?" asked DJ "Could you load the contents of that syringe into an empty tranquiliser dart and shoot Ryan with it." DJ turned to Hiroshi "Would that work?"

Hiroshi smiled: "Great idea buddy. That what we do! Can she make the shot from here?"

"Please!" Sarah snorted "I can do it with both eyes closed!"

Hiroshi emptied the vial into the dart that DJ handed him. Once it was sealed, Hiroshi handed it to Sarah.

Sarah loaded the dart into Daisy and prepared to fire.

Behemoth stepped out of the flames of the drugstore, burned and scorched but undefeated.

"You'll have to do better than that."

He looked around but couldn't see Ryan or Revenant. He was mildly disappointed that no one had heard his dramatic statement of intent.

"I'll find you. You can't hide from me." He yelled.

Ryan sat, propped up by Revenant against a fire hydrant. The hydrant was leaking. Revenant cupped her hands and collected fresh water to give to Ryan. Once he had drank his fill of water, Revenant busied herself by tearing up t-shirts from a ruined clothes store from across the street and used them to bandage the large cut on Ryan's chest.

"Are you OK?" she asked.

""I've been better. I don't think I'm able for all this."

"No one is, at first. It took a long time for your parents to become the heroes they ended up as. You've done great things today Ryan. If you hadn't fought him then he'd have levelled the area completely."

"I'm not sure how much more I can do, I've probably only got five more minutes of fight left in me. All he as to do is wear me down and he'll win."

"Maybe, maybe not. You still have to try... we still have to try."

They heard Behemoth bellow from down the street. A small group of tourists ran by. One of them delayed long enough to take a picture of Behemoth with a camera phone. Revenant looked around and then spoke to Ryan.

"I have to go. You need more time to recharge."

"Revenant, Aimee... don't... he'll kill you."

"If I don't go he'll kill us both. Stay here. Try to get your strength back and come help me when you can."

"I will."

Revenant walked down the street towards Behemoth. She unholstered her escrima sticks.

Behemoth was throwing cars around, picking them up to check if Ryan was hiding in or behind them when he saw Revenant approach. The street was a mess; trenches had been gouged out of the earth by the destruction Behemoth had caused. The glint of the sun off metal in one of the trenches caught Revenant's eye for a moment.

"That was a nice stunt girlie!" said Behemoth. "It almost worked as well. But I think you're all out of tricks."

"Maybe I'll surprise you. I'm the most dangerous nineteen year old woman in the world. I've spent the last five years learning how to maim people."

"Five years or five lifetimes. It won't save you. Nothing can!"

Behemoth thundered towards her. Revenant dived out of his path and struck at his feet as he passed by. Her sticks shattered against his muscular legs.

"Not so tough now are you?" Behemoth laughed. "I'm going to enjoy teaching you a lesson."

He charged at Revenant again. She drew her knife, aimed at his throat and threw it.

He used his hand to block the knife which embedded itself in his palm. He didn't slow down but continued his advance towards her at full speed. Revenant ran to meet him but, at the last second, dropped down and slid between his legs, like a baseball player reaching for the home plate. Behemoth slowed down and turned around.

"Two passes. You won't survive a third!" He said as he pulled Revenant's knife from his palm and tossed it away.

He ran at her again, managing to grab hold of her hair as she unsuccessfully attempted to stay out of his reach. He lifted Revenant up and wrapped his hands around her neck to throttle her. Revenant fumbled in one of her pockets, searching for one last weapon to use against him. Her fingers touched exactly what she was looking for; a small brick of plastic explosive attached to a timer. She pulled the weapon out and hit the switch to arm it.

"Any last words?" Behemoth said.

"Gaff... maig." said Revenant, her voice muffled.

"What?"

Revenant threw the device into the trench which contained the metal pipe that she'd seen earlier. The charge exploded, rupturing the pipe. The gas leaked and caught fire, the blaze expanded and spouted like a geyser of flame. Revenant braced her legs against Behemoth's torso and pushed as hard as she could. She fell backwards out of his grasp just as the inferno hit Behemoth square in the side.

"I said 'Gas Main', idiot." Revenant said as she dropped.

Revenant landed awkwardly on the ground and heard a loud snap. Pain shot through her left arm as she clenched her teeth in an effort to stop herself yelling.

"Agggghhh! That's broken!" she hissed through her closed jaw.

"Revenant!" shouted Hiroshi over the commlink.

"Hiroshi? Is that you?" said Revenant as she slowly backed away from the burning gas. Her arm was throbbing.

"Who else baby?"

"Did you bring the medicine for Ryan?"

"We going to shoot him with it now."

"What? Shoot him?"

"Not worry, it safe! She tell me she really good shot!"

"What? What are you talking about?"

Revenant heard the big crack of a rifle discharging.

Sarah aimed Daisy at Ryan. She took a deep breath and fired. The dart flew through the air and lodged in his bicep. Ryan clutched his arm in surprise and pulled the dart out.

"What the..." he began to say. He began to feel very warm. The afternoon sunlight poured into his body. He felt his strength returning by the second. The Nanotech was working.

Hiroshi stared at Sarah in admiration.

"That really nice shot." He said.

"Thanks." said Sarah.

"So, you doing anything later?" asked Hiroshi.

"Excuse me?"

"I asking if you doing anything later?"

"Hiroshi." shouted Ryan over the radio link. "Stop flirting. You're no good at it. What is this stuff doing to me?"

"I can't help it. I attracted to women who proficient in firearms. Nanotech fixing the problem different powers clashing in your nervous system. Powers won't work against each other all the time and will be able to co-exist. You won't expend your energy as quickly."

"Co-exist? Does that mean what I think it means?"

"Yeap! You will have all of your parents' powers. Flight, strength, energy blasts and super speed. Also, Nanotech will work to keep your teeth white and breath mint fresh always. I add that as a bonus."

"You can blast me, you can burn me, but you cannot kill me!"

Revenant watched in horror as Behemoth walked up the street, burning brightly like a funeral pyre.

"I can certainly try." Revenant said as she raised her good arm, ready to attack. Her left arm hung limply by her side.

"You don't need to." said Ryan from behind her.

She turned around. Ryan looked different. His eyes and hands shone brightly, bursting with energy.

"Ryan…" She said.

"Stand back Revenant. I'll finish him." Ryan rushed past her, faster than she could see. He thumped Behemoth backwards, sending him flying down the street. Behemoth landed, gouging out chunks of sidewalk which flew into the air.

Ryan rocketed down the street after Behemoth.

"Go get him." Revenant whispered.

"Curtis!" snarled Behemoth. "I wasn't aware there was any of your face left to smash open."

"Don't worry about me, I'm feeling much better."

"Caught your second wind, have you? Just you try and stop me. I'll obliterate you! Anything that's in my way: I go through."

"Really? You haven't shown much initiative so far. You're just a follower. You did what the ISA and Dr. Fleming told you and spent the last who knows how long in a dingy basement. You finally took your first proper decision in your entire life and all you did was badly copy what your predecessor did."

"You little jerk, you'll pay for that!"

Ryan smiled: "Make me, loser."

Ryan and Behemoth faced off, separated by twenty metres of roadway.

"This is the day the heroes fall, Curtis."

"Don't be so sure."

"I'll rip you apart. I swear Maria will have her revenge."

"Do you always talk this much before a fight? I'm beginning to feel like we're on a wrestling show. Let's finish this."

Behemoth smiled and opened his arms wide:

"Yes! Let the world see what happens."

Behemoth threw a jab that could have torn a hole in the side of a battleship. Ryan saw it coming and moved. Behemoth missed.

"What?" said Behemoth, "How could you have avoided that? You weren't that fast earlier."

"I've upgraded." said Ryan as he kicked Behemoth in the ribs.

Behemoth stood helplessly as Ryan hit him multiple times. Ryan's kicks and punches were too fast and powerful for Behemoth to either see or stop. Behemoth trashed around, trying to fight back. He put all his strength into one last punch, Ryan sidestepped it and pummelled Behemoth into the ground.

Behemoth rose slowly and lurched towards Ryan. The ground shook from the impact of his footsteps. Ryan planted his feet and unleashed an upper cut aimed squarely at Behemoth's chin. Ryan's glowing right hand caught him perfectly and flipped Behemoth forty feet into the air. Ryan leapt upwards into the sky and hit Behemoth again as he reached the apex of his flight. Behemoth shot backwards and crashed into the fifth story of an office block. Glass rained down as the windows shattered. Ryan hovered outside the building and charged a solar energy blast. He shot Behemoth, who zipped across the tiled floor and out the other side of the building. Ryan sped around the other side and caught Behemoth as he fell.

"We're going on a short flight, Behemoth." Ryan said. "I can promise that you're not going to like the destination."

"No! I can still beat you!" said Behemoth as he struggled to escape Ryan's iron grip.

"I don't think so."

Ryan flew higher into the afternoon sky. Behemoth continued to struggle but couldn't break free.

Ryan continued to fly, rising to twenty thousand feet before he stopped.

"It's over Behemoth. You're done. Surrender."

"No. Never. I'll kill you all!"

"Suit yourself." said Ryan, releasing his grasp on Behemoth.

Behemoth plummeted towards the ground, shouting curses as he did so.

Ryan hovered in the air for five seconds as Behemoth fell. He closed his eyes, relaxed and took in more sunlight. Ryan charged an energy blast and turned earthwards.

He aimed his fully charged energy blast at the falling Behemoth and fired. The orange beam hit Behemoth dead centre, burning him and pushing him faster towards the ground below. Behemoth accelerated towards a crash-landing. He impacted the ground in the foothills of Mount Charleston, just outside the Las Vegas city limits, creating a crater fifty feet deep.

Ryan touched down on the edge of the crater and charged another energy blast, just in case. He floated down into the crater to ensure that Behemoth was out of commission. The villain lay in the centre. Incredibly, he was still breathing but he didn't get up.

Ryan and Revenant had won.

Chapter Nineteen | The End Has a Start

Ryan, satisfied that Behemoth wasn't going anywhere, launched himself up into the air and landed at the edge of the crater. A helicopter circled overhead twice and touched down beside him.

Revenant, Hiroshi, Eva and three police officers got out and made their way over to him; each of them paused on their way to look into the crater to see Behemoth's body.

"Ryan! Good to finally see you!" said Captain O'Grady, shaking Ryan's hand. "He's not getting up again is he?"

"I don't think so."

"It over? Did we win?" said an over-excited Hiroshi.

"Looks like it" said Revenant, giving Ryan a careful hug to avoid further damaging her injured arm which was now in a sling.

"How's the arm?" Ryan asked.

"It's OK, I thought it was broken but it's just a fracture. I'll be fine in a couple of months."

"Glad to hear it."

"What do we do with this guy now?" asked DJ.

"We have equipment at the base that will hold him." said Eva.

"Will your boss mind?" asked Ryan.

"He's gone. I heard it over the radio during the fight. Half of the rest of the team abandoned the base and fled. Benning was amongst them. The remaining ISA agents will be here within the hour to take Behemoth into custody."

"So it's over?" said Ryan.

"Most of the city saw us fight an overgrown genetic mutant today. That sort of thing isn't easily forgotten. I think it's only just beginning." said Revenant.

Ed pulled out a tablet computer from his bag, pressed the screen and handed it to Ryan.

"Revenant is wrong about one thing: most of the world saw what happened today, not just those in the city. Look at this."

Ryan saw that one of the major news channels was already reporting from the site of the battle. The news ticker at the bottom of the screen read "Ryan Curtis involved in superhero battle in Las Vegas."

"I guess the world knows I've got super powers."

"Don't worry." said Ed. "We'll think of a way to make sure nothing bad happens to you."

The ISA technicians arrived an hour later and used a crane to load the unconscious Behemoth into a cryogenic tank as the heroes and police looked on.

"What will you do with him?" Ryan asked Eva.

"He's going to the base where we're keeping Maria Fleming." She replied. "I received a call from my bosses' boss. I've been made responsible for keeping him prisoner. Now that Benning and his men have disappeared, I'm the most experienced field agent that the ISA has left."

"What you do with him?" Hiroshi asked.

"Try to remove his powers if we can. The world doesn't need another mad villain."

"Do you think Benning is going to be a problem?" inquired Revenant.

"I have no doubt we'll see him again. But he's the ISA's problem now. I've also been tasked with tracking him down. He stole copies of Spencer's research when he left the base, but I doubt he'll use it straight away. Not now that he's seen what it did to Spencer. Benning will try to find someone to revise the mixture and solve the problems with it. I'll save a nice cryogenic cell beside Behemoth for him."

Behemoth's tank was loaded onto a flatbed truck, which drove away at high speed, escorted by a group of ISA agents in SUVs.

"Behemoth get to stay with the love of his life?" said Hiroshi. "That pretty generous of you."

"It's better than he deserves certainly." said Revenant.

"They deserve each other." said Ryan.

"No." said Eva. "I'm not putting Behemoth and Fleming together. It's too dangerous. Behemoth will spend the rest of his life away from her. He killed hundreds of people today. I don't want him getting any kind of happy ending."

"Wow. Vindictive much?" said Ryan.

"A little." said Eva.

"Can I ask you a personal question Ryan?" asked Revenant.

"Sure."

"When you saw Maria first, were you thinking of killing her?"

"No. My parents didn't raise me like that; they brought me up to do the right thing. I wouldn't kill a defenceless person."

"Glad to hear it."

"Can I also ask personal question, Ryan?" said Hiroshi.

"OK."

"Have you thought of superhero name yet? I got tons of suggestions. Sunnyboy, Sundude. Lots more!"

"I was thinking about it. A few names crossed my mind. I did really like one in particular though."

"So… don't keep us in suspense." said Revenant. "What was it?"

"I was thinking… maybe… Flare." he said anxiously

"Not bad." said Revenant.

"I guess it cool."

"So what now?" asked Eva.

Hiroshi replied: "I got to get back to Japan. Robot suits to build. UNSAFE probably want to court martial me too. You have my number if you want help again."

"Yeah," said Revenant. "I've got a real life to get back to as well. We'll talk soon Ryan… Flare. Hiroshi? I can organise flights home if you wish?"

"Sure! But only if it on a private jet. I don't fly commercial."

"I noticed." Revenant said.

Revenant hugged Ryan again and walked away with Hiroshi.

"Thanks for everything, Revenant. You too Hiroshi!" said Ryan

"It no problem" Hiroshi said. "Now you can fly really fast you can visit me anytime. Bring Milk Duds!"

"We'll speak again Ryan. You know how to reach me as well." said Revenant,

"I just have to find the world's most sparsely furnished apartment!"

"Well, maybe after today I can find the time to decorate it." She looked down at her broken arm. "It's not as if I'll be able to go out at night for a few weeks."

Ryan and Eva strolled over to a police car where Ed waited for both of them, leaning against the bonnet.

"How are things in the city?"

"We're still pulling survivors out of the buildings that Behemoth destroyed." Ed answered.

"It's nice to hear that there are survivors at least."

"Quite a lot; dozens more than we were expecting. You and Revenant saved a lot of people today. Your parents would be very proud."

"Thank you." said Ryan.

"Ryan." Ed said. "I've spoken to the Mayor. It's time for you to stop running and come home. We were thinking of offering you a job. How would you like to be the city's superhero? We also offered the job to Revenant but she said that we couldn't afford her."

"What would I have to do?"

"You'll train at the police academy on a part time basis, go to college and fight crime whenever we need your help."

Ryan thought for a few seconds: "I can think of worse things to do."

Ed noticeably calmed down: "That's what I'd hoped you would say. I've got to get back to the city."

"I'll join you, I guess the fire fighters in Las Vegas could use the help." said Flare.

Ed pointed at the passenger seat of the squad car: "Hop in and I'll give you a ride back."

"No need." said Flare. "I think I'll try out my powers again, if you don't mind."

"Be my guest." said Ed.

Flare took a running jump and rocketed into the evening sky. He smiled as he flew towards Las Vegas, happy to be finally going home at last.

Epilogue

Karl sat in an uncomfortable chair in a vacant apartment in the building directly opposite Aimee's. He'd been camped here for three days, waiting, trying to get an idea of her schedule. As far as he could tell she didn't have one. She wasn't at home, or anywhere. She had disappeared after the board meeting a few days back. Three days ago, she'd made a quick phone call to her office to say she wouldn't be available for a few days. Since then, he hadn't been able to find a trace of her. She wasn't at her apartment and hadn't booked into any hotels. She was nowhere. But Karl had a piece of luck late last night when Aimee had booked a flight from Los Angeles to New York using her credit card. He had no idea what she had been doing over there and he didn't particularly care. She had probably gone to Rodeo Drive to buy a dress or a blouse. Wealth was wasted on the rich.

Here he was; one of the world's finest killers reduced to eating take away food and drinking bad coffee as he waited to find out what he needed to put this spoiled rich girl out of his misery. Aimee's building was strange: no one had been in or out of it in days and yet lights turned on and off at all hours as if they were on a timer. Only someone who had watched the building continuously for a significant length of time would have noticed. Where were her neighbours? This was turning out to be both the most boring job he'd ever taken and the oddest. A cab pulled up outside her building as he watched through binoculars. Aimee got out of the cab, her arm in a sling. The cab driver then got out and ran to the trunk of the car. He opened it and pulled out a heavy looking suitcase. He carried it to the door for her and she paid him before entering the building.

Karl looked at the front page of the newspaper he had been reading earlier. The front page had a blurred picture of the two heroes who had been involved in the battle in Las Vegas. Karl looked closely at the masked vigilante called Revenant. Her arm had been broken in the battle, just like Aimee DeWitt's arm. The hairstyle was close enough too. Maybe this job was going to be more interesting than he had thought.

Eva sipped a cup of tepid coffee as the new lab technicians and agents ran through their ideas for the revitalised ISA. They had gathered in the main lab, the only space in the facility big enough to hold all of the new team members, freshly recruited from the CIA, FBI and other agencies. Overnight, the ISA had become the place to work. Eva had ordered that the main lab was to be turned into a temporary operations centre until they could find a new space to work from. Now that the ISA was public again and had a real budget, better offices were sure to follow. In the interim, the damage done to the lab by Flare and Behemoth's fight was quickly being repaired so that it could be fully operational. Eva didn't like the room. She had many reasons as to why that was. Dr. Fleming was still there, for a start. Eva's team would be moving Fleming to a specially constructed cell once it was completed.

Eva looked at Maria floating there for a couple of seconds as she finished her coffee, thinking of all the damage that the woman floating peacefully in the tank had caused over the years.

Eva was snapped out of her reverie by one of the new agents asking her a question.

"Ma'am? We'll need your signature on this requisition order." He said.

She turned her head to look at him as she signed the paper. Neither she nor any of the other people in the room noticed Maria's eyelids flutter.

Flare, Revenant & Mech will return in **Shooting Star.**

To know more about the Flare Series, please follow us in www.facebook.com/flarebook.

Name: Solarstorm AKA Jake Curtis
Powers: Flight. Strength. Solar energy blasts.
Affiliation: The Vanguard

Biography
(Extract taken from Warfare's personal tactical log)

Jake and Lisa Curtis (cf. file VG-002: Velocity) were the first two heroes I approached about forming a team of talented individuals to face threats that were beyond what we could hope to defeat on our own. Jake has been a superhero since he was eighteen years of age. He is the most experienced of the heroes and is seen as a figure-head of the hero community by the general public. He's often asked for his opinion on world issues by the media and he has a natural air of confidence that makes him particularly suited to a leadership and spokesperson role.

He and Lisa have been married since they were both twenty years old and had a child, Ryan (cf. file VG-006) shortly thereafter. Jake often feels guilty that he and Lisa do not give Ryan enough attention as their duties as two of the world's premiere heroes often interfere. This will need to be closely managed in future to ensure that they remain available when required.

Jake is one of the most powerful people on the planet and only team member Mountain (cf. file VG-003) would be of a similar power level. His powers are tied to the amount of sunlight that he has absorbed but I've yet to see him pushed to his limits and he regularly accomplishes feats of strength and endurance that would be impossible for most other heroes, never mind regular people.

Name: Velocity AKA Lisa Curtis

Powers: Super speed

Affiliation: The Vanguard

Biography

(Extract taken from *Superheroes today* magazine interview with Mage)

What do I think of Velocity?

This is off the record right? Good. It's no secret that she and I don't get on as well as the team's PR people would like you to believe. I put it down to a clash of personalities. Basically: I have one and she doesn't.

She sees herself as kind of a role model for the hero community. She's always like: "Mage, do this." "Mage, do that." "Mage; stop encouraging children to smoke."

Like she has the right to always question what I do just because she can run fast? Since when is that supposed to be a superpower? It's pretty lame.

She's a neat freak as well. You don't know pain until you've hung out with an OCD person who can move faster that the wind. In short, she gets on my nerves. Solarstorm and her seem to get on quite well though. I've heard a lot of people describe them as the perfect married couple. He must have the patience of a saint.

Name: Mage AKA Jonathon O'Toole
Powers: Level Nine Magician (self-described)
Affiliation: The Vanguard

Biography
(Extract from professional misconduct report
prepared by Velocity for the attention of Warfare)

Warfare, I'm not comfortable with Mage being on
the team. He is completely unprofessional and
often nowhere to be found when we need him. He's
much more interested in going to A-list parties
and hanging out with supermodels than attending
team meetings. What's going to happen if he just
decides to disappear to an awards ceremony during
a battle? We need team mates we can depend on,
not a spoiled child. Don't get me started on that
interview he gave recently.

I'm aware he has significant superhuman abilities
and a unique power set, but surely there's another
hero we can draft onto the team? Someone a lot
less childish and more dependable? I suggest that
during our next recruitment drive we look for an
actual teammate rather than a team member.

Name: Mountain

Powers: Strength, impervious to damage.

Affiliation: The Vanguard

Biography

(Extract taken from *Superheroes Today* magazine interview with Mage)

Big dude. Made of rock. Likes hitting things and, strangely: yoga. Kind to small children and animals. Not much else

to say really.

Name: Warfare
Powers: Gifted athlete, expert at numerous types of martial arts.
Affiliation: The Vanguard

Biography
(Extract from ISA file memo ISA11LRD6 written by Dr. Maria Fleming)

Warfare is the big unknown. We have sufficient information on all of the other heroes thus far encountered but we've been able to confirm little about The Vanguard field commander and tactician. He turned up out of nowhere several years back and made a name for himself in the Far East as a hero, travelling the region, learning many different fighting styles and righting wrongs. No pictures of him outside of his costume exist and he does not appear to have any close personal relationships outside of the other members of the team.

It should be noted that he has made it his mission to train younger heroes and encourages them to work together whenever possible. It is undoubted that the increase in effectiveness of many of the heroes that the ISA research team recently reported on (see memo ISA14PRD6W) owes much to him.

He is an excellent tactician and has led the team to victory against seemingly impossible odds on numerous occasions. He is far from the most powerful member of the team but he is clearly the most skilled when it comes to one on one combat. He is particularly adept in the use of edged weapons. Many of my team would give their right arms to study his electron sword. It's years ahead of our current technology, even with the numerous advances made by the project's armourers in the past eight years. The weapon is unique. Warfare can adjust the energy blade of the sword to allow him to change his fighting style to suit a particular situation. Confirmed options include a broadsword, katana, scimitar, rapier and, on one particularly messy occasion; a chainsaw. Leo Spencer has conjectured that the sword uses either a kind of 'hard light' or else a 'memory metal' technology to perform its numerous functions, but at the moment we cannot confirm these theories.

Name: Flare AKA Ryan Curtis
Powers: Strength, flight, energy blasts, speed.
Affiliation: N/A

Biography
(Extract from the diary of Eva Mann. ISA agent)
The ISA Director remains unsure of what to do with Ryan Curtis now that he has become a fully-fledged superhero. I'm willing to give Ryan the benefit of the doubt for the time being but I can understand why my boss and the government would be wary of him. He is now the most powerful inhabitant of this country. The power levels of the other surviving heroes just don't match up. If he went rogue I honestly don't think we could stop him. Hopefully we won't have to.

Personally, Ryan is a decent person. He's not as pure hearted as his father was but he still seems to want to do the right thing. He's a little socially maladjusted, quiet and very cynical. I suppose being an only child to absentee parents would cause you to be that way. For all that, he's not a bad person; he and I have become professionally close over the last few months. I intend to continue getting to know him. It may make him easier to manipulate if we ever need to do so.

Name: Revenant AKA Aimee DeWitt
Powers: Athlete, martial arts expert.
Affiliation: N/A

Biography

(Extract from the personal log of Hiroshi Saito)

Aimee crazy. She come over to me at a reception for the UNSAFE a year ago and ask me really odd questions about body armour, night vision lenses and other weird stuff. It not take me long to figure out she want to become a hero. I offered my help as I pretty bored with the budget restraints working on Mars project. Aimee came to me with blank cheque book and tell me what she wanted. I happy to oblige. Her costume a work of art if you ask me. It all top of the line tech. It designed to keep her safe as she prowl rooftops and hurt people. It have limits however.

She an expert in escrima, karate, Brazilian ju-jitsu and other martial arts I not sure of names of. She spend years training to take out her frustration at losing her mother on criminals. She very determined and focused. Maybe too much. I worry for her mental health as I think she goes too far in her actions sometimes, it like she spend years thinking up of nasty things to do to people and she love putting these into practice. She a creative genius at using whatever comes to hand and the surrounding environment to hurt an opponent. I doing my best to be her friend and keep her on straight and narrow, hopefully I able to mellow her out over time.

Name: Mech AKA Hiroshi Saito
Powers: Genius inventor
Affiliation: UNSAFE

Biography
(Taken from Aimee DeWitt's diary)
The word 'genius' is thrown around a lot lately. In Hiroshi's case it is completely justified, especially when it comes to mechanical engineering. He once turned an IPod speaker, two cell phones and a laptop computer into a sonic weapon capable of destroying a city block.

He quit being a hero after the cataclysm that almost destroyed Tokyo three years ago. He tried to stop what happened that day but was only partially successful. Half the city was destroyed but he single-handedly managed to save the other half. This perceived failure on his part led to him suffering a nervous breakdown. He decommissioned what was left of his Mech suit and took a job working for the United Nations on their space programme.

One of these days he is going to have to face his demons in order to overcome them. The world needs him functioning at the peak of his abilities. I have no doubt that his inventions could help to change the world for the better. I'll do my very best to ensure that as many of his ideas as possible come to fruition.

Obligatory 'About the author' page

Written **Paddy Lennon**

Paddy Lennon is the least creatively qualified person to have worked on this book (see bios below). He has an Honours Degree in Business from Dublin Institute of Technology and has worked in finance for many years, neither of which are relevant to writing novels. He watches an unhealthy amount of television, reads a lot of comics. He also loves martial arts, cooking, Transformers, G.I. Joe and Mass Effect.

Check out his blog at paddymlennon.blogspot.ie for short stories and articles on pop culture or follow him on Twitter: @paddylennon1.

Cover art **Ben Hennessy**

Ben Hennessy graduated from BCFE college with a B.A. Honours in Animation. Since he has graduated, he has worked as a character designer and a storyboard artist on computer games and TV productions. Games and shows he has worked on are available for iPad and the Nintendo Wii or can be viewed on RTÉ Jr, Cbeebies and Nickelodeon.

If you wish to contact Ben you can find him easily on Twitter @ Bennessy.

Design **Miriam Abuin**

Miriam Abuin studied Journalism at the University of Seville (Spain) and underwent further training as a translator at the Open University of Catalonia. She free-lances in English to Spanish translation and graphic design. She has experience working in the cultural arena. She's an occasional (and I mean occasional) blogger on walkercaminante. blogspot.ie, you can also find her on Twitter: @miriamabuin.

Cover Colours **Chris O'Halloran**

Made in the USA
Lexington, KY
27 March 2018